"Mattie." Kit DeChambelle's deep, masculine voice—possessive with its untoward use of her Christian name— rippled along her back with shivers of awareness. **"It is time to return to our box. The next act is about to begin."**

"Of course. Captain, if you will excuse us?

"Until our next meeting, Miss Fraser.

Kit clamped down the jealousy that spiked through him at Johnson's last lingering look.

One could hardly blame the poor blighter for his sudden obsession. Mattie's hair caught the candlelight and flamed, burning even Kit's reason to ashes. He drew her through the crush, focusing on the glittering assemblage instead of her nearness. A futile endeavor, that.

"You seem to have made a conquest, Miss Fraser."

"A novelty frequently attracts a fleeting notice."

"You do yourself an injustice, Miss Fraser." Indeed, he found her the most beautiful woman in the building. But his attraction extended beyond the physical to the uncommon loyalty that had induced h̲e̲ brother. And thoug ground—again—he himself.

C.J. CHASE

RWA Golden Heart Award-winning novelist C.J. Chase writes "Intrigue of the Past, Inspiration for the Present." It wasn't always so.

Armed with a degree in statistics, C.J. began a promising career in information technology. But after coworkers discovered she was a member of that rare species—a computer programmer who could also craft a grammatically-correct sentence—she spent more time writing computer manuals than computer code. Leaving the corporate world to stay home with her children, C.J. quickly learned she did not possess the housekeeping gene, so she decided to take the advice of her ninth-grade English teacher and write articles and stories people actually wanted to read. In addition to penning novels, she also wrote nonfiction for *The Banner,* a small Christian publication, for five years.

C.J. lives in the swamps of southeastern Virginia with her handsome husband, active sons, one kinetic sheltie and an ever-increasing number of chickens. When she is not writing, you will find her gardening, watching old movies, playing classical piano (badly) or teaching a special-needs Sunday School class.

C.J. CHASE

Redeeming the Rogue

Love Inspired

Recycling programs for this product may not exist in your area.

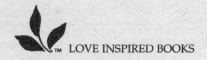

™ LOVE INSPIRED BOOKS

ISBN-13: 978-0-373-82882-1

REDEEMING THE ROGUE

Copyright © 2011 by C.J. Chase

www.LoveInspiredBooks.com

Printed in U.S.A.

Bless the LORD, O my soul,
and forget not all his benefits:
Who forgiveth all thine iniquities;
who healeth all thy diseases;
Who redeemeth thy life from destruction;
who crowneth thee with loving kindness
and tender mercies.
—*Psalms* 103:2–4

Dedication

For all men in my life:

My husband and hero, David, who believed in me
even on those days when I didn't believe in myself,

Calvin, my proofreader and fellow storyteller,
who will someday dedicate a book to me,

And Nathanael, my joy and delight,
who is nearer to God's heart than the rest of us.

And for Mrs. Betty S. Kantner, my ninth-grade
English teacher, who told me I could do it.

Acknowledgments

A special thank-you to my critique partners
who suffered with me to make this a better book:

Candace Irvin, for her diabolical mind and
willingness to take middle-of-the-night phone calls
when I plotted myself into a corner

And

Sue Mason, for keeping my focus
on the romance whenever I got too enthralled
with the suspense plot.

Chapter One

Wiltshire, England
September 1815

The Honorable Christopher James Michael DeChambelle staggered to the ancient sideboard and plunked down his empty glass. Perhaps with enough whiskey in his belly, he would at last achieve blissful oblivion—and hold the nightmares at bay for a few hours.

He'd started the evening with a single shot, just a little altitude to suppress the memories—the shrieks of terror, the tang of gunpowder, the rivers of blood.

When the first had proved insufficient to the task, Kit had added a second. And then a third and perhaps a fourth…he couldn't quite remember anymore. And yet the scene still haunted him, and guilt and remorse—his two ever-present companions these past months—remained lodged in his consciousness, their attendance overwhelming even the whiskey's power to let him forget.

He wrapped his fist around the neck of the bottle and commenced to refill his glass.

Familiar footsteps tapped against the hallway's wooden-plank floor. "What are you doing here, Harrison?"

"How did you know?" Lawrence Harrison slipped around the doorway and into the dim study.

"I could tell by your walk."

"A shame your sense of location isn't as proficient as your hearing. You might get more of that whiskey into your goblet."

Kit glanced at the puddle forming on the sideboard's dusty top. "I thought my choice of location rather inspired for one who wishes to be left alone. I didn't realize you would pursue me here. Now answer my question—why did you come?"

"Not because I desire to share your comforts." Harrison gestured to the hunting lodge's peeling paint and threadbare curtains. The heads of long-dead stags stared down from the walls, their moth-eaten fur since replaced by layers of soot. "Alderston has men scouring the country to find you."

"Alderston?" Kit tilted his head back and downed what whiskey had reached the glass. He hadn't seen the director of clandestine services in several months—Napoleon's defeat at Waterloo had suspended the government's need for Kit's special…talents. Or so he had thought. "The war's over. What does Alderston want?"

"You, obviously. What are you doing here?"

"Escaping my mother's lectures."

Harrison stared at him, reading him with an uncomfortable familiarity borne of their years of friendship. "I think you hide not so much from your family as from the world, from life. From God."

Kit ignored the too-astute observation and searched the sideboard for another glass. "Drink?"

"None for me." Harrison leaned closer and nudged the bottle just beyond Kit's reach. "And I think you've had your fill for the night."

Kit hurled the goblet at the cold hearth. The glass shattered and littered the floor, the pieces sparkling like stars against a dusty sky. "I came to escape my family, and it's as if my mother followed me."

"Perhaps like her, I care enough to end your unseemly indulgence in guilt."

"Spare me. Few speeches are more tedious than the sermons of a sanctimonious friend."

"And nothing so tiresome as self-pity."

"If my behavior bothers you, leave. I didn't invite you."

Harrison threaded his arm through Kit's and led him to a nearby chair. "Aren't you the least bit curious?"

"I want no more of Alderston's dangerous secrets."

"What do you want?"

Kit plopped onto the chair. A cloud of dust poofed from the upholstery as he rubbed his fingertips against his throbbing temples. "Peace."

"The war is over."

"Peace from…my past. So many times, I thought my life was over. I couldn't wait for the war to end. And now that it has, I feel lost. Purposeless."

"You can't change what lies before." Harrison pointed to the shards littering the hearth. "And whiskey will only make you a slave to its power—it won't bring the atonement you seek."

"But it does allow me to forget."

"At what cost? Your family? Your life? Your soul? Perhaps it is not forgetting you desire, but forgiveness."

Mattie Fraser wouldn't have suspected the headquarters of the formidable British Navy to hide such a tiny, briglike office. Not when the Admiralty's exterior—so grand in design and dimension—towered haughtily above the streets. The other rooms she'd visited had offered at least token obeisance to the occupants' status, but this musty cubbyhole boasted not so much as a window to let her view drenched, dreary London.

Though her damp stockings still squished inside her shoes, the frayed hem of her skirt no longer clung to her ankles. She drummed her foot against the floor as she twirled her umbrella on its point. The large puddle beneath it had almost dried, but for one stubborn spot that refused to disappear.

Like Mattie.

For two weeks, she had bounced from room to room looking for the elusive official who could answer her questions. Through the maze of government agencies, she had inquired, cajoled and pleaded—thus far, to no avail. Each stop had produced only the suggestion of another person, another location. Still, she persevered, refusing to let bureaucratic indifference halt her search.

A search that had led her…here.

After an hour or more in the cramped quarters, she recognized every crack in the plaster, every watermark on the ceiling. A clerk hunched over his desk and scrawled furiously. Unlike the others who had been only too pleased to send her posthaste to the next department, this one was strangely reluctant to dismiss her. On more than one occasion she caught the shrewd, speculative glances he cast her way, yet he guarded Mr. DeChambelle's door as if it were the portal leading to the crown jewels.

The oil lamp slumping on the clerk's desk belched more smoke than light—smoke that stung her eyes and choked her throat like the fires that had burned Washington the previous year. At least tucked away in this nook she no longer encountered the unnervingly familiar sight of English officers as they marched through the building's hallways, so like the way they stalked through her nightmares.

She hugged her coat, unaccustomed to such cold, damp days in September. Back home, the heat would have moderated to late summer warmth. Balmy breezes would stir the air and ruffle the sails of the ships on the Potomac, with only cooler nights to suggest the approaching autumn.

Her stomach growled, reminding her she hadn't eaten since her last foray outdoors at noon. The remaining half of her meat pie tempted her from the depths of her pocket. Impatiently, she tapped the umbrella point against the floor. The tip found a drop of water and skittered across the tile. She tightened her grip—too late. The umbrella slid out of her hands and fell with a clatter that startled an expletive out of the clerk.

Face flaming, Mattie slid from the chair and reached down to retrieve her fallen umbrella. She charged to her feet—

And ricocheted off something solid. Something that grunted.

Two strong hands clinched her upper arms, one on either side, and arrested her backward flight.

Something male.

Soap and leather tickled her senses, a pleasant but disturbing combination after a fortnight of London's foul air. She frowned and focused on the dark wool coat only inches from her nose. The fabric swept across broad shoulders and puckered slightly where the arms stretched to clasp her own.

"Laura?"

Laura? All that time waiting, and the miserable excuse of a clerk had her name incorrect. "I am not Laura."

Silence hung in the air like the smoke, then, "No, of course not. Are you injured?" The rich tones of the baritone voice drew her attention back to the man before her.

Her gaze wandered upward to a snowy cravat, then to his strong jaw with its shadow of afternoon stubble. Full lips thinned below an aquiline nose with a scar on the side that relieved his face of perfect symmetry—transforming it from mere prettiness to rugged masculinity.

Then she looked straight into eyes of the deepest blue, like the eastern sky at sunset. Their fringe of dark lashes contrasted with tawny hair that gleamed in the lantern's glow and fell in disarray across his brow.

"Madam, are you injured?" he repeated, concern darkening those mesmerizing eyes.

Suddenly aware of the hands wrapped around her arms, she drew back. He released her—nevertheless, his grip left an invisible imprint where the warmth of his palms had seeped through her sleeves. She gathered her composure and snapped her shoulders back. "Only stiff from my long wait."

"My apologies." He scooped a pair of spectacles from the floor—a casualty of their collision?—and settled them on his face, like a veil screening his eyes. The scar along his nose likewise disappeared from her view. "May I help you?"

"I am here to see Mr. Christopher DeChambelle."

"I am DeChambelle." He sketched her an elegant bow, then gestured to the gloomy room behind him. What with the dreary skies and approaching twilight, little light penetrated the soot-clouded panes of its single window. "Won't you come in?"

Kit waited as his visitor marched past him, then he glared at Baxter, his clerk. "Why didn't you inform me I had a caller?"

"Sir, it is Mr. Alderston's wish that he speak to you as soon as possible."

Kit gestured to the five empty chairs. "And yet, he is not here."

"We did not expect you to arrive so precipitously."

"Harrison said Alderston needed to see me about an urgent matter, so I came at once."

"The director has searched London these many days for you. This morning he left for Somerset."

Somerset. The DeChambelle estate. No doubt Alderston's questions into Kit's whereabouts would generate a new succession of worries for his parents.

"I sent a messenger after the director, informing him of your return. If the messenger intercepted Mr. Alderston before he'd traveled far, the director will be here forthwith."

"And if your messenger hasn't yet reached Alderston? Did you expect the lady to wait all night?"

Baxter's gaze slid toward Kit's office. "Sir, you should delay this meeting with the woman until you have met with the director. Mr. Alderston may return while—"

"Then let him take his turn waiting." Kit snapped the door shut on Baxter's protests and strode the three steps across the office where, so far as his family knew, he'd spent the better part of the war procuring supplies for Britain's mighty navy. "May I take your coat?"

His visitor ripped her gaze from its perusal of his desk and folded her arms over her chest. "No. Thank you."

"Well, then, please be seated." He grabbed a chair opposite his desk and held it for her.

Definitely not Laura, despite her sun-and-spice-scented hair of the same cinnamon red. This woman was too short, with a nose too pert and lips too generous—and a disconcerting way of staring into a man's thoughts. He swallowed, aware that any who looked too closely found…nothing. Only the empty hole left from guilt eating away his soul. She gracefully settled to the seat, the back of her unfashionable coat brushing his hand and drawing him back to the present.

He slid around the desk and dropped onto the chair. "Now then, Miss…"

"Fraser." Her voice held a hint of a drawl. "Martha Fraser."

"Welcome to England, Miss Fraser. You are from…Virginia?"

"Washington."

"Not so far from Virginia then." Or perhaps not far enough, given the recent hostilities between their countries. "Were you in Washington last summer?"

"Yes." She raised her chin and probed him with a challenging brown stare.

"That must have been a frightful experience. I am sorry about the destruction of your city. Was your home spared?"

"General Ross designated an officer to guard my house from any too eager members of your army."

"Ross was a good man. I was sorry to hear of his death. Now how may I be of help to you, Miss Fraser from Washington?"

"I'm inquiring into the fate of my brother." The knuckles of her fingers whitened as she twisted her hands into intricate knots that suggested some other, less assured side to Miss Fraser. "The officer I met last year—a Major Andrew Harley-Smith—offered to see what he could learn from a friend who worked at the Admiralty. However, it has been a year and I haven't heard from him."

Kit pushed up his drooping spectacles, their frame now loose and possibly bent from the impact with Miss Fraser. "I am probably the man you seek. Drew and I attended Oxford together, though it had been an age since I last saw him."

Hope lightened her gaze to a charming shade of amber and eased the determination in her mouth. "So then you know…"

"No, I fear not. Major Harley-Smith was killed in September of last year—in the fighting near your city of Baltimore."

Her back snapped straight until it no longer rested against the chair. Her eyes smoldered to umber again, the golden flecks glowing like sparks in their depths. "I'm surprised and dismayed that in two weeks of tramping from one office to another, no one has informed me of this until now."

Carriage wheels bounced against the cobbled streets outside, echoing through the room. Kit glanced out the window at the darkening sky that reflected his mood, so black since... "Miss Fraser," he said at last, "our country has been at war a long time. The names of our dead are many."

"But you knew Major Harley-Smith."

He turned away from the gloomy view of London and met the challenge in her eyes again. Freckles sprinkled her nose, adding to the sense of girlish innocence. "Drew began a letter to me—one he unfortunately never finished, leaving me with no means of contacting you—before his last campaign. It was among his personal effects when they were returned to his brother and didn't reach me until months later. By then, our war with America had ended." And Napoleon had escaped, and Kit was reassigned to France for one final mission.

"But my brother?"

"I fear I have more bad news, Miss Fraser. All the American prisoners were sent home some months ago. If your brother was not among them, you must assume the worst."

"But my brother wasn't a prisoner. At least, not that I am aware of. He was a sailor on a merchant ship when a British frigate stopped them and took several of the men, including my brother, for service in your navy."

"Ah. I fear Drew did not include that information in his note. When was your brother pressed?"

"A little over three years ago."

"Our officers were only supposed to enlist sailors originally from our country. Was your brother born in the United States?"

"Yes. Major Harley-Smith thought there would be no problem getting him released because his citizenship is undisputed."

Kit snatched a sheet of paper from the corner of his desk. "What is your address here in London?"

"I'm staying at the Captain's Quarters."

"The *Captain's Quarters?*" He jerked his gaze from the paper and met her eyes. A face like that, in a place like that, could only effect trouble.

"I don't know the name of the street—it's near the docks."

"I know where it is, Miss Fraser. *You* should not. If I may be so bold as to say, that—"

"Is none of your concern." She glared at him with that steely determination.

"But that place is filled with patrons of the worst sort— drunkards and ruffians and the like. It is no place for you."

"I have supported myself for some time. I know how to manage an inebriated man or two."

"I begin to understand why our countries' differences could not be solved amicably."

Her lips twitched at the corners and once again her eyes gentled, this time with suppressed humor. A solitary ray of light speared through the murky clouds in his mind.

The tic still throbbed in his jaw, but he returned to his notes without further comment about her choice of residences. "What was the name of the American merchant ship?"

"The *Constance*."

"Do you know if any of the other men who, ah, spent time aboard our ship went home?"

"No. That is, I don't know."

He raked his fingers through his hair. "Miss Fraser, since your brother has not yet returned, I suspect that we shall learn he suffered a fate similar to that of Major Harley-Smith."

"I understand. It's just the…uncertainty of it all." For once the forthright Miss Fraser fixed her gaze on a point above his head.

A sudden grimness consumed his compassion when she wouldn't meet his gaze. Perhaps she was only a grieving sister in a faraway land, but war bled the idealism out of a man and replaced it with cynicism. "Do you know the name of the frigate that stopped the *Constance?*"

"The *Impatience.*"

He stilled, his hand frozen above the paper. "The *Impatience?*" No wonder Drew had asked for his help. Did she know?

"So Captain Ramsey informed me when the *Constance* returned to Alexandria."

"What is your brother's name?"

"George. George Fraser."

"Very well, Miss Fraser. I will try to have an answer for you tomorrow." His chair scraped against the floor as he pushed it back. "If that is everything?"

"Yes." She rose and nodded, and he stood as well.

"Until tomorrow then." He wrenched open the door and gestured her out.

Her bright hair flashed a final, mocking gleam at him as she exited his office.

Kit set aside Miss Fraser's address and scrawled a hasty note. "Baxter? See that this is delivered immediately. If Alderston returns, tell him I will be at Hogarth's."

"But sir—"

Kit brushed past the clerk and charged out of the office. He needed none of Alderston's drama and danger in his life tonight.

Outside the Admiralty, gaslights threw a mellow glow onto the wet bricks of London's streets. Mattie shoved the umbrella under her arm and rammed her hands into her coat pockets. Her fingers brushed steel—round, hard, cold.

Only one day away from learning her brother's fate. She ought to be thrilled.

So why the nagging doubts?

The soft voices of Evensong drifted through the open door of a nearby stone chapel. Drawn by the music and a memory of a happier time, Mattie edged closer. Large choirs and loud organs were rare in Washington, and her attendance at such services rarer still. Around her, Londoners bustled about their business but she lingered on the street while the melody meandered through her mind and assuaged her apprehensions. The glowing candles inside the church cast colorful light through the stained-glass windows and onto the cobblestones at her feet.

The last notes of the chorus faded, then the sonorous voice of the reader rippled across the twilight. "'For if ye forgive men their trespasses…'"

Forgive? Tension tightened across Mattie's shoulders, as if she'd been tricked by the sweet cadences of the song. She lurched away and continued on her journey.

The rain had abated, but the misty air condensed the odors. The unpleasant smells intensified the farther she traveled from the Admiralty to less affluent neighborhoods where humanity crowded together in concentrations she had never imagined.

And the smoke! That was the worst, evoking memories of that fateful night a year ago when the British army had invaded Washington. The blaze had lit the sky while the explosions rocked the ground. The acrid stench had hung heavy on the air for days after the flames consumed America's new capital and reduced its beautiful buildings to rubble.

Washington's warmth was an ocean away, yet despite the London chill seeping through her clothes, sweat trickled down her back. Forgive? Never. Not the English who had burned her city. Not the father who loved whiskey more than his children. And especially not the God who abandoned her to the vagaries of drunkards and invading armies. She clenched her fingers around the tempered steel, willing the terrible memories to recede.

The streets grew darker, the buildings more squalid, the stench more foul as she drew closer to the inn she had chosen for its affordability and proximity to ships sailing in and out of London.

She turned into an even darker alley.

"All alone, pretty leddy?" A derelict stepped into her path. His clawlike hands lunged for her coat.

"No, I brought a friend." She withdrew her pistol and pointed the barrel at his chest.

The man froze, except for the oily smile that smeared his face. "Now lovey—"

She cocked the hammer. The click of metal striking metal reverberated through the street and momentarily surpassed even the ever-present noise of people, animals and vehicles. "Go."

Her would-be assailant raised his hands and backed away, eyes glimmering in the muted light, until he slithered into a crevice between the buildings.

"Gor, that was a good 'un!"

"Nicky?"

An urchin stepped from the shadows. The blade of a knife winked as he tucked it into his clothes.

"What are you doing here this late?"

"Been waiting for ye, Mattie."

Her heart warmed despite the chill. 'Twas a long while since anyone had missed Mattie Fraser. Or cared enough he would draw a knife on a man four times his size. She uncocked the hammer and returned the pistol to her pocket. "What did you take?"

"Just a few coppers. Bloke didn't 'ave much on 'im." The

boy's eyes sparkled and his smile flashed white, except for the void created by his missing front teeth.

At what age did boys lose their teeth—seven perhaps? Or had Nicky's been prematurely removed by an unkind fist? He didn't seem as old as George was when their mother had died, when life had begun to go so terribly wrong. No, Nicky seemed so much smaller—because of his poor meals or her poor memory?

She shoved those disturbing thoughts into the dark recesses of her mind. "I really oughtn't reward such behavior. However, since in this case he deserved a bit of his own medicine..." She reached into her pocket and retrieved the remains of her lunch, now slightly squashed by her encounter with Christopher DeChambelle.

Unmindful of the puddles, she squatted to Nicky's height and offered him the bundle. He tore it open and bit off a sizable portion of the food.

"What do you say, Nicky?"

"Thank ye, mum," he mumbled around the food. He rammed the rest of the meat pie into his mouth, handed her the handkerchief and scampered into the shadows.

She watched him disappear to a destination probably even he didn't know. London was filled with such children, orphans who lived on the streets, who grew old too soon and died too young. She wanted to whisk Nicky away, but much as her heart ached for him, she had no future to offer.

Eyes stinging, she rose and shoved the napkin into her left pocket, then patted the right where her American-made stubby pocket pistol, primed and loaded, waited for her to learn the truth of her brother's final days aboard a British frigate.

The Treaty of Ghent had brought the recent conflict with England to an inconclusive end, but her private war had only begun.

Years earlier her mother had entrusted Mattie with the care

of another lad, but she had failed them both. If only she'd been a better sister, a better caretaker, a better person. Perhaps George would have grown to be a better man.

She wouldn't fail this time. She wouldn't allow this British official to discount her search for her brother's fate. And she wouldn't stop until she had taken action on whatever she learned.

She *would* win justice for her brother.

Kit took another sip from the snifter in his hand. The brandy's lackluster quality rivaled the lethargy of his mind. He had been off-kilter all evening, like a child's top with a lopsided spin.

At another table in the exclusive club, men wagered their fortunes and futures on cards, their voices boisterous with bravado and their eyes bright with belief in their own invincibility. No doubt some of them would lose their joviality before the night ended, or perhaps in the morning when they sobered enough to realize their mistake. Too late.

At least Kit knew better than to combine his recent predilection for alcohol with gambling. He stared into the drink, its rich brown hue reminding him of Miss Fraser's eyes. Regrets weighed on him, made him wish for simpler times when mistakes weren't so costly. So deadly. A man might earn another fortune, but where did one go to regain a lost soul?

"I was surprised to get your note." The familiar voice ripped through Kit's reverie. Captain Julian Thomas Robert DeChambelle, Viscount Somershurst—and Kit's older brother—stood beside the table, an imposing figure in his resplendent naval uniform and its many decorations. The chandeliers glittered on his gilded head, like the Heavens' smile of approval on the golden son.

"Good evening, Jules. How is peacetime treating you?"

"It is…an adjustment. I didn't know you were in London."

"Just arrived today." Kit gestured to a footman to bring a second glass—and a second bottle—as Julian dropped into an adjacent chair. "Drink?"

"None for me. I can't stay."

"Then I'll be brief. I have a question about your old ship."

"My ship?" The creases around Julian's frown deepened. Years of exposure to the elements had weathered his face before its time, and his eyes had hardened since Kit had last seen his brother a year ago. But then, consider how much he had changed in that time. "The last I knew, the *Impatience* moored at Portsmouth."

"I'm seeking information about an American named George Fraser. You pressed him into service on the *Impatience* three years ago."

Had Kit not been so attuned to reading others' reactions, he would have missed the slight tensing of Julian's shoulders and the subtle narrowing of his lips. "George Fraser, you say?" Even the pitch of his brother's voice rose a half step.

Kit nodded.

Julian shook his head. "Wish I could help you, Kit, but I never heard the name."

Never?

Kit wanted to believe him for the sake of their parents—and the chums he and Julian had once been as children, before school and work and war had separated them. Unfortunately, he no longer trusted his brother. He couldn't.

And yet, the disloyalty engendered by those doubts hit him surprisingly hard.

In recent years he and Julian had been compatible, if not precisely affectionate. Indeed, they scarcely knew one another anymore, Julian having joined the navy nearly two decades ago. Save for their blood ties, they might well be strangers now. However, family loyalty demanded Kit accept his brother's word, despite his senses' deduction to the contrary.

A portly gentleman, perhaps a score years or more Kit's senior, paused beside their table. He gave Kit a brief nod, then focused his attention on Julian. "Somershurst. Heard you were in London. Regretted to hear about your brother's demise. How are your parents?"

"Good evening, McKeane." Julian returned the other's greeting. "As well as one might expect. They'll be coming to London shortly."

McKeane lingered by their table a few seconds longer, as if angling for an invitation to join them. When none was forthcoming, he offered a hopeful smile. "Be certain to give Chambelston my regards."

"I'll tell my father you asked after him."

"Good. Good. Perhaps I'll see him when he arrives in town." McKeane shuffled away to join several of his contemporaries.

Julian waited until the man had passed out of earshot. "Spare me any more fathers with eligible daughters."

"A complicated position, to suddenly be so popular."

Julian was silent several moments. "Are you jealous?" Their brother Gregory's sudden death last year had promoted Julian from second son to heir apparent. Once Kit and Julian had stood shoulder to shoulder, two younger brothers in a society ruled by primogeniture, before Julian's naval service and Kit's secret life working for Alderston in France had sent them different directions. Now as the eldest surviving son, Julian stood to inherit lands, wealth, prestige and power while Kit had to make his own way on wits and talent alone. Their relationship would be forever, irrevocably altered.

"You contributed more to the family coffers than any of us. I don't begrudge you the estates."

"Good to know. Especially since you are my heir."

"Only until you marry and produce a child of your own." Kit leaned back in the chair and smirked. "I understand Mc-Keane could assist you with procuring a bride."

"Thank you, no." Julian shuddered. "If you have nothing else to ask, I am expected elsewhere."

His words, another reminder of the distance between them, brought Kit back to his original purpose. "This American, George Fraser—his sister is in London. If you would meet with her—"

"Wish I could, but I have other plans."

"I meant—"

But Julian shoved his chair from the table and jumped to his feet, leaving Kit only a view of his escaping back. And a host of questions about his brother's strange reticence. Kit had lived with secrets for too long not to recognize obstruction.

Chapter Two

The London streets should have been less frightening by day than at night. However, the morning drizzle exacerbated the smoke stench, and the fog created a peculiar feeling of isolation.

Mattie unfurled her umbrella and peeked over her shoulder. The inn's door remained closed. The drunken tars who frequented it at night had staggered to their beds to sleep off the cheap ale and women.

A shadow streaked from a crevice between the buildings and brushed against her coat.

Her breath locked in her chest. She shoved her hand into her pocket and whirled to face the threat behind her. Her umbrella bounced against the cobblestones.

"'Morning, Mattie." Nicky materialized out of the fog. His eyes glimmered with welcome and the undisguised desire for approval.

"Oh, Nicky," she gasped his name on the breath that swooshed from her lungs. "You startled me." She uncurled her fingers from the pistol. Her heart still thudded against her ribs as she accepted the fallen umbrella from his outstretched hand.

"Sorry to scare ye, Mattie."

"I'm a little skittish this morning."

Nicky fell into step beside her, under her umbrella. "That Stumpy bloke bothering ye again?"

"Not since last night." She had arrived at the Captain's Quarters after the patrons had begun to fill the tap room. Being a young female in a roomful of sailors accounted for only half her problem. Sentiment against Americans ran strong among those English mariners whose pride and flesh had been put to rout by the upstart American Navy, especially now that peacetime had cast so many adrift into London's slums.

"I'm afeared for ye, Mattie."

"He's all bravado and no bravery." Still, she had forgone the evening meal and barricaded herself in her room rather than endure Stumpy's vulgarities about her sex and citizenship. As with her father, drink intensified the malice on Stumpy's tongue.

"Ye don't belong 'ere, Mattie."

She didn't belong anywhere. Not anymore.

They paused at the corner near another squalid but quiet tavern. She squatted until she could look directly into Nicky's soft brown eyes, nearly hidden under the wet, shaggy hair that fell over his face. "You don't belong here, either, Nicky."

"I got no other life to go to, mum. Ye do. Go 'ome, Mattie, back to America."

His hand reached toward her, as if to touch. She held her breath, but he backed away. She snatched the bundle from her pocket. "Toast?"

"Thanks." The too-long sleeves of his green coat, illegally requisitioned from another's clothesline, slipped back to expose hands even dirtier than his face. He crammed the toast into his mouth in a single bite, then wiped the crumbs from his face with one of those sleeves. "Got some news for ye last night."

"News?" Anticipation tingled at the nape of her neck.

"I 'eard there was a bloke at the Duck and Dog that used to be on the ship yer looking for."

At last! "Can you arrange for me to meet him?"

Nicky cocked his head and studied her with eyes far too old for his face. "I'd rather ye tell me what ye want to ask, and let me meet 'im."

"No, I need to do it, Nicky."

As he opened his mouth to protest, a lumbering farmer's cart splashed into a puddle. She hauled the boy close to avoid a dousing.

Nicky jerked from her hold. His wide eyes shimmered with longing and uncertainty as he paused two steps away. "I 'ave to go. I'll talk to 'im."

Mattie shuddered to think what had caused this lonely boy who so wanted friendship and approval to so fear contact. Her heart ached to show him love and kindness. Instead, she rose. "Don't get into trouble."

"Ye, too, Mattie. Be careful." Within seconds he had disappeared, swallowed by the fog.

Her heavy shoes thumped in rhythm with her heavy heart until at last the Admiralty rose before her. Her target was within range, but her heart and conscience conspired to create misgivings. She squashed her feelings of compassion and tried to conjure her brother's image, but it transformed into Nicky's face.

She sighed and reordered her scrambled emotions, then entered the building.

"I'm here to see Mr. DeChambelle."

The same clerk wrenched his attention from the papers on his desk. "Indeed, miss."

He disappeared through the nearby door and the murmur of his voice, followed by the deeper tones of Mr. DeChambelle's, drifted to Mattie on the room's dank air.

"You may go in," the clerk announced scant moments later.

Mr. DeChambelle stepped from behind his desk. The gray skies reflected on tawny hair that already looked finger-raked. The insubordinate lock fell farther than at her prior visit and brushed a perfectly arched, light brown brow. "Miss Fraser. May I take your coat?" he asked in his clipped, aristocratic speech, so different from the coarse accents and frequent vulgarities one heard along London's docks.

Though the room was of a size, perhaps larger even than the outer office, it felt suddenly as suffocatingly close as August in Washington. "No, thank you." Her voice cracked.

"Well, then, let us proceed." He positioned his hand on her back and steered her toward the empty chair. She started at his touch, just like Nicky moments earlier—and her umbrella crashed to the floor again.

She dropped onto the chair. While Mr. DeChambelle crossed to the other side of his desk she arranged that wretched umbrella under her seat, then clenched her hands together in her lap.

He settled back in his chair, and with that action the room grew larger. "I spoke to the recent captain of the *Impatience*."

"The captain is here? In London?" The *Impatience* wasn't—the sailors residing at the Captain's Quarters had assured her the ship was berthed in Portsmouth.

Mr. DeChambelle's gaze bored through the thick screen of his spectacles. Sympathy, concern, even pity infused the brilliant blue depths. "I am afraid he has no recollection of your brother."

So, they were going to lie to her. Had she expected less? "But I know George was on that ship. He wrote me a letter."

"Please, Miss Fraser. I am not saying your brother was never aboard the ship—only that the captain doesn't remember him. A fully manned frigate has hundreds of men. Factor in those who must be replaced for...various reasons, and a typical captain commands thousands of men over his career. It may be that your brother was not on the *Impatience* long enough to create an impression."

The greasy eggs and toast—customary morning fare at the Captain's Quarters—churned in Mattie's stomach and surged to her throat. "You are suggesting my brother may have died shortly after his impressment."

"I fear that is the most likely scenario. We have been at war these many years, and the *Impatience* was involved in numerous engagements."

"But the letter—"

"Probably given to someone else—perhaps one of the other men taken from the *Constance*. I'm sorry, Miss Fraser. I wish I could offer you more hope."

Strange how his words—not unexpected—affected her. Or perhaps not, given that with his condolences the last potential for reconciliation, her remaining chance to restore her family died. "I...thank you." The words hitched in her throat. "May I speak to the captain?"

"He declined to be present at this meeting."

"An extraordinary example of English courage."

This Englishman leaned back in the chair and hefted a paperweight from the desk. His gaze never met hers as his long, well-formed fingers toyed with the object. "Miss Fraser, I agree that you have a right to know your brother's fate. An American of undisputed citizenship on one of our ships was inexcusable. Such a lapse should never have happened."

But it had. Simple misfortune, or had the *Constance*'s captain seized upon a way to simultaneously rid his ship of an American troublemaker and an English threat by surrendering George to the *Impatience?* She clenched her jaw, unwilling to voice her disloyal suspicions.

"We must consider other channels to discover your brother's fate."

"Such as?"

"You mentioned a letter. Did it contain any useful information? Perhaps the names of other crew members or bunkmates?"

"Not exactly. Would you like to read it?"

"You have it here?"

"Yes." Mattie extracted the oft perused note from her reticule and passed him the page.

"'My dearest sister,'" Mr. DeChambelle read aloud.

"I pray this note finds you in good health. My life at sea has taken a peculiar turn, and I now find myself aboard an English vessel, the *Impatience*. The food is as bad as I'd feared, but I have made a few friends and collected a few trinkets I hope to someday share with you. I miss you and Papa and even my cramped quarters above the store, which I have come to realize were actually quite spacious compared to a ship. If I do not return, I pray you will forgive me the troubles I caused you and look back on the good times with fondness. Affectionately, your brother, George."

Her brother's words in that unfamiliar speech caused a ripple of disquiet to skip along Mattie's spine. "He mentioned some friends."

"But not by name, unfortunately." Mr. DeChambelle refolded the paper and returned it to her. "But we have confirmation that he knew several others aboard the *Impatience*, though where they might be now is difficult to guess. I shall continue to make inquiries, both here and in Portsmouth. In view of the limited chance of success and the extended amount of time such an investigation will involve, I suggest you return to America."

"America?" Not without achieving her objective.

"I will write you when I have a confirmation, one way or the other." He grabbed a paper from the corner of his desk, then paused, his lips swagging to a frown as he snatched the quill and dipped it into the inkwell. "How can I contact you in America?"

"I sold my house in Washington."

The quill fell, spattering ink across the desk and dappling his cravat with black specks. Mr. DeChambelle leaned back in the chair and folded his arms across his chest. The movement stretched his coat over his arms, and the bulges under his sleeves suggested a strength one would be foolish to discount. What other secrets lurked behind that facade? "You no longer have a home in America?"

"I used the money to finance my journey to London."

"What about your parents or other relatives?"

Mattie averted her gaze to the window. The clouds had parted and a few scattered patches of blue peeked between them, filling the skies with a brightness that mocked her loss. "No."

"I see. Then let me give you my address." He seized the quill again along with a clean sheet of paper. As his hand slashed across the foolscap, a few valiant rays of sunshine pierced the gray clouds and gritty window to reflect on his spectacle lenses. "Write me once you return to America, and I will make you aware of any progress I have made."

He shook off the sand and slid the paper across the desk, his fingers brushing hers as she plucked it from the surface. She folded the note without examining it, and tucked both pages in her reticule. Unlike her brother's last words, Mr. De-Chambelle's address would undoubtedly remain out of sight and out of mind while she conducted her own investigation. The captain was here in London. She would find him.

She slid her hand into her pocket where her fingers kissed the pistol. "You didn't tell me the name of the *Impatience*'s captain."

"Viscount Somershurst."

A viscount?

"Now, if I may see you to better lodgings until—"

"No. I shall be fine where I am."

His stare measured her. "Miss Fraser, as I mentioned, the inns near the docks are inhabited by ruffians of the worst sort. For one such as you they are quite dangerous."

And quite where she was most likely to acquire useful information. "I have fended for myself for some time now, ever since my brother disappeared. I will be fine." Despite those regular insults from the sailor who had lost his arm to an American cannonball on Lake Champlain. Thoughts of Stumpy's bitterness to all things American once again raised the question that had plagued her for three years. "You said the *Impatience* was involved in numerous engagements. Where did the ship operate?"

Mr. DeChambelle sighed, but ceased his futile protests. "If you are worried your brother was forced into a confrontation with fellow Americans, let me assure you the ship served along the coast of France during much of the war."

She managed a weak smile. At least George hadn't met his death at the hands of his own countrymen.

"Indeed, due to the *Impatience*'s proximity to Ghent last winter, she was charged with the delivery of the treaty to America. It was quite an honor for her captain and crew."

A shame George hadn't lived to share that *honor*.

Mr. DeChambelle flattened his hands on the desk and stood. "Unless you have other questions?"

"Not at this time." She rose and ceded him a curt nod, then

whirled and marched out of the office. Her coat billowed with the movement, and the pistol in her pocket whacked her leg.

Kit slid open his desk drawer and snagged a paper. He clenched it in his hand for several long moments while he stared out the grimy window at blue autumn skies. Finally, he dragged in a deep breath and unfolded the stained, creased parchment. Drew's untidy scrawl covered the page, but Kit's attention focused on one name—the same name he'd so recently heard from Miss Fraser's lips.

George Fraser.

The note begged Kit to use his contacts to learn the fate of the American sailor, brother to a lady Drew had encountered during the campaign.

Dated 1 September 1814, the letter cut off in mid-sentence with no further particulars about the request or details of George Fraser's service. Kit leaned back, pondering what great event had interrupted his friend before he finished. A battle? Drew's death?

What had been the nature of Drew's relationship with Miss Fraser? A mere two days' acquaintance forged in fire? Kit sensed something amiss in her story. A lie? An omission? He glanced at the empty chair opposite his desk as he—

Froze. A dark and peculiarly shaped object on the floor captured his attention. Every muscle in his body tensed, then relaxed when he identified the article as nothing more threatening than Miss Fraser's umbrella, overlooked in the luxury of the clearing skies. He abandoned Drew's letter, skirted the desk and knelt to retrieve the object, not at all surprised by its questionable worth.

Heels clicked against the floor in a familiar tattoo. Kit glanced over his shoulder at a pair of riding boots, their black sheen dulled by the mud of a hard ride. His gaze flickered up over the nondescript coat to the equally unremarkable face.

An advantage in their line of work that let one assume many a disguise.

William Alderston latched the door shut. "Where have you been, DeChambelle? I've had men searching the countryside for you."

"So I heard, though I cannot imagine why." Kit straightened, Miss Fraser's umbrella still in hand. "As I keep reminding everyone, the war is over."

"Not completely, it seems. I understand a young woman called upon you." Alderston leaned against the door frame and folded his arms across his chest. "An American."

Kit didn't bother to question the man's sources. Alderston knew everything that happened in London—even all of England and the continent, too—most often before it happened. Information was, after all, his profession and his passion. "Miss Martha Fraser, from Washington. She came to inquire after her brother, a sailor pressed into service on the *Impatience*. I spoke to Julian last night, but he has no recollection of the man or his fate."

"Do you believe him?"

Kit strove to imbue his voice and features with a lightness he didn't feel. "I fail to understand how that—"

"Do you believe him?" Alderston's pale eyes blazed with patriotic intensity as he repeated the question, his stare piercing through Kit's pretense.

"Miss Fraser makes a compelling argument for her allegation. The letter purported to be from her brother—"

"A letter? Do you know when it was written? What it says?"

"Nothing out of the ordinary, only that he missed her and hoped she would remember him fondly if he failed to return home." Kit braced a hand against the desk as he studied Alderston's features—the tight line of his jaw, the shadows of anxiety not quite hidden behind the fierceness of his gaze.

"Why the peculiar interest in an American nonentity—when our war with them ended nearly a year ago?"

Alderston paced to the window and stared at the tableau outside. "Your brother lied. He did indeed know George Fraser—the man stole a paper while on board the *Impatience*. A paper whose very existence was a secret—*should* have been a secret—to all but four men."

"When was this?"

"February."

When the *Impatience* delivered the treaty to New York. "And where is this paper now?"

"We don't know." Alderston whirled around to face him, head cocked to one side. "But I find it most fascinating that Miss Fraser has come to London. To you. How many Americans would venture so far, particularly unmarried females traveling alone, unless the reason was…compelling?"

"Perhaps Miss Fraser considers her brother just such a significant cause. She asked a mutual friend to investigate his fate last year." Kit slid Drew's note across the desk. "He wrote me—I suspect due to the nature of my relationship to Julian. I hardly see how her inquiries begun so long ago could involve an event from February."

"You seem quite taken with the young lady." Alderston seized the unfinished letter and skimmed the contents. "Be careful, DeChambelle."

The not-so-subtle reminder of his folly lanced straight into Kit's stomach. He had allowed a pretty face to dupe him, and while he had unmasked the traitor selling secrets to the French, the victory had come with a price.

The death of an innocent woman. And Kit's soul.

Kit swallowed, but the ever-present awareness of failure remained in his throat. "I am only suggesting that Miss Fraser's arrival in London may be unrelated to her brother's actions on the *Impatience*."

"Be that as it may, as she has initiated contact with you, we intend to use this connection to learn what she knows— or what she might discover."

"What, precisely, was this…stolen paper?"

"Your brother's orders concerning the treaty's delivery."

"He was to present the treaty to the Americans for ratification."

"The orders were a bit more…complicated than that."

"Rumors abounded last winter that the American president might reject ratification and demand further concessions."

"I will only say there are delicate issues involved that we do not want to see made public. And neither would your brother." Alderston tossed Drew's note back onto the desk. "You will find those orders and give them to me, and then you will immediately forget everything you know about them. Had your brother been anyone other than Chambelston's heir, he would have been tried for treason."

The frothing in Kit's belly now surged to his throat.

Treason.

No wonder Julian was so closemouthed last night. Kit fought to keep his face impassive though his mind whirled with the implications. "The crown couldn't try him for treason without admitting to the contents of those orders." Contents Alderston seemed reluctant to share even with him.

"Your brother's saving grace. So long as the orders remain missing, his claim that he destroyed them upon arrival in New York stands—though I know better. But should they resurface, no power in England will save him."

"You cannot ask this of me. Julian is my brother."

"And that is precisely why I know you will do whatever you must. I suggest you situate Miss Fraser in the path of those most likely to get us that paper. It is to Julian's benefit. To your family's benefit." Alderston spun and jerked open the door.

"Wait. George Fraser—"

"Dead. May his secret die with him—once I have that paper."

Kit stared at the door as it banged shut behind his old mentor, the man who now ordered Kit to use another woman—an innocent woman?—to further his ends.

He couldn't.

He had to, if only to prove Julian innocent. Not only for Julian, but for his mother's welfare. For his sister's future. Was there enough drink in the world to wash away his guilt should this situation go terribly wrong?

His fingers curled, drawing his attention to the object still in his left hand. As he stared at the black oilcloth, an idea formed in his mind. Miss Fraser's umbrella provided him the perfect excuse for an unexpected visit. He reached for her London address, which he had left...

Where? Drew's letter perched amid the clutter of his desk, but a quick search failed to produce his notes from yesterday. He had been so certain he had left them on the corner of the desk.

No matter. Kit quite remembered her questionable address—the Captain's Quarters—no doubt chosen for its economy, if one were to judge by the commonplace quality of Miss Fraser's coat. He tugged the door open. "Baxter, find me clothing suitable for a venture to the docks—perhaps a coat and shoes of more subdued color and quality. I shall return for them within the hour." No need to call attention to himself before he understood the situation. People tended to be more forthcoming with those of like station, a human trait he'd exploited to his advantage during his decade traveling about France.

"Very good, sir."

Outside the Admiralty's tall doors, Kit squinted against the cheery autumn sunshine that sparkled on the wet cobblestones and mocked his mood.

"DeChambelle." A rear admiral in full regalia—the row of gold lace on his jacket cuff winking in the light—greeted him before Kit could escape to Mayfair. "Sorry to have missed Chambelston the last time he was in town."

"I believe he intends to return soon. I will tell Father you asked after him."

"Do that. And give my regards to your brother." The admiral marched to the entrance.

His brother.

Anger and fear frothed in his gut as Kit pointed his feet toward Mayfair. A warm breeze wafted across his cheek and rippled on the surface of a lingering puddle.

Lured outside by the blue skies, a nurse escorted her young charges—a demure girl and two rambunctious boys—to a nearby park before winter's chill drove them indoors until spring. Their antics tugged Kit into the past, to a time before school and the navy and war had separated Julian from him— forever, he now feared. Once they had chased squirrels across the lawns, fought imaginary pirates by the pond, stood together against their older brother and sisters.

And now that same brother sought to obstruct Kit's investigation.

At Piccadilly, a carriage bearing a ducal crest splashed through a rut and sprayed Kit's coat. He brushed water drops from his sleeve and tried to focus his thoughts, but not even the warm sun could melt his suspicions as he pounded on the door of Julian's townhouse.

"Is my brother home?" Kit strode past the butler.

"His lordship is in a private meeting. Would you care to wait?"

Muted voices drifted to the foyer. Kit did not particularly care if Julian were entertaining a fellow officer, a widow of dubious reputation, or the Prince Regent himself. He thrust his hat at the butler. "No."

"Sir—"

"I shall announce myself." He pivoted and marched down the hall. His shoes thumped against the floor in tempo with the anger pulsing through his veins.

Stale cheroot odors caught in his throat as he paused before the library's shut door.

"No!" Julian's curses thundered to the hallway. "I will have the blunt tomorrow."

Debts? Kit paused, fingers curled around the knob. True, the end of the war idled many an officer and reduced him to half pay, but as a frigate captain Julian had collected a fortune in prize money. Or so Kit had always assumed.

Another voice—words muffled by the heavy wood but with tones low, calm, and male—drifted into the hallway.

Kit twisted the knob and nudged the door.

"Ah, Christopher." Not an irate creditor. Neville Fitzgerald smiled and greeted him with smooth charm. No longer in British naval uniform, Julian's former first lieutenant flaunted an elegant coat above fitted breeches.

"Kit!" The look Julian hurled at him embodied little warmth despite his flushed face and fiery eyes. He radiated tension, anger, and…fear? The room crackled with it despite the chilly dampness.

"Aren't you going to offer me a chair?" Kit's gaze darted from Fitzgerald's seated form to Julian's erect one pacing before the empty fireplace. The two had served together since they were midshipmen, and their relationship, so far as Kit knew, was underscored by professional respect and personal regard.

So what didn't he know?

His gaze slipped to Fitzgerald's bland smile, then back to his brother.

"Two visits within as many days." Julian had once again adopted his imperturbable mask, yet shunned to offer Kit a seat in the other, empty wingback. "To what do I owe this great honor?"

"Your reticence. I came to demand some answers. The woman I spoke of last evening has a letter purportedly from her brother, and he mentions the *Impatience* by name."

Julian paused before the barren mantel and arched a brow. "She must be a singularly fine-looking woman."

Kit clenched his jaw but ignored the subtle insult in Julian's remark. He was not doing this for her—he was involved to protect *Julian*. "You could meet her and judge for yourself." Kit folded his arms across his chest and leaned against the door post as he fixed a pointed stare at his brother.

"Not interested." Julian's lips flattened as he looked away.

More ugly suspicions invaded Kit's mind. He glanced once again at Neville Fitzgerald. It was the first officer's responsibility to procure sailors—by whatever means necessary—and to complete the mission in the event of the captain's incapacity. How much did he know about George Fraser? And the orders? "Perhaps you can help me, Lieutenant. I met a woman, an American, who claims her brother was impressed onto the *Impatience*."

"Kit, I told you we never had such a man," Julian interrupted.

"No, you told me you 'never heard the name before.'" Kit kept his focus on Fitzgerald as he dissected that man's response, but the former officer's controlled expression revealed nothing. When his accusation aroused no response, Kit continued, "You were her first lieutenant. Do you recall an American seaman named George Fraser? I agreed to help Miss Fraser learn his fate."

"George Fraser?" Fitzgerald shook his head. "No, sorry, Christopher. I didn't press any American citizens."

Kit sensed the lie in the too-mild tone. "But you did stop American ships."

"Of course, Kit," Julian interrupted again. "We were at war. We boarded dozens of ships."

Kit spun around and glared at his brother, his shoe beating a challenge against the floor. "Then meet with Miss Fraser and give her your answer."

"Perhaps…when I have more time."

An officer on half pay with more leisure than funds?

Fitzgerald rose to his feet. "I have other business to attend to, Somershurst," he said as he sidled towards the door. "Do remember what we discussed earlier. I await your response."

"Of course." Julian smiled despite the implicit threat lacing the other man's words.

Satisfaction gleamed in Fitzgerald's eyes, then he whirled and strode into the hall with steps more akin to an infantry sergeant's march than a mariner's swagger.

"What was that about, Jules?"

"What?"

"Fitzgerald. You said something strange just before I opened the door."

The flush deserted Julian's face, leaving it a green that clashed with his coat. "Oh, I lost some blunt to him at cards."

"Cards?" Kit almost believed him. "How could you be such a nodcock?"

"It was no great amount."

"If that is true, then why is Fitzgerald so anxious to collect his winnings?"

"My affairs do not concern you, Kit. You aren't my mother

to lecture me about my vices." His insolence echoed Kit's of two days prior.

"Maman has grief enough without you adding to it." Even as the words shot from his mouth, Kit wasn't certain whether he spoke of Julian or himself.

Julian crossed to the desk and scooped up a long-neglected book. He flipped through the pages in an infuriating display of bad manners, yet the hands that held the dusty book trembled. "If you are quite finished?"

No, Kit was not.

But obviously he couldn't trust Julian to help absolve himself.

Chapter Three

An hour later, Kit once again slipped out of the Admiralty and pulled the floppy brim of an old felt hat low over his brow. A fleet of senior officers—including his admiral friend of that morning—sailed past him without deigning more than a flicker of a glance in his direction. Kit smothered a chuckle and hailed a hackney with the requisite distinctive markings. The driver pulled his plodding horse to a stop.

"The docks."

Turner muttered something unintelligible under his breath, but obligingly prodded his horse into a shuffle and steered the conveyance in the chosen direction. With the animal's every step, the view deteriorated and the stench heightened. Drunken sailors—idled by the war's end—slept in the streets. Slovenly women loitered on the rotted stoops of dilapidated buildings while broken window panes watched them from above.

The hackney passed a ramshackle structure with a faded sign sporting a handsome man o' the sea. Below, a crudely painted caption indeed proclaimed the enterprise to be the Captain's Quarters.

Kit knocked on the cab. "Stop."

Turner reined the horse to a halt. The narrow road required him to park in the middle of the street.

"Wait for me." Kit leaped to the ground.

"A few minutes only, then I'll leave whether ye are 'ere or not."

"No ye won't."

The door of the building gaped wide, a ragged, dark-haired urchin of indeterminate age peering through the entrance. Kit walked up behind him. Despite his quiet steps, the boy slunk out of reach and stared at him with wary eyes.

"I want ye out." The strident tones blasted out of the building and startled the hackney's swayback horse out of its doze.

Ignoring the curious waif, Kit ducked under the low doorway.

"I paid through the end of the week." Ice edged Miss Fraser's soft, slow speech, and anger colored her cheeks a dusky peach that complemented her fiery hair.

The dank, dark room was devoid of occupants save Miss Fraser and another woman, but Kit could well imagine what kind of company would frequent this place come nightfall. Their odor lingered despite their absence by day.

Annoyance at Miss Fraser's female obstinacy bubbled in his gut.

"Ye ken 'ave your money. I want ye gone."

"How inconvenient. I need my room."

"Well ye can't—"

"Miss Fraser," Kit interrupted.

The women started, guarded gazes flicking in his direction. The three of them stilled for several moments, like figures in a wax museum.

"Miss Fraser?" he repeated. He waited additional seconds for recognition to replace the confusion in her eyes. Brows the same remarkable shade as her hair drew together in a frown as her gaze registered his changed attire.

"Mr. DeChambelle. I don't suppose you have information for me so soon." Despite the coldness still infusing her tones, her husky drawl sliding over the syllables of his name filled him with…foreboding? danger? longing?

He held out the umbrella. "Ye left this." His finely tuned hearing—and years of practice—allowed him to slip into local dialect as easily as he had adjusted his attire.

"Thank you." She accepted the object and waited for him to depart.

His gaze flickered to the stone-faced woman who watched them, fists braced on her hips. "A problem?"

A spark of suspicion flashed in Miss Fraser's eyes, then she shrugged. "It seems I am without a room for the night."

How convenient for him. Too convenient. Kit would have smiled had his instincts not produced ugly suspicions about the nature of Miss Fraser's sudden eviction. Who would want Miss Fraser at his mercy?

None but the all-knowing Alderston.

An explanation, perhaps, for the paper missing from his desk?

Kit glanced about the unappealing room lest she detect the speculation in his eyes. Weak sunlight shone through cracked window panes and reflected on the ale spills that splotched the floor. Watermarks stained the warped walls and hinted as to the condition of the rooms above. He arched a single brow at the old woman who shifted her bulk from one foot to the other. "Not much loss, eh?"

For a moment, amusement softened Miss Fraser's face, then her expression resumed its customary aloofness. "I can take care of the matter."

"Get yer belongings."

Distrust swept across her features. "That's—"

"Common sense, unless ye intend to leave them behind."

Resolute brown eyes clashed with his, sparking a bit of life into his emptiness. She shoved a hand in her coat and stared at him before aiming her fire at the innkeeper. "I expect you to refund my money."

She pivoted and marched from the common room with the precision of the Foot Guards.

Kit sidled toward the innkeeper, intent upon discovering whom—

A man's heavy tread echoed against the stoop. "Ale, Polly!" The already inebriated customer lurched into the room accompanied by the stench of cheap rum, powerful enough to intoxicate the hardiest sailor. An empty sleeve brushed the man's corpulent waist with his tremors.

The proprietress pointed to the open door. "Ye 'aven't paid me from this morning, Stumpy."

"Got me some funds now." Stumpy jingled his coins, then his watery eyes focused on Kit. "'Ere now, told ye I'd take care of it."

Kit retreated a step. A wisp of unease, of premonition, curled through him at this forewarning of life as a slave to drink. "I'm sure ye 'ave."

Stumpy swayed again, his bloodshot, red-rimmed eyes straining to focus. "Aw, 'e ain't the same bloke. See that, Polly? Now, ye gots me ale?"

Thunk. The wall reverberated from the *thwack* of a hard, heavy object, then Miss Fraser's slender form appeared on the steps, a bag in each hand. Her carriage had lost its customary poise, and as she drew closer Kit observed uncharacteristic apprehension shadowing her eyes.

"Well, if it ain't our American cousin," Stumpy slurred, a sneer curling his puffy lips. Malice emanated from his every pore with as much intensity as the rum fumes.

Kit strode to her side and plucked a bag from her grasp.

He tugged on the other one, but she refused to yield it. "Are there any more?"

Her eyes smoldered as she turned them on the innkeeper. "I *think* this is everything. At least, it's everything I could find in my room."

The innkeeper scowled but produced the requisite refund. At Stumpy's snicker, Miss Fraser whirled to face him.

Kit fastened his hand against the small of her back and nudged her away before she responded with a provocative comment. Warmth seeped through the shabby coat and into his palm. As he propelled her out of the gloom, he whispered, "Ignore him. He's too drunk to know his name." He slammed the door behind them.

"Mattie?" The lad who'd lingered by the door scooted towards her.

"I have to leave, Nicky."

"I 'eard." The boy jutted his narrow chin. "Glad for ye, too, I is."

Nicky did not look happy for himself though. He swallowed twice, and his lower lip trembled. Kit tried to guess his age. Six? Seven? The boy's stained, oversize coat and Kit's limited experience with children hampered his judgment.

The inn door flew open and smashed against the wall. The drunken sailor staggered into the boy, his bulk knocking the child to the ground.

"Finally realized ye ain't wanted 'ere, Yank?" He spat at the ground, narrowly missing Miss Fraser's foot. "And don't come back, neither."

His single, filthy fist reached for Miss Fraser's coat, but as his fingers closed over her sleeve, Kit launched himself at the man, his spectacles flying off his face for the second time in as many days. Stumpy's extra weight was no match for surprise, anger and sobriety. The drunk crashed against the side of the building with force enough to crack the rotted timbers.

Kit coiled Stumpy's shirt collar around his fist and pinned the man against the wall. "If I catch you disturbing women or children again, I will see you too impaired to drink." He unthreaded his fingers from the tattered shirt, and Stumpy slumped to the ground.

While the wheezing man pushed himself to his knees and slunk away, Kit retrieved his spectacles and the bag he'd dropped, tossing Miss Fraser's luggage to the hackney's still-waiting driver. Her questioning gaze burned through his back, but when he turned to face her, she had crouched down to comfort the boy.

"Nicky?"

Already a welt formed on the boy's forehead, visible through his unkempt hair. "Ain't nothing." The lad stiffened as her arms wrapped around him, then he melted against her.

She burrowed her face against his neck and stroked his coat with graceful, soothing fingers. Whereas before Kit had found her admirably daring and uncomfortably direct, now he witnessed a new aspect of her character, that of kindness and concern. The sun reflected on the two heads, so dissimilar—one as dark as ebony and rank as a cesspool, the other shiny as polished copper and piquant as spring. Yet Kit sensed a camaraderie of spirit that excluded him.

He shoved the thought away as he hefted her other bag and passed it to the driver. "Miss Fraser, we must leave before yer friend discovers a couple of comrades and another bottle of courage. Unless ye would rather I found ye a ship bound for America?"

She shoved a hand into her pocket, a steel core of resolution glittering in her eyes. "I came to discover my brother's fate, and I will not leave until I've achieved satisfaction."

* * *

Dismay twisted Mattie's stomach as Mr. DeChambelle spoke to the driver. The vehicle dipped as he ascended the cab, then rocked with more violence when the driver prodded the dozing horse into action. "Where are we going, if I may be so bold as to inquire?"

"Boldness, Miss Fraser, is a feature of yours I have rather come to expect."

"Whereas I have come to expect evasion from you. Where do you take me?"

"To lodge with a friend." He shoved his spectacles over his face again, causing those disturbing eyes to retreat behind the glass. For one moment, the movement revealed the strength beneath the oh-so-ordinary brown coat before its ill cut once again concealed his form.

"A friend?" Mattie looked from the hackney's stained upholstery to the charming neighborhood beyond the window. Already the narrow alleys and shabby buildings had transformed to wider streets and modest shops. Young misses and their chaperones strolled ahead of package-laden maids while a gentleman escorted a brazenly dressed woman into a milliner's establishment.

And where did she fit into this tableau?

She glanced at the rear-facing seat. Knowing eyes stared back at her, into her mind. Was that amusement sparking in their blue depths? She'd seen enough of his countrymen not to trust a congenial manner.

And this man warranted particular caution after that display of strength back at the Captain's Quarters. Obviously Mr. DeChambelle was no ordinary clerk. So exactly what was he?

She slipped her hand into her coat pocket. The pistol barrel welcomed her fingers and provided her a measure of security. "I would prefer another inn."

He shook his head. His hair fluttered with the movement and fell across his brow, but even that bit of boyishness did not mitigate the marked implacability of his unyielding stare. "No."

"But I—"

"Need a place to stay that is warm, dry, and safe. The Harri—"

"Safe? But surely Stumpy won't have the assets or ambition to follow me elsewhere."

"Miss Fraser, you are a woman alone. I fear you will encounter others of Stumpy's ilk. The Harrisons are completely respectable. You will find the accommodations tolerable, the company congenial and the food excellent." He crossed his arms and stretched long legs out in front of him. His foot brushed her skirt.

She stared at the scuffs that littered his worn shoes. Not the same apparel he'd worn earlier. Why the change? And exactly how had he arrived so precipitously to her rescue? She swallowed and sidled closer to the hackney door. "The Harrisons?"

"Lawrence Harrison, er, works for me."

"I can't impose on strangers."

"Mrs. Harrison is a fine Christian woman. She won't turn you away."

"No indeed, as a 'fine Christian' she will feel obliged to assist the poor American." Mattie had experienced her fill of Christian charity—"Lady Bountifuls" who swooped in after her mother's death with a token meal for the motherless children and a self-congratulatory smile for their own beneficence. And then after a week of good works, they'd gone back to their lives, leaving her eight-year-old self to struggle along as best she could.

"The Harrisons would never consider a guest an obligation." He straightened and reached forward to brush the hand that rested on her lap. Shock jolted through her, supplanting her indignation with confusion.

His sympathetic caress burned through her skin, through her resentment. But was it really sympathy? Mattie wrenched her hand away before misgivings tempered her determination. He withdrew and leaned against the squabs again, eyeing her form as if he could peer through the bulky coat.

She shifted under his scrutiny, for once too warm in the heavy wool despite the damp chill. She stroked the cool barrel of her pistol and forced her mind to the innkeeper's bizarre behavior.

For what reason would a woman in such straits evict a *paying* customer?

Had she been the recipient of threats from Stumpy and his like? No, the paper Mattie had found in her room expressed too much sophistication to have originated with the likes of an illiterate sailor.

The horse plodded to a stop before a tenement squashed between two other structures of similar modesty. A young boy, smaller even than Nicky, observed their arrival through wide blue eyes, then dashed into the building.

"Shall we?" Mr. DeChambelle jumped from the vehicle and extended his hand. "If you don't feel comfortable with my friends, I will find an inn for you. But meet them before you decide."

She hesitated, then placed her palm against his. Strong, warm fingers encased hers, holding them fast. As soon as her feet reached the ground, she tugged her hand away and wiped it surreptitiously on the back of her coat as if she could scrape away her perturbation. The driver tossed her bags to Mr. De-Chambelle, who set them down and searched for the fare.

His eyes glittered like ice as he patted his coat.

"Gov'na?" The hackney driver waited.

The lines around Mr. DeChambelle's mouth tightened. "Ah…" He reached inside the coat again.

Mattie stifled a giggle. That imp. She had a few things to say to Nicky if they met again. "I'll pay the fare." She extracted several English coins from the dwindling collection in her reticule.

"Thank ye, miss." The driver glared at Mr. DeChambelle.

"Yes, thank you, Miss Fraser. I fear a pickpocket lifted my purse."

"I've heard London is a dangerous place, filled not only with drunken sailors but also thieves and cutthroats."

"Indeed. I fail to understand, though," he continued as he hefted her bags with a single hand, "how this particular thief missed your reticule."

She coughed and cleared her throat. "Perhaps he assumed your purse would provide the greater bounty."

The tenement door squeaked open to reveal a short woman with a wide smile and wider belly. Even her eyes were wide, their blue depths conveying trepidation as she offered a nervous curtsey. "M-Mr. DeChambelle? Is something wrong? Is Lawrie…?"

"He's fine, so far as I know. I came to request a favor."

A frown furrowed her brow. "A favor?"

"This is Miss Fraser. From America. May we come in?"

"Oh, why, ah…yes, of course."

She stepped back from the doorway and gestured to the dim interior.

Mattie's misgivings scratched in her stomach. She seized Mr. DeChambelle's sleeve before he could follow. "You can't ask this of her. It is too much."

"If it will ease your mind, I'll see the Harrisons receive some remuneration for their troubles. After all, you are here to put right our government's error." He shook loose from her grasp and followed the other woman inside.

For several more awkward seconds, Mattie lingered on the stoop. But with her belongings already inside, she shrugged and joined the others.

The tang of stale bacon fat and wet wool hung in the air. Clothes in an assortment of sizes dangled from the rope that stretched the length of the room. Children in sizes corresponding to the laundry bounced about the guests with such a flurry of activity so as to make counting them difficult if not impossible. Mattie ducked under several small stockings and joined the other two adults by the stove.

"Where is Harrison today?" Mr. DeChambelle was asking Mattie's potential hostess.

"At the docks, unloading a ship."

"Do you know which ship?"

"The *Laughing Mary,* I believe." Her mouth softened as she spotted Mattie draw closer. "Good morning, Miss Fraser. I am sorry to learn of your difficulties. Of course we would be delighted to have you as our guest."

"All is good, Miss Fraser." Mr. DeChambelle reached down and patted the top of a tow-headed toddler who was tugging on his coat. "Not today, Peter. I can't stay."

The lad's lower lip began to curl. "Pwease?"

"Very well. But only to the door." A smile—the first of Mattie's observation—flashed across Kit's countenance. He crouched low to the floor and assisted the lad onto his back. As he rose, he focused those startlingly blue eyes on Mattie. "I'll continue my investigation tomorrow."

"I want to come with you."

The silence stretched for several moments, long enough to make the young boy on his back wiggle impatiently. "Very well, I'll come for you at nine." He galloped away, ducking clothes and dodging chairs and trailing giggles until he reached the door. Then he slid the boy from his back and slipped out of the building.

Mrs. Harrison shook her head as she watched him leave behind a whirlwind of energetic children. "He needs several of his own. Lawrie said—" She pursed her lips. Her throat moved with the swallow that consumed the remainder of her thought.

Mattie waited, but the other woman offered no further confidences.

"Come, let me show you to your room." She snatched the handle of Mattie's bag.

"You mustn't carry that!"

Mrs. Harrison's laughter tinkled like a fistful of silver coins. "This is my lightest burden of the day. I have four children, Miss Fraser. Indeed, I hope you don't mind sharing space with my daughter."

"Of course not. I only hope she doesn't regret having to share with me. And please, call me Mattie." She followed her hostess into a tiny room whose only furnishing, a none-too-large bed, filled the available space.

"And my name is Alice." Mattie's unexpected hostess set the bag at the end of the bed. "I'll leave you to a few moments of privacy. I'm afraid you won't get many."

Alice exited and pulled the curtain across the doorway. The fabric swished over the opening, separating the room from the remainder of the house and shielding Mattie from curious eyes. Quickly she withdrew the pistol from her deep coat pocket and caressed the polished curly-maple stock, stroked the smooth barrel.

But where to stow it in the meantime? Particularly in a place where curious little fingers wouldn't discover the weapon. She glanced about the unfamiliar room. A black wool scarf shrouded the tiny window and draped the room in gloom and privacy. Mattie retrieved a dark stocking from her bag and dropped the gun inside. Reaching behind the curtain, she tied the stocking to the nail holding the corner, then moved the fabric back in place. A faint bulge, only visible under close scrutiny, hinted at the curtain's dual purpose.

Then Mattie hauled another item from the other coat pocket. Elegant script contradicted the vile sentiments on the paper she'd discovered in her room at the Captain's Quarters a mere hour ago.

"Go home, Yank, lest you meet with an unpleasant end."

Chapter Four

Kit exited the hackney where he'd spent the better part of this glorious day. If only the building before him reflected some of the afternoon's splendor. He ducked and entered the ramshackle pub once again.

"What do you want?" Polly marched forward to guard her domain from his entry.

"No one evicts a paying customer unless she 'as a better offer."

"Now see 'ere, that woman created a disturbance."

"Aye, she appeared the sort to get drunk and rowdy."

Polly tilted up her chin. "Women like that don't need to cause the trouble. It follows them naturally like in a place with lots of men."

"But Miss Fraser's trouble stemmed from a single man, one who offered coins." Kit extracted two silver pieces—for which he'd traversed the length of London—from within his coat and flashed them before the woman's eyes. "One for a description. Double if you give me a name."

Interest flared on the woman's face. "What's that Miss Fraser to ye?"

"Business. Do ye 'ave a name?"

"Some red 'eaded chap. Never seen 'im before."

"A plain enough depiction to describe a hundred men. Was 'e tall? Short? With a beard? Did 'e walk like a sailor?"

"I didn't notice nothing—'e was…ordinary."

Kit clamped his teeth together and shoved the coins back in his coat. "You waste my time."

"See 'ere, I gave ye a description."

"No, you gave me generalities. Give me something useful."

Polly scratched the top of her head. "Blue eyes. Not tall, but powerful. Scar on the back of 'is hand."

Kit tossed the woman a single coin, then stomped back to the waiting cab. "Belgrave Square."

As the vehicle lurched forward he leaned back against the cracked upholstery, plucked the bent spectacles from his face and rubbed his throbbing brow. Without the spectacles' assistance he observed no clear delineation amongst the various buildings, no way of determining decrepit ruins from charming homes. A little like what he was doing now, trying to make sense of an ambiguous situation.

Who would want Mattie Fraser evicted from her humble lodging—enough to part with good money to make it happen?

The cab slowed to a halt before the imposing DeChambelle mansion. He pushed his spectacles over his nose again, bringing the faint signs of adversity and neglect into focus. The roses in wont of pruning. The trim calling for a new coat of paint.

"'Ere ye are, Mr. DeChambelle."

Kit stepped onto the street. "Come early tomorrow. We have more work to do."

"Aye, gov'na. And be certain to refund the lady's money."

As the hackney pulled away, the front door swung open to reveal the butler's prim and proper form. "Good evening, sir. Will you be dining here tonight?"

"No, tell Cook not to trouble herself. I'll eat at my club. Have the carriage brought around in fifteen minutes."

"Very good, sir."

Kit mounted the stairs two at a time to the room he'd occupied since childhood—past the daunting portraits of celebrated DeChambelles who reminded him that a man of eight and twenty should have his own lodgings.

His siblings, all but his youngest sister Caroline, had homes of their own. Families. Futures. Kit had a past…a past of which he couldn't speak. A past that included a profession disparaged in polite company.

Espionage.

Alderston had made the scheme sound so exciting ten years ago when he'd come offering adventure wrapped in mantle of patriotism—an opportunity to outwit the French in service to his country. And Kit had chosen excitement over stability only to discover disillusionment—a life in the shadows where black and white didn't exist, only shades of gray.

He kicked off the bulky shoes and shrugged out of the homely jacket. Once properly attired as a gentleman of means, he departed. Minutes later, he faced Julian's door for the second time that day.

But despite his increasingly emphatic knocks, no butler answered his summons with even so much as an admonishment to depart. Kit stalked away, anger bubbling low in his gut.

He needed to speak to Julian. But if he couldn't have that, he would settle for a drink.

"Would you get the stew, Mattie?" Alice nodded to an enormous pot that contained a little meat and a lot of potatoes. "I hear Lawrie arriving. At last."

Mattie moved dinner to the center of the table. Shouts and giggles reverberated from the other room, then Mr. Harrison hitched around the corner. A towheaded tot wrapped his arms around one leg, an older girl with brown curls tugged on an arm and a third child climbed on his back.

"Sarah tells me we have a guest." Mr. Harrison wasn't tall or imposing or particularly handsome, and his clothes matched the undistinguished condition of his house. His receding hair lengthened his forehead, leaving his aquiline nose too prominent on his face. And yet, a peculiar joy glowed on his smile.

"Miss Mattie Fraser, from America. Mr. DeChambelle suggested she stay with us for a few days." Alice gestured the family to take their seats on the benches that stretched the length of the table. "Mattie, somewhere buried under all those children is my husband, Lawrie."

"Welcome, Miss Fraser from America." He peeled the child off his back, then assisted the smallest one onto the bench. "Sarah would like to sit beside you, if you don't mind."

All eyes in the room—six pairs, to be exact, focused on Mattie. Unaccustomed to so much attention, she stiffened. The tiny room seemed to contract even smaller around her.

"Perhaps Mattie would prefer—"

"No, no. I don't mind. Indeed, I would be delighted." She slid onto the already crowded bench.

Sarah smiled then slipped her hand into Mattie's. Alice grabbed her other one as the entire family created a chain around the table.

"Our Father, we thank thee for thy bounty—for providing us with good food, good friends and good fellowship." Lawrie Harrison's voice rose over the rustlings of wiggly children. "We ask thy blessing upon this family and upon our guest. Amen."

The family dropped hands, and the noise began in earnest. A lump caught in Mattie's throat as she glanced at the oldest child, a lad within a year of two of Nicky's age. Poor Nicky, who suffered more than physical deprivations. He lacked even what the Harrisons had—good food, good friends, good fellowship.

A good family.

Perhaps if she finished her business quickly, she would have funds remaining. Would the Harrisons accept yet another child if Mattie provided his financial support?

"Some stew, Miss Fraser?" Mr. Harrison held up a hand for her bowl. "It's long on potatoes and short on beef, I'm afraid."

"She knows." Alice snagged Mattie's dish and passed it across the table. "Mattie helped me with the meal. And the laundry. And the children."

"How long did you say she was staying with us?" Harrison scooped out a healthy portion of stew. "Four years? Five?"

"Only a few days, I hope." Mattie set the bowl on the table and waited while Harrison served the remainder of the family. "Long enough for me to enjoy your company, but not so long you tire of mine."

The Harrisons laughed as if she had shared a great witticism.

"'Better is a dinner of herbs, where love is, than a stalled ox and hatred therewith.' You are welcome at our table any time, Miss Mattie Fraser from America." Harrison filled his bowl last. "Is Mattie short for Matilda?"

"Martha."

At the other end of the table, two boys elbowed each other. Their father aimed a stern look at them, then focused his attention on Mattie again. "A good Biblical name."

"My mother's father served in the war under General Washington. Afterward, he opened a shop in Alexandria, so my mother had occasion to meet both the president and his wife." Images of her mother flickered in Mattie's mind, the pictures growing ever more hazy and indistinct with the passage of time. A wave of loss—burgeoned by the presence of a happy, loving family—surged through her. "And thus, she named her children Martha and George."

"Peter! Stop that." Harrison reached across the table and plucked the spoon from the tot's hand before it became a missile. "And Andrew, if you tease your brother again—"

"I won't."

Alice rested an elbow on the table and sighed. "Please excuse us, Mattie. My heathens have yet to learn the finer points of good table manners."

"Only the finer points? You give them too much credit, my dear." Lawrie Harrison stood.

Mattie grabbed her bowl and started to rise, only to realize the rest of the family remained seated while the husband and father pulled a large black book from a shelf. Mattie lowered herself back onto the bench.

"We're reading the story of King David," Mr. Harrison explained as he resumed his seat.

"About how the king's son went to war with his father so he could become king instead." Andrew's eyes glowed with the excitement of a boy listening to tales of war and glory.

"But tonight's chapter is the most important because it is about the king's forgiveness toward those who wronged him." His father drew the candle nearer and opened the Bible to the marked page. "Second Samuel, chapter nineteen."

As his voice rose and fell with the quaint passage, forgiveness felt as foreign as ever to Mattie. No, resentment and regret swelled in her throat at the difference between the end of this meal and those she'd experienced in her childhood when the three Frasers went their separate ways—Mattie to scrub the dishes, her brother to engage in mischief with his friends and her father to find comfort in his whiskey. Another spurt of determination shot through her to provide something better for Nicky.

* * *

The door of his parents' townhouse closed behind Kit as he climbed into Turner's hackney. Church bells chimed in the distance, while closer to home a lark sang her approval of the beautiful morning. A morning Kit wouldn't enjoy until he completed this onerous task.

What would happen when he introduced Miss Fraser to his brother? And what about when she discovered his own secret, his relationship to the man responsible for George Fraser's death?

"Where to, Mr. DeChambelle?" Turner gathered up the reins.

"Harrison's."

"Ah, meeting the young miss again, are ye?"

The hackney rocked as Kit settled on the seat without answering. Across the street, a man in Sunday-morning finery loitered near a garden gate.

Kit leaned back against the upholstery and closed his eyes. The twinges of the previous night's overindulgence dulled his thoughts. As the vehicle jostled from one rut to the next, misgivings murmured deep within his mind. How strange, when he'd thought the last vestiges of his conscience long since destroyed.

The hackney crawled to a stop and Kit jumped out, wincing at what the jolt did to his head. The tenement door swung open even before he reached it, revealing an eager face.

"Mr. DeChambelle!"

"Good morning, Miss Sarah. You look especially pretty today. Would you inform Miss Fraser of my arrival?"

Sarah smiled and tripped away as Kit stepped over the threshold.

"Did you find Alderston?"

Kit looked down to where Harrison sat on the floor, fastening shoes on Peter's wiggly feet. "Spoke to him yesterday."

Sarah danced back into the room. "Miss Fraser is putting on her coat."

"Thank you."

A smattering of freckles dotted the girl's nose, rather like Miss Fraser's. Alas, the resemblance ended there. Sarah's jaw lacked the brittle edge of challenge nor did her chin tilt with wary pride. Instead, her eyes danced with joy and happiness and the knowledge she was loved. An ache formed in his chest as he contemplated what circumstances had hardened Miss Fraser's responses. The loss of her brother, of course. But more?

Harrison gave Peter's laces one last jerk and rose to his feet. "I don't suppose I could convince you and Miss Fraser to attend church with us."

"No, Miss Fraser and I have business to attend to this morning."

"Certainly your business could wait a few more hours on such a fine Lord's Day."

Bitterness lodged low and deep as Kit considered the discomfort such a venture would engender. "This morning is the best time." Besides, Julian could hardly claim a pressing appointment elsewhere at this hour on a Sunday morning.

"Do what you must, but Sarah will be most disappointed, won't you, darling? She is quite taken with your Miss Fraser."

His Miss Fraser chose that moment to stroll into the room, her pursed lips indicating her displeasure at the designation. The same drab coat swallowed her form except for the fingers that locked around her reticule.

"Precisely on time, Miss Fraser." Kit jumped to his feet and offered her a bow that did little to thaw her annoyance. "Though I doubt you will need your coat."

"Nevertheless, I prefer to keep it with me." The tension in her rigid jaw clipped short her drawl.

"As you wish." Kit ruffled Peter's hair and offered Sarah a bow deep enough for royalty. "Please excuse our departure, Miss Sarah."

"Only if you promise to return forthwith."

Kit chuckled. "Are you—" He looked to Miss Fraser, only to discover a moment of undisguised longing darkening her eyes to the color of warm chocolate. And then, aware of his regard, wariness slammed across her mouth and shuttered her gaze. He turned to Harrison while she composed herself. "Thank you for opening your home to Miss Fraser."

"Yes, thank you. You have a wonderful family." Gratitude softened her face as she directed a smile at Sarah. "I will see you in a few hours."

Kit fixed his hand to the curve of Miss Fraser's slender back and guided her to the waiting hackney. Despite the layers of wool too warm for the fair day, the muscles beneath his hand stiffened to match the frown that drew her lips into a tight line.

The streets in this part of town bustled with people. Some few, like the Harrisons, traveling to services in their Sunday best. Others simply enjoying a few hours of respite from their weekly labors.

Turner smiled as Miss Fraser climbed into the cab. "Good to see ye again, miss."

Kit grasped the frame, then hesitated. His nerves jangled with the sensation of being observed. He glanced over his shoulder but could pinpoint no threat. Still, he motioned Turner closer and whispered, "Watch for someone following us."

Turner nodded and prodded the horse into motion.

Silence settled over the cab. Miss Fraser's brown gaze stared out the window at a few fluffy white clouds hovering in a blue sky.

"It really is a fair day—much too nice for such warm apparel."

She turned her face toward him. "Perhaps your notion of a fair day differs somewhat from mine."

The peel of church bells ringing out a joyful hymn floated on the balmy air. Kit gestured to St. Paul's dome, gleaming golden in the sunlight. "Come now Miss Fraser. You are not being disloyal to your American sensibilities to enjoy the beauty around you. Even in London."

She relaxed slightly against the seat, her lips tweaking up at the corners. "You do have some charming sites. Provided one doesn't look too closely."

"I hope you will take the opportunity while you are in London to visit our most famous landmarks."

"I've seen nearly every inch of the Admiralty."

He allowed a smile to slip onto his face. "Beyond that. We must get you elsewhere before your return to America." The hackney pulled to a stop before Julian's townhome. "Unfortunately, we have to start here. Business before pleasure."

Mattie descended from the cab and gawked at the mansion before her, scarcely registering Mr. DeChambelle's gloved assistance in her excitement. Trepidation.

Resentment.

At last. At last. At last.

She was *here,* at the home of the man she had crossed an ocean to meet.

And possibly kill.

Anger swept away her awe as her feet trudged toward the door. That this captain should enjoy such wealth and status and privilege while her brother...

Mr. DeChambelle pounded on the door. The knock reverberated hollowly inside the building. "He's gone."

"Gone?" She jerked her gaze to the man beside her. Today

he sported a fine morning coat of soft gray. A high-crowned hat covered much of the tawny hair.

Another knock yielded them the same nonresults. Mattie peeked in a nearby window but the reflection of the blue sky stared vacantly back at her. Her disappointment melted her knees. Mysterious. And oh, so coincidental. "Could he have another appointment?"

"On a Sunday morning? Not likely."

"Perhaps he went to church."

"Less likely."

"Well, then, perhaps he is sleeping off a night of carousing."

"More probable—but his staff would be here, if only to order us to knock more softly lest we disturb his recovery." He grabbed her by the elbow. "Come, there is no sense wasting further time here."

Mattie instinctively yanked her arm away. Her coat billowed out then tumbled back into place, the heavy pistol brushing against her thigh. "But we can't leave." Not when she was so close.

"And what would you have us do, Miss Fraser? Judging by the abandoned nature of the house, we could be setting ourselves up for a very long wait." He gestured toward the cab without touching her. "In the meantime I'll take you back to the Harrisons'."

"Do you suppose we could walk? It's such a beautiful day, and after all those weeks at sea I relish the freedom."

"Yes, one's mobility is rather limited on a ship." He paused beside the hackney and murmured to the driver, then turned to her as the cab pulled away. "Well, then, shall we enjoy our stroll?"

Mattie fell into step beside him and gestured to the row of magnificent buildings. "What is this place?"

"Mayfair."

"Ah." She studied the stately homes with their cheerful flower boxes below palatial windows—hoping to memorize her location so she could return.

Without her oh-so-diligent escort.

"So what will you do next?" she asked.

"About the search for your brother?" He paused before a rose-covered wall and plucked one of the late-season blooms. "I have some other avenues I'll try while I wait for Ju—the captain to return."

"You think the captain will return then?"

"Oh, yes. He is on half pay." He passed her the flower. "The color matches your cheeks."

Mattie stroked the soft petals as they moved on. Heat rushed to her face, no doubt painting her skin several shades darker than the rose. "Half pay?"

"Maintaining a large navy is an expensive proposition for any country, but a necessary one during war. There are sailors to be paid, supplies to be bought, ships to be maintained. During peacetimes, we berth some of the ships and furlough their men. Officers collect half their pay in exchange for their willingness to be recalled in a time of emergency."

She considered a mansion whose wrought-iron fence walled out commoners like her, and tried to imagine the captains of her acquaintance in such fine circumstances. "Being a captain in your navy does seem to pay well."

"All men on a ship share in any prize money, but yes, the largest portion goes to the captain of the victorious ship."

"So this captain, Viscount Somershurst, is older? He must have been a captain for quite some time to amass so many prizes."

"He has great skill, not years." Pique—or patriotism—sharpened the edge of his consonants.

"You probably say such about all your country's officers."

He tilted his head rakishly to one side as if giving the matter great consideration. "No, certainly not all. Merely most."

They continued in silence—a surprisingly congenial and companionable silence—wandering through ever-changing neighborhoods, each like a town unto itself, until they passed rows of tenements like those where the Harrisons lived.

Nicer than the dockside taverns but not so fine as Mayfair, the buildings huddled together, sometimes brushing against one another, sometimes separated by narrow alleys. As she neared one such opening, a flash of green caught Mattie's attention.

Nicky? Had the imp followed her, yesterday and then again today? A warmth owing nothing to the fine day filled her heart as the form retreated into the shadows.

"This one." Mr. DeChambelle's voice stopped her when she would have continued down the street.

"Do you think the Harrisons have returned?"

"You would hear them if they had."

Mattie allowed a smile to escape. "They are a noisy horde, but so much happier than anyone else I know."

Mr. DeChambelle stiffened.

What had she said…? Mattie's shoulders tensed and her fingers tightened around the rose stem until the thorn's prick registered in her mind. She dropped the flower and tucked her hand into her pocket. Her fingers traced the pistol's stock to the trigger as her gaze followed the hard line of Mr. DeChambelle's stare to the door.

The door that now gaped—ajar.

Chapter Five

Danger!

Kit's mind shouted a silent warning as an autumn draft trembled on the door. Harrison would never be so careless. Habits that kept a man alive in war did not easily die in peace.

He nudged Miss Fraser behind him, motioning her to silence as he pressed himself against the wall next to the entrance. The bustle of the street faded from his consciousness as he concentrated on the threat before them. Interminable seconds ticked away.

Nothing.

Quietly he toed the gap open farther. The door's rusty hinges screeched, a warning to any villain yet lurking within. Kit braced for danger to explode out the opening, like that horrific night in Marseilles when everything went so atrociously wrong.

And yet…still nothing.

A cart lumbered along the cobblestoned street. Its rattling wheels mingled with Miss Fraser's rapid breathing and the pulse pounding in his ears. Kit raised a silent hand, motioning Miss Fraser to wait.

After several more tense seconds he stretched one foot over

the threshold, shifting his weight gradually so as to prevent any squeaky boards from announcing his entrance. Then he repeated the motion with his other foot. Step. Pause. Step. The slow progression moved him farther until at last he stood in the narrow parlor, blinking his eyes against the gloom.

Sunlight sifting through a faded muslin drape revealed the slashed upholstery and broken frames of the room's humble furnishings. He slid to one side, keeping the wall to his back, and his foot brushed against a book. The shelf above lay bare, its prior contents now tumbled onto the floor in a heap. Kit edged farther into the wrecked home, noting the overturned benches, the shards of broken crockery.

Not a thief then, but a vandal.

Anger mounting, Kit slipped into the bedchamber, only to find the coverlet slashed to ribbons and the tick beneath similarly abused. Straw littered the wood planks like a barn floor while glinting slivers of glass from the broken window sparkled among the debris. The thug's means for gaining entrance? Kit stalked to a smaller bedchamber, a child's room—this time hoping to yet find the brute in residence, but knowing him to be long gone.

An image flashed in the back of his mind. A man loitering across the street from his parents' home this morning as he departed. Following him? To find Miss Fraser?

"You said I needed a safe place to stay. This happened because of me, didn't it?"

His anger spiked even as he identified the voice behind him as Miss Fraser's soft American drawl. "I believe I ordered you to wait outside."

"And I believe I followed you in. Truly, if your man is not in here then he is somewhere out there. I'm in more danger lingering on the stoop."

That her words held a modicum of truth did not temper his

anger. Or his fear. "And you know that how? He could have slit my throat and been waiting in ambush."

"I can't stay here. With the Harrisons." She reached down and retrieved the dismembered remains of Sarah's ragdoll, her fingers combing its shorn yarn hair and then tracing a path over the mutilated cheek. "Yesterday you said I needed a safe place to stay. You didn't mean from Stumpy or his like, did you? The threat is against me, and my presence here puts the Harrisons in danger."

First an eviction, now sabotage. Specters of Emilie Boucher's bloody body—haunting images of the young woman caught between the vengeful Laura and his duty to his country—coalesced in Kit's mind.

He had to move Miss Fraser somewhere else, somewhere safe. And yet, would safety lead him to his goal? The attention Miss Fraser had attracted would please Alderston, and he'd expect Kit to use her as an enticement. To trap whom? Who would want to end Miss Fraser's investigation? Only someone with knowledge of the missing orders.

His own brother?

The irony nearly choked Kit. Julian had no secret to protect if Alderston already knew about the orders' disappearance.

Childish voices drifted through the doorway, followed by lyrical tones of Alice Harrison and the deep chuckle of her husband.

"Wait here." Kit glared as he repeated his order of only moments ago. The one she'd disobeyed seconds later. "The children mustn't see this."

"No, of course not."

Kit darted outside and intercepted the family in the street. "There you are. Did the service go long?"

Harrison stopped and grabbed Sarah by the hand, his eyes narrowing. "DeChambelle?"

"Miss Fraser and I concluded our business somewhat

sooner than expected. Alas, when we arrived, we discovered the fire had gone out." He targeted Harrison with a look. "I fear the stew is quite inedible."

"Oh, no!" Alice toddled to the door. "How could—"

"Dear me." Harrison threw his other arm around her shoulder and arrested her progress. "I must have forgotten to stoke the fire in all the excitement this morning. I'm so sorry I ruined everyone's meal."

Four small pairs of gloomy eyes looked at Kit. He tweaked one of Sarah's curls. "It's a fine day for a picnic."

"A picnic! Oh, do say we can, Papa."

"Now why didn't I think of that?" Harrison withdrew several coins and passed them to his wife. "You know that widow lady down the street who makes the best meat pies? You and the children go. I will speak with Mr. DeChambelle and join you shortly."

Andrew tilted his head and studied the adults through suspicious eyes. "But what about Miss Fraser?"

Kit forced an unconcerned smile. "Not this afternoon. Miss Fraser has to leave. She has a family situation requiring her attention." Namely, that her search for her brother threatened those who assisted her. "But perhaps she'll be able to visit again before she returns to America."

Trepidation flickered in Alice's tired eyes as she grasped Peter by the hand. "Come, children."

Kit waited until the children had skipped away, then lowered his voice for Harrison's ears alone. "I never meant to endanger your children."

"Can you tell me?"

"No. Only that I am worried. And now my brother appears to have vanished." Willingly—or not? In his annoyance, Kit hadn't considered that aspect of Julian's disappearance. "I would appreciate your help."

Questions percolated in Harrison's eyes—questions he

would never ask. "Of course. You protect Miss Fraser. Leave your brother to me. Where did you last see him?"

Mattie reclaimed another shredded stocking from the wreckage on the floor. Unfortunately the vandal had reduced all her belongings—even the bags she carried them in—to ribbons. Another warning, like the note and eviction? Or had someone searched for something specific—something he thought she possessed?

A shadow reached across the doorway. Fear fisted in her belly and clawed up to her throat.

"Mattie?"

Her head snapped up, even as Nicky's voice registered in her conscious. "How did you get in here?"

He shrugged, and the too-large coat drooped off a scrawny shoulder. "Probably the same way as the wretch who did this to ye. Broken window in the other room. Mattie, ye've got to leave."

"Yes, I know. I'm going to find somewhere else to stay." She considered her dwindling collection of coins. "I don't suppose you know of any place—"

"No, not 'ere. Ye got to go far away. Back to America."

"Soon, I hope. Did you talk to that bloke you mentioned?"

"Not yet. If I find 'im for ye, then will ye go?"

"Meet me tomorrow afternoon at…where would be a good place?"

"St. Paul's."

"Isn't that a church?"

"One even an American can find. I'll be under Big Tom—the clock." With a jaunty wave, he crept away, leaving her strangely alone.

Lonely.

Footsteps tapped against the floor of the parlor, then Mr.

DeChambelle stood in the bedchamber doorway, lips pressed into a stern line. "Come, we must leave this place."

"The Harrisons?"

"We sent Alice to get the children some meat pies for a picnic. Harrison will find someone to tidy the mess, then join them. That should spare the children the worst." His head tilted as he regarded her for one overlong moment. "A shame we can't join them—a frolic would do you good. But we must get you settled elsewhere."

If only his country's army had shown such concern when they'd occupied—destroyed—her country's cities. "I..." She extracted the bent remains of her umbrella from the wreckage, suddenly aware she had nothing but the clothes on her back and a few coins in her reticule. And the pistol in her pocket.

"Leave it. I'll replace what was ruined."

"I can't accept charity from you."

"Must you debate my every attempt to help?"

"I don't."

"No?" The curve of his mouth warmed to the kind of roguish grin that could make an ordinary woman feel beautiful and his soft chuckle crawled under her coat, sweeping shivers up her spine. Perhaps she should be thankful he didn't smile more often. He clasped her elbow and hauled her to her feet. "Come."

She cast one last look at her ravaged belongings, then followed him into the warm sunshine. "And to think, had I taken your advice I would have lost my coat with the rest of my clothes."

His brow rose as he eyed the ancient wool. "No great loss, that." He matched his steps to hers and guided her back in the direction from which they had so recently come.

"I hope you don't intend for me to stay with any more of your friends. Not after what happened."

"As a matter of fact, Miss Fraser—no."

They continued in silence while she waited for him to elaborate. The buildings transitioned from modest tenements to fashionable shops and then to ever finer homes. "Are we returning to Mayfair?"

"Near there, Miss Fraser."

The noon sun, beautiful for its scarcity, glittered on spacious houses that towered over the wide road like a row of castles. Behind garden gates, solemn statuary guarded lush greenery.

"I doubt my purse can afford such luxury."

"Fret not, Miss Fraser. I have the perfect place in mind—comfortable, secure and economical. Do you trust me?"

Did she? He had listened to her when all others had ignored her petitions, and assisted her during troubles and threats. And yet as she stared into the blue eyes behind their glass screens, suspicions lurked in her mind as if she sensed hidden depths. Hidden dangers. Nicky's warning echoed in her mind.

Mr. DeChambelle paused in front of a glorious mansion of gleaming white. Below the arched windows, flowers bloomed in boxes and scented the air with perfume. Square columns flanked the portico's three steps that led to a door. "The chez DeChambelle, mademoiselle."

"The what?"

"My parents' London residence."

"Your *parents'* house!" A hundred orphans such as Nicky could find refuge in a house as large as this one. And Mattie would be as out of place as every one of them. "I can't intrude on your family."

"You won't. My parents and youngest sister are in Somerset."

The import of his words washed over her. Wealthy landowners involved in American politics often had multiple residences, one in their home state and one in the new capital. They had shopped at her father's store where their daughters bought imported silks. They had *not* shared their tables and beds with the likes of Mattie Fraser. "Your youngest sister? How many brothers and sisters do you have?"

"One brother and four sisters, but only Caroline and I yet live with our parents."

She schooled her features to betray nothing though her bitterness grew. He had five siblings and two parents—and she had herself.

"It will be perfect. There are rooms aplenty, a well-stocked larder and an army of servants to prevent further attempts at intimidation."

The door of the mansion opened to reveal the general of that army—a proper English butler. His impeccable attire, far superior in quality and style to anything she owned—or rather, had once owned—exaggerated the drab color of her coat. "Good afternoon, Mr. Christopher."

"This is Miss Fraser, Higgins. From America."

Mattie turned to the man beside her, the clutch on her composure ready to shatter. "I…you…"

"She will be staying with us for a few days." Mr. DeChambelle clamped his hand to her back and whisked her through the door.

"Very good, sir," the butler intoned as if such occurrences were altogether natural. He gazed down his long nose at Mattie, but his cool eyes betrayed no surprise at the ragamuffin before him.

Once inside she stopped, the haughty butler and even Christopher DeChambelle forgotten. A hundred lofty window panes welcomed the sun into the airy foyer where a smiling man and woman in larger-than-life portraits exaggerated her inadequacy.

Gold-and-white-papered walls stretched to high, high ceilings replete with intricate scenes molded onto the plaster surface, and the floor gleamed where it peeked out from under the colorful rug that led to a monstrous staircase.

"Have Mrs. Parker take Miss Fraser to her room."

The butler never so much as raised an eyebrow. "The yellow chamber, sir?"

"That will be fine."

"May I take your coat, Miss Fraser?"

She shoved her hands into her pockets, and her fingers once again encountered her cherished pistol. With no way to remove the weapon and unobtrusively convey it to the mysterious yellow room, she dared not relinquish the garment. "No, thank you."

She shifted under Mr. DeChambelle's intense stare. His eyes narrowed, then softened. He gave her shoulder a squeeze more disquieting than reassuring and she ripped her gaze away to the portraits who watched her with censure in their lifeless eyes.

Then the door thumped shut behind her like the stone rolled in front of the tomb, and her poise died. She cramped her fingers around the pistol stock as she seized control over her response.

"Mrs. Parker will see to your needs. I am going to see a man who might be able to answer some of our questions." Mr. DeChambelle's breath stirred loose tendrils of her hair and whispered against her face. "Don't surrender yet, Yank."

She touched her fingers to her burning cheek, his whisper echoing in her mind as he strode away.

Yank.

The same designation as in yesterday's threat, another reminder of who she was—an American who need bow to no one. Not impervious butlers. Not mysterious gentlemen. And most especially not anonymous cowards.

As Mattie stared after him, shoes clicked against the floor, then whispered against the rug.

"Miss Fraser?"

She turned to confront a formidable woman in gray, from the top of her silvery hair to the hem of her pewter skirt. Her cold, steely gaze pierced Mattie like a saber into flesh. "Yes?"

"I am Mrs. Parker, the housekeeper. I will show you to your room." She wheeled and marched toward the wide, curving stairway. The profusion of keys around her waist jangled like a chain.

Mattie drew in a deep breath of rose-scented air, then followed the rattling up the stairs and through the maze of hallways. How would she ever find her way out of here? She glanced backward, already confused as to which of the myriad passageways returned to the entrance.

"This way." Mrs. Parker indicated a door identical to the others they'd passed. She pushed it open and gestured Mattie inside. The keys at her waist clanked in protest as she rapped her toe against the floor.

Mattie entered, half expecting the woman to slam the door and lock it with one—or more—of those keys. Instead, Mrs. Parker swished across the rug, then paused before the large bed that dominated the room. Its yellow damask coverlet, matched by the upholstery on the two chairs, complemented the deeper golds of the walls.

The inviting scene would have offered warmth and welcome but for the chilling, gray plume of Mrs. Parker's presence. "I will send Betsy with water so you may wash. Have you any bags?"

Heat surged to Mattie's cheeks. "All my belongings were… stolen."

Mrs. Parker's leaden gaze melted ever so slightly. "Ring if you need anything, Miss Fraser." She spun and charged to the hall.

Mattie deposited her reticule on the bed, then removed her

coat and draped it alongside, the color appearing even more dreary than usual next to the cheery coverlet. The wool bulged at a peculiar angle over the lump of pistol.

That would never do.

Gathering up the coat, she slid the gun from her pocket and checked the flashpan to verify the powder level. Sufficient, but the touchhole was clogged. She tugged a pin from her hair and poked it through the hole. Then she raised the gun and aimed as Major Andrew Harley-Smith had taught her thirteen months ago.

Memories poured back of one kindly Englishman and three days of horror. Already time muted his features to a vague impression of green eyes and a shadow of a smile. He'd marched out of her life with the same rapidity as he'd arrived, but he'd left her a most valuable gift—the ability to defend her honor and to exact her vengeance.

She examined the room again, ruling out the most obvious hiding places as being too apparent to the staff. She crawled under the bed and groped along the planks. Aha! A niche between a slat and the soft down mattress. She tucked the pistol—

A timid knock announced Betsy's arrival.

Mattie scrambled out from under the bed. "Come in."

The door swung in to reveal a maid encumbered with a pitcher. She was young, probably not more than eighteen years, and rather pretty despite her plain black frock. The maid placed the pitcher on a stand.

"Thank you, Betsy."

Betsy scooped the coat from the bed. "I'll clean this for you, miss." She curtsied and left, the door latching behind her with a soft click.

Mattie stared after her, then glanced at the empty spot on the bed next to her reticule—where her coat had so recently sprawled. Privacy, it seemed, diminished in proportion to the number of servants in an establishment. How did one maintain secrets with so many servants having access to one's most personal details? Perhaps she would stash her brother's letter in the same hiding place as the gun.

"Brandy, DeChambelle?" Colonel Bedell asked after the preliminary greetings.

Kit nodded, cheered by the notion of a drink before the forthcoming interview. "Yes, thank you, sir."

The colonel poured two glasses and passed one to Kit, then returned the decanter to the sideboard and gestured to the chairs that flanked the fireplace. "What can I do for you?"

Kit settled himself on the closest seat and sipped his brandy, disappointed to discover it was as impotent as the king's mind. "I understand Andrew Harley-Smith served under you last year in America. Drew wrote me a letter last fall, forthwith before he died."

Bedell grunted as he dropped into the other chair. He took a long draught of his brandy, its poor quality notwithstanding.

"Drew asked for my help concerning a woman he met in Washington. I believe he guarded her home to prevent inflamed soldiers from extending the conflagration to private residences. As he never mentioned her by name, I thought perhaps you could help."

"Yes, as we were only to target the American government's property, General Ross assigned men to protect civilians and their possessions. Sad bit of business about Ross," Bedell said with another gulp. "Great soldier. Great man. He will be missed. More brandy?"

Kit shook his head.

Bedell quaffed the contents of his goblet. "Yes, Harley-Smith was assigned to the woman."

"Woman?" Kit leaned forward.

"Pretty little thing." Bedell rose and refilled his sifter with more brandy. "Several of the men were quite envious."

Excitement zinged along Kit's spine. "Did you see her? Would you know her if you saw her again?"

"Likely not. She spoke to Ross, and I sent Harley-Smith. Never met her myself."

"Do you remember anything that would help me identify her? A name? A description?"

"Small lass with deep red hair, the color of trouble. I believe she lived alone."

"Do you suppose I could speak to any of the others who might remember her?"

The officer gulped more liquor, as if the drink assisted his memory. "Adams died at Waterloo. Winston sold out—probably hunting at his family's estate in Northumberland. Harley-Smith is dead, of course. Don't remember that Eyre ever saw the girl."

Bedell's description matched closely enough that if Martha Fraser was a fraud, she was too good for anyone within three days of London to distinguish. No, mostly likely she was as she claimed, a young woman searching for her brother. "Thank you, sir." Kit rose to leave.

"Sure I can't offer you more?" The colonel hefted the decanter.

"No, you have already provided me all that I can use."

Mattie paced to the yellow-draped window and peered longingly at the garden below. The sun hung low on the horizon, painting the late-blooming roses with a gold that matched her new chamber. A nap had restored her composure but now left her with a surfeit of energy. Despite the luxury of her surroundings, she felt unnoticed, unneeded, unwanted.

Unwelcome?

She traipsed to the other side of the room and tested the

doorknob. Unlocked. She slipped into the hallway, leaving the door ajar so she could identify it on her return.

"Can I help you find something, Miss Fraser?" Mrs. Parker's icy tone suggested Mattie searched for the silver.

"I thought perhaps I might obtain something to read."

"I will show you to the library." Mrs. Parker led her through the halls and down the stairs until they arrived at a large room with shelves that stretched to the ceiling.

"My goodness, what a lot of books!"

Mrs. Parker's gray bodice swelled with pride. "His lordship has one of the finest libraries in London."

Lordship? Lordship! The shock jolted Mattie back a step. Then anger stirred in its place, amplified by the housekeeper's superior airs. "My home city of Washington once possessed a fine library, too. Until British troops burned it last year."

"Perhaps in your browsing you will find some advice about the futility of waging war against superior powers. Indeed, his lordship might even offer to donate such a work to your countrymen. To replace what was lost." Mrs. Parker pivoted and marched away, leaving Mattie with a thousand books and her growing trepidations.

A British lord? The man in the portrait?

Mr. DeChambelle's father. What did that make him? Hardly the clerk she had first assumed. Idly she searched the shelves, her mind whirling with the implications of the housekeeper's words. She browsed past a book of sermons and a few volumes printed in Latin before deciding on a slim collection of poetry. She carried it to a window seat where the afternoon sun provided enough light to immerse herself in the works of Herrick.

An hour later, as the waning light made the words difficult to decipher, footsteps pattered against the corridor floor outside the library. Mattie strolled to the door and peeked out to where a crowd gathered in the foyer. To welcome Mr.

DeChambelle's return? She abandoned Herrick on a table and set forth to investigate.

As she reached the corner, her gaze skimmed the assembly. Mrs. Parker the housekeeper. Higgins the butler. And... not Mr. DeChambelle, but two people—a man and woman who looked suspiciously like the subjects of the portraits.

Chapter Six

For several long moments everyone froze as Mattie and the new arrivals stared at each other. Awkward silence as thick as any London fog hung in the room. Mattie's muscles tightened around the empty hole in her stomach, replacing her earlier hunger with sudden nausea. Nothing in her mother's gentle teachings had covered the protocols for introducing oneself to unwitting hosts, and Mattie was quite at a loss for what to say.

Then a girl of perhaps two and ten years slipped forward and eyed Mattie with unconcealed curiosity. "Who's that, Maman?"

The younger sister? As Mattie scrutinized her, she realized the arrival had a young woman's development despite a height that barely reached to Mattie's chin. The tilted eyes—set in a round face—revealed a childish innocence at odds with her years.

Then Higgins opened the door for Christopher DeChambelle's perfectly timed entrance.

"Kit!" The girl-woman abandoned her study of Mattie and raced to his side, throwing her arms wide to embrace him.

"Caro." His genuine, unguarded delight subtracted years from his face and cynicism from his eyes.

Shards of jealously sliced Mattie's midsection. Her own brother's features as she had last seen them—sneering, contemptuous—flashed through her mind. No congeniality was to be found in the memories of *her* brother. Indeed, his enraged voice reverberated again in her ears.

"I've missed you, Poppet." Mr. DeChambelle's soft, very British voice poked through the bitter memories.

"Missed you, too, Kit."

Mr. DeChambelle—Kit, his sister had called him—leaned over to kiss the straight brown hair on the top of her head. Then his gaze swept over the crowd filling the foyer. "Father, Maman, I didn't expect you today."

The sardonic glint in the older man's eyes looked so very familiar. "So it would seem."

"I see you have already made Miss Fraser's acquaintance."

"Not…exactly." The in-the-flesh lady wore more years than her portrait. Lines of maturity now framed her deep-set eyes.

"Well, then. Let me rectify this situation." Kit DeChambelle's smile remained in place as if he found nothing extraordinary about the circumstances to which he'd consigned Mattie. "Father, Maman, this is Miss Martha Fraser from America."

The tension lingered. What must they think of her, a woman who'd taken up residence in their house with their son—and only their son—as host?

As Mattie hesitated, the older version of Kit DeChambelle stepped forward, his face as unrevealing as his butler's. "How do you do, Miss Fraser. Please excuse our rudeness. Kit didn't warn us he'd invited a guest."

"My apologies, Father." Mr. DeChambelle focused a rare smile on his parents though he kept his arm wrapped protectively around his sister. "Miss Fraser arrived here this afternoon. She has of late come into difficulties during her visit to England. Miss Fraser, these are my parents, the Earl and Countess of Chambelston. And this is my sister Caroline. Caro to her friends and family."

The countess—countess!—nodded, cool reserve still intact. "Perhaps we can discuss this further after we have refreshed ourselves, Christopher. Caro is quite fatigued, and no doubt Miss Fraser wishes to change for dinner."

A grand dinner? The last of Mattie's hunger fled and a pulse throbbed in her temple as a bad situation turned worse. "I, ah, I fear my belongings were…stolen while I was out this morning."

"Oh, dear. You have come into difficulty." Lady Chambelston's voice betrayed a hint of accent unlike that of the other English people of Mattie's acquaintance—a slight stress on the vowels that was at once intimidating and charming. "I will have my maid find something for you. Perhaps with a few alterations we can concoct some appropriate garments for you, yes? Come, Caro, Miss Fraser."

Mattie followed the other two women up the daunting staircase without looking back.

Kit strolled to a sideboard of the same mahogany as Miss Fraser's eyes and poured a liberal quantity of brandy. The sight of his guest sans her ubiquitous coat had rocked him to his heels, despite her being garbed in the most hideous gown he'd ever seen. Her form matched the dainty facial structure—deceptively delicate and overly thin. The drab color did nothing to enhance her complexion, and yet when she'd followed Maman and Caro up the stairs an hour ago, the ugly gown had swayed in a dance of tantalizing movement.

Now as he waited for the rest of the family, Maman perched on a chair—back straight, head erect and hands tightly clenched on her lap. Her blond hair complied with perfect order as befitted a woman of her station. "I hope you have a very good reason for entertaining an *étranger*—a young, un-attached *femme* at that—in our home. In our absence." Agitation always intensified Maman's accent.

He downed the drink in a single gulp. "Captain Andrew Harley-Smith referred her to me." In a manner of speaking. After years of lying to England's enemies, this one small falsehood to his family tripped from his tongue with surprising difficulty. And yet, to reveal too many details implicated Julian of incompetence, cruelty or evil. And possibly put him at risk.

"Harley-Smith—Lady Irene's son? I thought he died."

He ambled to a chair and dropped onto the upholstery. "Yes, last year."

"How did this Miss Fraser meet him?"

"During the war in America. General Ross assigned Drew to protect her during the attack on Washington. He didn't want the army…"

Lady Chambelston rested her chin on her fist and pondered the blaze in the fireplace. Old horrors tightened along her jaw. "So why is she in London now? I should think she would avoid all things English after such an experience."

The brandy's siren call beckoned. "She, ah, seeks to know the fate of her brother. She relayed the situation to Drew last year, and he offered to assist her. Alas, Drew died before he completed the task."

"I surmise she has no other relatives?"

"No, she doesn't."

"Poor child. When I learned of my family's fate…" Maman's eyes stared across the room to another country, another time, another tragedy. "Such a waste."

Kit hauled his gaze away, unable to witness Maman's pain when she alluded to France's Reign of Terror. Thousands died at the radicals' hands—including Maman's entire family. What unfortunate events had left Miss Fraser alone in the world? "Unfortunately, Miss Fraser has had a run of bad luck since her arrival, culminating in losing her belongings this morning. Not quite knowing what to do, I brought her here."

"So she only arrived here today?"

"A few hours before you." Kit rose and retreated to the other side of the room where he refilled his goblet.

Maman frowned as she followed his movements.

"I'm surprised Father is not here yet. I've never known him to be late for dinner."

But Maman would not be deterred. "How much of that have you imbibed?"

Not enough. Not yet. "Anyway, I would appreciate ever so much, Maman, if you would make Miss Fraser feel welcome."

"What do you want me to do?"

"For one thing she needs new gowns, but she is a proud woman. You will have to be clever with your suggestion."

"As long as she is considerate to Caro, Miss Fraser is welcome in my home."

An image of Miss Fraser comforting a homeless urchin formed in Kit's mind. Whatever her feelings toward his countrymen, whatever her true motivations for coming to England, the woman had displayed compassion toward a lonely child and earned the loyalty of a lad who could offer her nothing in return. "I think Caro will be safe."

But Julian? Perhaps not.

Caroline flitted into Mattie's bedchamber, a lovely sight in pale pink silk—a fairy-tale princess who lacked only a crown. "Dinner, Miss Fra-Fra—"

"Please, Caroline. Call me Mattie."

"Mat-tie." The young woman formed the name and smiled.

Mattie analyzed her own reflection. Betsy had arranged her hair into a knot of intricate elegance, but already a few rebellious tendrils escaped. Lady Chambelston's icy blue gown washed the color—except her ubiquitous freckles—from her face and emphasized the shadows of uncertainty in her eyes. Still, Mattie took pleasure in the change from her customary brown wool. The gossamer fabric gleamed in the candlelight and shimmered when she moved. She twirled, watching the skirt swish out, then whisper against her again.

Caroline laughed and clapped her hands. "Mat-tie's dancing."

"Mattie's giddy." Over the next upcoming ordeal. Dinner. She held out a hand to the girl-woman. "Will you lead me? I'd get lost in your house and never be seen again."

Caro smiled and obligingly fitted her small hand in Mattie's. Together they traipsed down the grand staircase. Mattie clutched the front of the too-long skirt as she stomped in the unsightly shoes that contrasted so peculiarly with the ephemeral gown. Caro clung to her hand, and as Mattie realized the difficulty stairs posed for the young woman, she slowed her steps.

For the second time in as many evenings, Mattie discovered someone who valued her company. In many ways Caro was of an age with Sarah—both displayed the same unconcern for Mattie's American heritage and homely attire. For several moments her heart warmed at Caro's easy acceptance, until she reminded herself she had not come to England to form friendships. No doubt her brother had found the English of *his* acquaintance less congenial.

Fleet seconds later Caroline guided them into a room that exerted a formal, masculine intimidation. Candlelight gleamed on the dark wood paneling and created dancing shadows in the corners. A fire blazed in the grate, its sparks igniting awareness along Mattie's spine and on the back of her neck.

Kit DeChambelle leaned indolently against the mantel and studied her over the rim of the sparkling crystal goblet. With the tight, formal clothes, his transformation to stiff English aristocrat was complete. He touched his glass against his lips, making her suddenly aware of the dryness of her own mouth. No doubt he preferred a more sophisticated liquor than the second-rate whiskey her father had used to achieve his nightly stupor. But did he consume a lesser quantity than her perpetually inebriated sire? He lowered his drink and curved his lips into a smile as warm as the appreciation gleaming in his eyes. Warning bells clanged in Mattie's mind, and a chill prickled along the skin of her bare arms. Drunk, her father alternated between amicable and irritable, but painful experience had taught her that drink heightened some men's amorous natures. Including her host's?

"Good evening, Miss Fraser." The earl's voice disturbed her musings. He was a gray-haired version of his son, but without the scar along his nose.

"Good evening, sir—my lord."

The clock on the mantel chimed eight o'clock.

The earl proffered his elbow to his wife. "Shall we?"

Lady Chambelston inclined her perfectly coifed head and glided from her seat.

"Caro? Miss Fraser? Shall we go in to dinner?" Mr. De-Chambelle's baritone caressed her ear.

A whiff of his drink stirred her senses and sent bitter memories washing through her. Mattie turned her head and found those mesmerizing eyes only inches away from her face. Clear eyes, without a hint of drink-induced haze. Eyes that probed her thoughts, her emotions, her secrets. "I…ah…"

"Kit!" Caro clasped her brother by the arm.

His face softened and he focused one of those rare smiles at his sister. Then he extended the other elbow to Mattie as he leaned closer—so close his breath brushed her hot cheeks. "Thank you for your kindness to Caroline."

Was it merely simple kindness that stirred his approbation? Mattie's vanity shriveled, only to be replaced by a kindling gratification deep within. She touched the sleeve of his coat, careful to avoid embracing the form beneath. Still, his warmth burned through to her fingers.

"Relax." His whisper stirred the unruly hair on the back of her neck. "You'll survive the mad DeChambelles."

She—penniless, pedestrian, provincial—must have been mad to have agreed to stay here.

Rather than risk another glance at him, she studied the dining room. A large table served as the focal point of the otherwise plain room. A floral arrangement decorated the table's center, circled by five place settings.

Rows of silver were arranged at each place, like soldiers lined up for review. Their intimidating presence waited for her to choose wrongly and commit an unpardonable social gaff.

Two days ago she'd resided in a crumbling tavern typical of London's slums. Last night she'd dined in the humble home of a poor English family. What was she doing here? In this house? With this family? Beside this man? She stumbled on the hem of her too-long skirt and tightened her grip on his dark sleeve. Cut crystal twinkled in the candlelight as she dropped into the chair he held for her.

Once Caroline assumed her seat, the men sat, too. To Mattie's horror, the earl sat at the head of the table to her left while Kit DeChambelle took the chair on her right. She gulped. Across the table Caro smiled, unconcerned by the frightening array of utensils certain to reveal Mattie's place.

And then three of the DeChambelles—all save Kit—bowed

their heads for several silent moments, raising them only after Lady Chambelston crossed herself and murmured an "Amen" that was echoed by her daughter.

Who wouldn't thank God if blessed with such an elegant home and fine furnishings? And a loving family?

Bitterness filled her belly as Mattie peeked at the man beside her. His eyes gleamed behind their spectacles, and she ripped her gaze away before learning the correct member of the silver army for this course.

The countess cleared her throat. Mattie glanced her direction, then noted the faint curve of her lips. When the lady chose a utensil with deliberate care, Mattie aped her movements.

"So sorry to have surprised you today, Kit." A twinge of… disapproval? laced the earl's aristocratic tones. At finding her in residence?

"I'm sure Miss Fraser appreciates the presence of other ladies in the house."

"Your mother wrote Julian to let him know we were coming to London."

"Yes, he told me." Kit DeChambelle's gaze flickered to Mattie, then he lifted his goblet and sipped the contents.

"You saw him?"

"We arranged to meet at his club one evening."

Caro tilted her head. "Jule?"

"Yes, dear. Julian." Lady Chambelston patted her daughter's arm affectionately before turning her attention back to her son. "I would have contacted you, but I did not know your whereabouts. When did you arrive in town?"

"Only two days ago, Maman."

"We thought we would visit before winter. Caro could use a few new gowns, and you know how much she loves music. I planned a night at the opera for her. Finding you here makes our journey all that much more worth the effort."

Mattie studied her plate while the conversation about unfamiliar people and places swirled around her. A servant—what was he called?—brought in the next course. She waited for Lady Chambelston to start before she reached for the silver.

"I will send Julian an invitation to join us for dinner Tuesday," the countess said to her husband.

Beside her, Kit DeChambelle tensed to stiff-shouldered posture, his fingers circling his glass with dangerous force. A telling reaction for the habitually unflappable gentleman.

"Miss Fraser, my son tells me you are in England to learn the fate of your brother." Lady Chambelson's expression sobered in sympathy. "You are welcome to stay with us as long as you need."

"Thank you, ma'am." But would the lady be so generous if she knew the other purpose for Mattie's journey? Agitation tightened around her heart. She took another bite of heavily sauced fish.

"I hope we can prevail on you to cast off your cares now and again to join us in a few amusements. You should see some of London while you are here."

Caught with food in her mouth, Mattie swallowed hastily but the fish mired in her throat. "You are very gracious, ma'am."

"Perhaps you would enjoy the opera."

"The opera, Maman?" Kit DeChambelle's deep voice rumbled beside her, melting her composure to the consistency of the sauce. "Are you certain…?"

"But of course." Lady Chambelston touched her napkin to a corner of her mouth. "We cannot be so rude as to abandon our guest while we indulge ourselves. The opera would give Miss Fraser a chance to see another aspect of London. I expect musical entertainment is different in America, no?"

"Ah, yes. Quite different." Mattie stabbed the fish dish

with her fork and summoned the fortitude to smile despite the turmoil that bubbled within her.

"For which you would be grateful if you knew what awaited you at the opera." The earl looked to Mattie with a nod. "Four hours of wailing the same words over and over—in a foreign language, no less. I always find an excuse not to go. Stick with your American entertainments."

"My father served in America during the war," Kit De-Chambelle explained. "Ah, that is, the previous war."

"A messy business, that." Lord Chambelston's eyes clouded as if he looked back at some painful memory. "I liked the Americans. A few who fought with us were more concerned with vengeance on their neighbors than loyalty to the king, but most were decent, hearty folk with strong convictions. A pity we couldn't have resolved our differences amicably."

Mattie stared at the glowing white tablecloth. "I...thank you for those kind words."

The earl harrumphed.

"War is the worst way to settle a dispute." A shadow crossed the countess's deep-set eyes.

Mattie pondered the plentiful fare, the hovering footman, the elegant furnishings—and realized that despite all the De-Chambelles' wealth and privilege, they had experienced loss and pain.

Kit stretched forward and plucked his glass off the table. The movement, like the dozen or so prior, brought him within range of Miss Fraser's—Mattie's—fragrance, discernible beneath the stronger aromas of roast duckling and mushroom timbales. Her cinnamon hair had been tamed into a formal chignon, but missed sleek perfection by escaping tendrils that danced around her face. He limited himself to a small sip to avoid otherwise certain inebriation by the end of the interminable evening.

He needed to be stone cold sober around this woman.

Under the guise of returning the goblet to the table, he glanced at her and caught the censure that sparked in her eyes before she turned her head and shifted ever so slightly away.

No, beyond censure. Disappointment.

Even…sorrow?

Maman gestured to the footman to bring the next course. Though darkness still lingered under her eyes, she forced a hopeful smile onto her face. "I thought perhaps I might invite Mrs. Sinclair and her daughter to our dinner with Julian."

Father rubbed his forehead. "Julian wants your company, my dear. He would appreciate his time with us more if you did not present him with all manner of female candidates for his inspection. He spent years fighting, Agnes. Let the boy enjoy his holiday."

"He is not a boy, and enjoying himself is precisely the reason he ought to find a wife."

Mattie leaned closer to Kit, torturing him with a whiff of her scent. "Who is Julian?"

Of all the times for his parents, for *Caro,* to come to London. With both Mattie Fraser and his parents in residence, he could hardly expect to keep his relationship to Julian a secret. Another reason to be dismayed by their unexpected appearance.

Mattie reached for her fork—the *wrong* fork.

Not that he cared about forks, but he knew the faux pas would mortify her when she realized what she'd done. "The other one," he murmured for her ears only.

A touch of pink caressed her cheeks, but her composure never faltered as she smoothly switched utensils.

In that moment, Kit ascertained Miss Fraser's allure. It was not great beauty that made her unforgettable, but a composure she wore with an assurance that other women only achieved with diamonds. That remarkable poise hadn't faltered in the face of indifferent clerks, insensitive innkeepers or even a pernicious vandal. Indeed, if the idea of meeting a countess in a worn gown or attending a formal dinner with unfamiliar dishes bothered Miss Fraser, she masked her abashment flawlessly.

He glanced across the table in time to intercept the silent curiosity in Caro's eyes as she studied his guest. He'd begun by using Miss Fraser and now he'd involved his family in this…charade. Threats had already followed Miss Fraser to Harrison's home. What if his efforts to absolve Julian brought harm to his parents—or even Caro? He snatched his own fork and crammed a clump of the dry rice dish into his mouth.

After dinner. He had to tell Miss Fraser the nature of his relationship to Julian. If she discovered the truth on her own, he'd lose whatever of her trust he'd secured. Trust he needed to exploit for Alderston, for Julian.

Premonitions roiled through his gut. He dropped his fork and grabbed his goblet, gulping the contents to stem the rising tide of bile in his throat.

The movement once again attracted Miss Fraser's attention. Her disapproval. Her pale, freckled skin contrasted with those hard, glittering eyes of darkest amber—now drawn narrow in a frown.

What he would not give to read the thoughts that germinated behind them.

"Miss Fraser, you mentioned having all your belongings stolen today. James," Maman nodded toward Kit's father, "and I would like to make amends, if you will allow us."

Her shoulders stiffened under the borrowed gown but Miss Fraser managed a serene smile. "Oh, I can't ask that of you when you've already been so kind as to open your home to me."

"It would be our pleasure. I intend to take Caro to the

modiste tomorrow, anyway. Your presence would be so help-
ful in keeping her entertained while I am being fitted. And
Kit did suggest you get out and see some of London. Perhaps
we could arrange an excursion to one of our famous sights
after our fittings."

Miss Fraser's eyes flickered. Interest flashed in their dark
depths, like sparks kindling in dried leaves. "I'd like to see
St. Paul's."

Kit's fingers tightened around his fork. He wouldn't have
pegged Miss Fraser for one of those evangelical types like
Wilberforce or Moore or even his mother. Not when their
guest had shown no compunction about disregarding Sunday
services this morning in favor of meeting with the *Impatience*'s captain.

But Maman's smile widened. "I so esteem St. Paul's—
every time I go there, I feel God's glory and majesty around
me. But I fear that is rather some distance from Bond Street.
Perhaps we could make time for services there later in the
week, yes?"

"Ah, that would be most gracious of you, ma'am." Miss
Fraser's mouth flattened into a dubious line.

"Excellent. But for tomorrow, why not a visit to Hyde Park
after we finish with the modiste?" His mother patted Caro's
arm. "What color gown would you like?"

"Blue."

Maman chuckled and glanced at him. "Blue is Caro's new
favorite color."

Kit's gaze swept his forever-childlike sister as the weight
of love and responsibility crushed against him. Julian had carried the family financially with his years in the navy. Now
it was Kit's turn to protect them. He would have to see Miss
Fraser followed tomorrow—for her own safety and for Caro's.
Harrison was his preferred choice, but Miss Fraser would

become suspicious if she chanced to see him in such an odd milieu.

Baxter. Miss Fraser already assumed the worst of him after he'd left her waiting so long in the office—in the hopes Alderston would return before their meeting. If she noticed Baxter's presence on Bond Street, peering into shop windows when he should be clerking at the Admiralty, that would only confirm her belief in his ineptitude.

His mother rose, their signal to end the interminable dinner.

Kit pushed to his feet and looked to their guest. "May I speak to you in private, Miss Fraser?"

His mother's hand fluttered. "Kit, is that...?"

"I need to confer with Miss Fraser about the search for her brother."

Maman's frown eased. "I suppose it is acceptable then."

Kit circled the table and embraced his sister, pulling the small, fragile body against him. The day of travel was taking its toll. Caro's mouth drooped with fatigue and her eyes had lost their brightness. "Get some rest. You have a long day of shopping tomorrow. I can't wait to see your pretty blue gown."

She nodded. "Good night, Kit."

Kit waited while Maman escorted Caro out, then he turned to his guest.

Miss Fraser tilted her head to one side and arched a single brow. "You have something to ask me?"

He snatched a candelabra from the table and gestured towards the salon they had vacated for dinner. "Perhaps we could adjourn?" And minimize interruptions from the hovering servants intent on tidying the dining room.

The blue skirts swished with Miss Fraser's purposeful walk as she vacated the room. His feet plodded behind, reluctance making them heavy and slow. She paused next to a chair, one hand resting on its arched back as he pulled the door shut.

The crystal decanter hailed him from the sideboard, promising courage for the forthcoming interview as well as relief from the memories of when another woman had upended his world. He joined it on the other side of the room, situated the candelabrum beside it and lifted a goblet. "Would you care for a drink?"

Her shoulders snapped back. Golden flames smoldered in the depths of her eyes, and her regal bearing conferred an illusion of height. "Surely you didn't invite me here to offer me a drink."

"Not exactly." Although mellowing her sharp mind and tongue had its merits. But perhaps it was just as well she refused. No need to arm her with a crystal weapon before his confession.

Despite the quantity of alcohol he'd already consumed, Kit filled a goblet for himself. Unfortunately no drink would drown the inappropriate and dangerous feelings he was developing for their guest. Guilt and remorse, of course.

But something else? Something more?

Something worse?

He quaffed the brandy despite her disapproval. Or perhaps because of it. A bit of rebellion against the woman who threatened his world, his peace, his family. And yet, the fine liquor tasted of bitterness in his mouth and burned like acid in his stomach.

"You asked the identity of Julian."

"Yes."

"He's my brother."

The brown gaze flickered to him. "And he lives here in London."

"Yes. Yes, indeed. My brother—Julian Thomas Robert DeChambelle, Viscount Somershurst. Of late, captain of His Majesty's Ship, the *Impatience*."

Chapter Seven

Mattie gripped the chair while the earth rolled beneath her feet. Her dinner churned and rushed to her throat, threatening to disgrace her right here. Right now. Right in front of this… the man she'd trusted, who'd seemed so eager to help.

All a lie. There was indeed another persona behind Kit DeChambelle's obliging disguise. A deceitful scoundrel more adept at deception than even her brother.

Why had he waited to impart this little nugget? And why tell her now?

"So after three days, you've finally decided to confess this little oversight? I don't suppose you considered this important until tonight?" When his parents arrived. Oh, he'd intended to continue the lie—would have continued the lie—but for the summary arrival of his family.

He poured himself another drink. At the rate he was consuming, he'd be in a stupor before he answered her questions. If he even intended to do so. "I feared the truth would only bring you additional grief. I hoped to get your answers without exposing you to any more pain."

"How kind of you to be thinking only of me." She didn't even try to soften the sarcasm sharpening her words.

"I didn't think it would matter. I'd get your answer and you could return to America none the wiser."

"And now? Does it matter? After I've been evicted? Received a threatening letter? Had all my possessions destroyed?"

"What threatening letter?" Agitation clipped his words, giving them same edge as when he'd interrupted her eviction at the Captain's Quarters.

"The one ordering me back to America—the same sentiments you seem to share. I've been in London over two weeks, yet only after I met you—and asked uncomfortable questions about a man who is, as it so conveniently turns out, your brother—have such troubles befallen me."

"I had nothing to do with any of those."

She ignored his protest as comprehension hammered through her mind. At last she understood his reluctance to introduce her to the *Impatience*'s captain. He'd never intended her to meet Viscount Somershurst or learn the truth about her brother's fate. Why? What was there to hide beyond George's death? "Did you even speak to this *Julian?*"

"Of course. I told you, I spoke to him that first day."

"And yet you have no answers for my questions, nor will you let me ask them myself." Her brother's blood cried out to her, demanding she take action.

He smacked his goblet against the table. She stared at the sparking crystal, at the fingers wrapped around it with dangerous tension. The tendons on the back of his hand rose in taut ridges. "I've told you the truth."

The entire truth? But she didn't challenge him, not when his past conduct already imparted his answer. "Under the circumstances, I think it would be best if I found another place to stay."

He held up a hand, suddenly—suspiciously—conciliatory. "I understand, and I apologize for the way my actions appear.

However, please reconsider. You have limited resources, especially now, and you want answers from my brother. Well, Miss Fraser, I want answers, too. I want to know why Julian avoided you and now me—why he has disappeared from London so precipitously without a word to anyone, even my parents."

She flexed her fingers against the back of the chair, tightened her grip on her temper and hardened her heart against the last niggling of her conscience. Moments ticked by as she considered her options—her extremely limited options, given the dismal state of her finances. Kit DeChambelle possessed the knowledge she needed to complete her mission. Perhaps she would be best served remaining here. Near him. Using him, as he had used her. "Very well, I concede your point. I accept your apology and your offer to remain here."

"I ask but one thing of you."

She lifted her chin. "Yes?"

"Whatever happens, whatever you learn, be kind to Caro." A shadow crossed his face and filled his eyes with...emptiness. And yet she sensed a honed edge—indeed, almost a threat—on his words. "She doesn't deserve your wrath."

Mattie gave him an abrupt nod. Whatever she might think of his evasions—whether out of his purported consideration for her or for some ulterior reason—she didn't doubt his concern for his sister. "I can make that promise."

The hands of the clock raced through the minutes as the fitting dragged. Mattie drew in a deep breath. A pin in the gown's bodice protested the movement and scratched her side.

"Hold still, mademoiselle."

Mattie locked her aching shoulders into place while the woman with the French accent—fake, Lady Chambelston had whispered with no small amount of amusement—pushed, prodded and pinned.

"Eez beautiful, non?" Madame Celeste praised her creation with modesty as feigned as her accent.

Beautiful? Exquisite. Never in her life had Mattie worn its equal. Despite the gathering gloom outside the window, the golden-yellow muslin radiated sunshine, its burgundy ribbons fluttering when Mattie shifted tired muscles yet again.

"At least she don't look like a beggar in that." A seamstress muttered her comment loudly enough for Mattie to overhear.

Well, she *was* a beggar, dependent on the charity of others for her shelter, her sustenance and even her skirts and shifts.

"You look lovely, Mattie," Lady Chambelston complimented.

"Thank you, ma'am, but another brown frock would be more practical."

"You do not need more than one brown gown."

Truly Mattie didn't need anything *but* bare, boring brown. She was a simple shopkeeper's daughter, after all. And yet, the countess had ordered her four gowns—four!—in assorted colors with all the associated accoutrements. Even the new brown boasted a finer fabric and fit than anything in Mattie's prior experience. "Practical colors suit me." Indeed, Mattie could see only a future bleaker than her ugly American gown stretching before her. Either a return to a life of drudgery in America or a stay in an English gaol. And probably a short stay at that, followed by an even shorter rope.

The modiste unpinned the bodice and Mattie breathed normally again. "I shall have zis for you in a week, madame," Madame Celeste said to Lady Chambelston.

"The dark green and the opera gown tonight, this one

tomorrow and the brown on Wednesday. And Madame, I appreciate *all* your effort."

"It eez a very great effort, non?"

"Of course."

Understanding zinged from one woman to the other. Shopkeeper's daughter that she was, Mattie knew the countess's appreciation would accompany extra financial remuneration.

The modiste shrugged, the avarice glittering in her eyes like gold and giving lie to a nonchalance as feigned as her modesty. "As my lady wishes."

The mantel clock chimed a cheery count of the hour, an impatient reminder of the day's growing lateness. Mattie must be on her way or Nicky would worry.

Carefully yet quickly Mattie removed the gown—only scratching herself three more times in the process—and dressed again in the coarse woolen clothes she'd brought from America, the sole survivors of the attack. The color, a blend of drab and dull, looked even worse by comparison to her fine new gowns. She covered the hapless wool with one of the countess's pelisses—a stylish gray garment with fur trim—shoved the matching bonnet over her hair and pulled on a pair of gloves. Suitably attired, she joined Lady Chambelston and Caro as they prepared to leave.

"Come, Mattie. Caro." The countess wrapped an arm around her daughter's shoulders and guided them outside. The maids, Betsy included, gathered the boxes of their purchases and followed.

A raw wind whipped the assembly with threats of rain as soon as they exited the building. Gusts yanked at Mattie's bonnet ribbons and lunged under the pelisse's collar, sending a blizzard of shivers skating down her spine. She shoved her hands into the shallow pockets and encountered the orange she'd saved from last night's dinner.

The fine wrap had been designed for women such as

the countess—women with maids to carry their purchases, women who had little need for the deep pockets Mattie found so convenient in her father's shop. She hadn't wanted to leave behind her old coat that so neatly hid her pistol. But how could she explain her acceptance of a new dress—or four, as Lady Chambelston insisted—and then be so churlish as to refuse the offer of an old pelisse? And it wasn't as if she needed the weapon today. Not without further information.

"A pity the weather proved so uncooperative for our outing. Did you wish to see Hyde Park? I am afraid it will not be at its best." Lady Chambelston seemed determined to treat Mattie as an honored guest—much to Mattie's discomfiture. How could she maintain her justifiable anger in the face of such consideration?

For the first time, doubts crept into her righteous certainties as she realized the man she sought to kill might very well be Lady Chambelston's son. "Oh, I couldn't trouble you further. Besides, I have some personal business to attend to, and as I don't want to inconvenience you, I'll just go alone and return when I have finished."

Lady Chambelston hesitated. "Very well. I shall send Betsy with you. You must not parade about London alone."

Why ever not? Mattie had supported herself for years alone, had faced an invading army alone, had crossed an entire ocean alone. But how to slip away without being detected?

"Oh, my dear Lady Chambelston!" The greeter's overly effusive smile revealed a row of ill-fitting false teeth. "I'm so thrilled to meet you here."

"Good afternoon, Mrs. McKeane." Lady Chambelston tilted her chin the merest degree.

Mrs. McKeane rested her gloved fingers on the countess's arm, her simpering smile growing impossibly wider. "My husband said you would be coming to town. He met Somershurst at his club several days ago, you know."

"Did he indeed?"

"I'm so thankful you arrived in time for our little musicale Friday. I shall send you an invitation—and one for Somershurst also."

"I await the evening with pleasure, as do Caroline and our guest, Miss Fraser, of course." The countess nodded in their direction. Affront glittered in her normally serene blue eyes.

Mrs. McKeane's frown screened her teeth. Her gaze flickered past Caro and Mattie with all the attention she spared for the maids. "Of course. We shall look forward to seeing all the DeChambelles." She fluttered away, leaving Lady Chambelston to mutter under her breath.

"My apologies for subjecting you to my tiff, Miss Fraser. My behavior was not very Christianlike."

"But it was perhaps humanlike." Mattie glanced at Caro, who fortunately remained oblivious to Mrs. McKeane's subtle scorn.

"Perhaps, but we are called to emulate godliness, not succumb to our human nature."

They encountered more ladies with their entourages of men and maids, many of whom looked askance at Caro—though they nodded their deference to the countess. And then once not-quite-discreetly out of earshot, they whispered behind fans, their glares sharp with censure.

Another wave of doubt surged over Mattie as she realized all the DeChambelle wealth and position couldn't procure Caro's acceptance among the so-called enlightened class. An image of Kit DeChambelle embracing his sister flickered in Mattie's mind. Whatever suspicions she might harbor about his intentions, he cherished his sister despite Caro's limitations.

"Oh, Mr. Tubney." Lady Chambelston halted to speak to

a short, squat man approaching from the opposite direction. "How delightful to see you."

"Lady Chambelston." He removed his hat and bowed low at the waist. And then in a first for the afternoon, he aimed watery eyes directly at Caro. "Lady Caroline, how are you?"

The young woman's face lit with her smile. "Tub-bie."

"A pity the weather is not so fine as yesterday, but there is always sunshine in my heart when I encounter you lovely ladies."

"And you always bring a smile to my face with your droll praise." Lady Chambelston gestured to Mattie. "This is our guest, Miss Fraser. From America."

"Welcome to London, Miss Fraser. I hope you enjoy your visit." He shoved the hat back on his head and returned his attention to the countess. "Will you be coming to the next meeting of the Society?"

Mattie shifted from one foot to the other. If she didn't leave soon she would miss Nicky. And then, how would she ever find him? She turned to Betsy, but the maid directed a sly smile toward a vaguely familiar man.

Strange, because Mattie knew almost no one in London. She searched her mind to recall where she might have prior acquaintance with the moderately dressed, middle-aged fellow with the round spectacles. No matter. She had other business to concern her.

The soft voice of the countess and the drone of Tubney's responses continued for several moments longer, then Mattie hedged away. When no one noticed, she crept farther and slipped around the corner.

She was free. Alone. She drew a deep draught of London's damp, smoky air into her lungs and searched the sky above the gathering of roofs for St. Paul's distinctive dome.

* * *

The door squeaked in protest as Kit pushed it ajar. He paused to glance down the silent hallway—being observed now would pose all sorts of complications should Miss Fraser learn of his foray into her apartment. No one there. He released his tension with a whoosh and slipped into the tidy room, then shut the squawking door.

What did he think to find in Miss Fraser's chamber when she'd lost all her possessions to a vandal? And yet, once before he'd believed in a woman's innocence and that miscalculation had cost him dearly. And cost another even more.

His gaze circled the room twice—a bed, a wardrobe and two chairs that framed the window. He crept across the rug to the wardrobe and slid open the drawers, unsurprised to find them bare. The lackluster wool coat dangled from a nearby peg. He ruffled through the pockets and discovered a handkerchief, the solitary occupant. A few crumbs drifted to the floor, but otherwise…nothing. No note. No secret stash of funds. Nothing to indicate Mattie Fraser was otherwise than what she claimed.

The Aubusson rug lay flat on the floor with no suspicious bulges. He checked the fluffy pillows on the bed. Still nothing. He lifted the bedskirt, but the darkness revealed only the chamber pot. With a sigh, he stretched out on his back and shimmied under the mattress, groping the frame.

Just as he concluded he would find the usual—nothing—his fingers brushed a cold, hard object nestled between the mattress and a slat. He plucked the article from its hiding place and slithered back to the center of the room.

There, cuddled against palm, rested a pistol.

"You are a prime piece." He ran a finger along the stock that gleamed with the same polished brown as Mattie Fraser's eyes.

A fine pistol, American made.

It seemed his guest had managed to save one possession from the villain who threatened her. The well-oiled barrel and unclogged touchhole suggested an owner with a purpose. So where and when did Mattie Fraser intend to fire this weapon?

Mattie wove through the tangle of streets—streets that gave way to ever more streets and connected buildings to more buildings, as thick as the forests back home. St. Paul's dome towered above them all, the cross at its pinnacle disappearing into the darkening clouds like the distant, unapproachable God it symbolized.

St. Paul's bells began a discordant song, continuing some minutes until the last peel rolled across the London landscape. And yet the church seemed as far away as ever. She passed a parked hackney, but after a quick calculation of the ride's cost she continued her walk.

As she neared the famous cathedral, her confidence plunged. St. Paul's was built on the same massive scale as London itself. This was like no church of her experience. Why, all of Washington could worship here and still there'd be space aplenty for many more.

All around her the jostling, boisterous sea of humanity moved with a steady purpose that didn't include one slightly lost and very confused American. The biting wind tossed a cautionary raindrop against her cheek.

How would she ever find Nicky? She hiked the length of the building and around a corner. There. A tower with a clock atop whose hands read half past one. She quickened her steps along the facade.

"Mattie!"

She whirled to greet the lad's broad, enthusiastic smile. "There you are, scamp."

He had found her. Her loneliness diminished.

Somewhat.

"Where ye staying, Mattie?"

"You'll never believe. Mr. DeChambelle's father is the Earl of Chambelston." And his brother was the captain of the *Impatience*. Her temper began to simmer again. "I'm staying at his home." She stripped off her gloves and set them down, then shoved her hands into the pelisse's pockets. "Wait 'til you see what I brought you."

His eyes gleamed. "Is that a new coat, Mattie?"

"In a manner of speaking." She passed him the orange.

"Coo! Share it with me, Mattie?"

They found a quiet niche in the garden—out of the path of harried travelers and curious onlookers. Mattie peeled the orange and passed half of it to Nicky.

"Umm." Juice trickled down his chin and blended with the dirt that grayed his once-green coat.

Mattie took a bite of her piece. As the sweet-tart liquid filled her mouth, she closed her eyes and savored the taste.

"Are they treating ye well?"

"Yes. Despite," she drilled him with a look, "your misdeed the other day."

He flashed her an impish grin. "Aw, Mattie, 'is purse 'ad less in it than ol' Stumpy's."

"You took Stumpy's, too?"

"Same day. Deserved it, 'e did, treating ye that way."

"I should reprimand you, but I won't."

"Never could figure out what got into ol' Stumpy. 'E weren't usually so mean."

"I'm American." And that was enough for a man impaired and embittered by war. Mattie shoved another section of the orange into her mouth.

"I wish I could see America sometime."

Homesickness for Washington's sultry summers and crisp winters gnawed at her stomach. Even its muddy streets teemed with optimism rather than the despair so predominant on London's east side. "I do, too."

Nicky had about as much chance of traveling to America as to the moon. Transportation to Australia or violent death on the streets loomed most likely in his future.

She swallowed the lump in her throat. Once. Twice.

"Mostly, though, I wish ye'd go back to America, Mattie."

She'd never intended to leave London until she'd completed her mission. But now? "Soon. I've enjoyed seeing London. And meeting you."

"I've seen plenty of London, and it ain't pretty."

Another doubt took root in Mattie's conscience and a hole opened in her heart. She ripped her gaze from Nicky's dirty face to the spectacular facade of the cathedral that towered over them. What kind of God would abandon a child to London's cruel streets or to a drunk's lax care? "I have to finish my business here first. Did you learn anything?"

"Found where that bloke is staying."

"The one who remembers my brother from the ship?" Bitterness replaced the nectar in her mouth. "I need to talk to this man. Can you arrange it?"

"I'll send word once I talk to 'im."

"But you don't know where the house is."

"You said 'e's the Earl of Chambel—Chambelston, Mattie. 'Ow 'ard can it be to find an earl's 'ouse? Ain't like there are a lot of them."

"Thank you. Can you do one more thing for me?" A gust of wind tossed another raindrop under her borrowed bonnet and against her face, warning her to hurry. "I'm trying to learn the whereabouts of a navy captain, Viscount Somershurst. He's the son of the Earl of Chambelston, and he's supposedly left London. I'm less certain." After all, he wouldn't have actually left the vicinity if he sought to stop her search, would he?

"Where think ye 'e might be?"

Where would such a man go to hide? Not to the nobles in his community. To the rough sailors who owed him loyalty or favors? "Perhaps the docks."

"Swell like that shouldn't be 'ard to find."

"So you'd think." She glanced at the darkening sky. "I ought to return."

His smile drooped, and he peered at her through his haunted dark eyes. "Take care of yourself, Mattie."

He looked so dejected, more than she felt even, that pain snapped like a vise around her heart. She reached into her reticule and withdrew several coins. "Here, take these. I can't have you going hungry in the meantime."

"Still 'ave some from that swell's purse. And Stumpy's." Despite Nick's jaunty grin, disappointment shadowed his eyes. "Keep it, Mattie. I 'ave a feeling ye'll be needing it worse than me someday."

With that chilling prediction, he slipped away into the maze of the city. She stared at the spot where he had disappeared. His words prickled along her spine as she turned the opposite direction and started for the Earl of Chambelston's residence.

As Kit tucked the pistol back into its niche, he encountered three semicrumpled sheets of paper. Curious, he withdrew them, but the darkness under the bed prevented an examination.

Once again he crawled out, papers in hand. He paced to the window and held them to the faint light filtering through the gray clouds. Flipping through the pages, he identified the first as the address he'd provided Miss Fraser and the second as George Fraser's letter to his sister. He read the words again, analyzing each phrase for hidden meanings.

When had Fraser written this note? And for that matter, who'd seen to the letter's delivery? An ordinary sailor, perhaps another pressed American concerned for a loved one left behind? Or an accomplice to Fraser's theft?

The muster books.

The Admiralty required captains to maintain detailed records of every sailor's service. After all, the central Pay Office needed to know who was due compensation. The *Impatience*'s muster books would list the exact dates of George Fraser's tenure on the ship—and those of the others pressed from the *Constance*—from the date of their impressments until they ended their service through desertion, discharge or death. A quick visit to the Admiralty and Kit would discover his first clue as to whom Fraser might have entrusted with his ill-gotten prize.

He started to fold the notes when he remembered Miss Fraser had tucked another page in her hiding place. He glanced—

And stopped, staring at the hateful threat.

"Go home, Yank, lest you meet with an unpleasant end."

Anger sizzled in his blood, heating the fingers that clutched the note Miss Fraser had mentioned in passing last night. By her own admission she'd been at the Admiralty two weeks before she located him. Anyone could have learned of her search for her brother—presuming this was indeed related.

Except she'd asked about Andrew Harley-Smith. Few would have made the link between one Martha Fraser of Washington and lowly sailor George Fraser of the *HMS Impatience*—only those with a vested interest in the missing seaman. Alderston. Julian.

Kit refolded the missives, wriggled under the bed and—

"Higgins! Is Kit home?" His mother's frantic cry reverberated through the house.

Kit's chest tightened around his lungs. A thousand ominous possibilities created dire imaginings in his head. Caro, hurt by the malevolent fiend who had targeted Mattie Fraser. Mattie, injured...or worse. He shoved the papers back into their niche and scrambled out, whacking his head in his haste.

Ignoring the throbbing lump forming on his brow, he vaulted down the stairs. "Maman?"

"Kit!" Caro ran to him, her cheeks streaked with tears.

He stroked her fine hair and looked at Maman over her head. "What happened?"

"Is Mattie here?"

"Here? No, she was with...you." But she wasn't. Not now. Fear melded with anger as his past slammed into the present. Had she left of her own accord? Or not? He glanced out the window at the menacing clouds and gestured Higgins to bring his greatcoat. "Tell me what happened."

"We chose gowns—all tree of us." The accent of her native Normandy thickened Maman's words. "Zen we left and I asked Mattie if she wished to visit Hyde Park."

"What did she say?"

"She mentioned other business. I suggested she take Betsy. But then I stopped for a little tête-à-tête with Mr. Tubney, and I do not remember seeing her after that. Neither does Betsy."

Kit weighed the benefits of questioning the maid but decided such course provided nothing further to gain and risked much time to lose. He squeezed Caro's shoulders and patted Maman's arm. "I'll find her."

"Will you tell me what this is about, this situation with Miss Fraser?"

"I...can't."

Maman touched his cheek as if he were once again a six-year-old boy with a scraped knee and bruised pride. "I will pray for Miss Fraser's safe return."

"I'm sure she would appreciate the sentiment."

"Come, dear one." Maman gathered Caro in her arms. "All will be well."

If only he could believe that were so. Kit shoved an arm into his coat sleeve—then paused. "Maman, is Julian coming for dinner tomorrow?"

A couple of wrinkles ridged her forehead as her brows drew together. "I sent a messenger, but he returned and told me there was no one home."

So both Julian and Mattie had gone missing. Last night she'd mentioned St. Paul's. Had she journeyed there, perhaps for reasons other than a tourist's curiosity? Wherever she'd gone, she was unarmed.

In a situation that seemed to grow ever more threatening.

Chapter Eight

Mattie could no longer deny the obvious—she was lost.

She forced her exhausted feet on—and on and on—but every street, every turn increased her confusion. After she'd wandered past Sebastian's Tobacconer Shop for the third time, she stopped to analyze her location. The cathedral's tall dome disappeared into the darkening clouds. She knew the De-Chambelle residence to be west of St. Paul's, but those same clouds obscured the sun and prevented her from determining the direction.

Around her the throng of Londoners scurried to and fro about their business. A woman in maid's attire bumped into her once, then hurried away without apology or even curiosity as to why Mattie would dawdle in the busy thoroughfare.

Worse, she was being followed. She'd seen that man in the black beaver and gray coat even more times than Sebastian's. He lingered about twenty feet away, feigning interest in a window now that she'd paused.

She ducked into an alley and followed the dark corridor to another street. Two more quick turns and she no longer observed her mysterious companion. She ambled a while longer, then paused once again before the ubiquitous Sebastian's Tobacconer Shop. The window reflected the street scene behind her as shopkeepers shuttered their windows and locked their doors.

A hackney lurched past. Casting pride aside, she checked her reticule to locate the address Mr. DeChambelle had provided her—and discovered only the sad state of her coinage. She'd left the address, along with her brother's letter and the menacing note, under the bed with her pistol. What she wouldn't gladly give to have them all with her now.

Somewhere near Mayfair, Mr. DeChambelle had said. Nicky had assured her he could find the earl's house based on his name alone. Would the hackney driver know its location? She lifted her hand to—

"Well, if it ain't the little Yank." The familiar menace in the strident tones buffeted her like the strengthening wind.

Mattie spun around so fast the pelisse billowed. What was Stumpy doing here? Now? She rammed her hand into the pelisse's pocket—its shallow, *pistol-less* pocket—as the hackney clomped away. The few pedestrians kept eyes on their feet or stared ahead, studiously avoiding the incident about to happen. "Did the Captain's Quarters refuse to serve you drink?"

Stumpy's harsh laugh echoed against the walls of Sebastian's ominously quiet shop. "I thought ye'd be 'alfway across the ocean by now."

"While you are more than halfway to inebriation by now." She sidled away from the sour breath he spewed across her face. Fear wrapped ice around her heart but she wouldn't let this bully see it. She really could use that pistol hiding under the bed though. "If you'd thought at all, you'd have realized I don't respond to threats."

"Then I'll 'ave to do more than threaten." Stumpy thrust his thick-set body against hers. She stumbled back, her nostrils filled with his rancid odors.

He grabbed her arm with his single paw, his fingers bruising her through the pelisse.

"Let go!" She jerked against his grasp. The ripping of fabric blasted her ears, but the tar's hand remained embedded on her sleeve as she fought to free herself. Where was her beaver-hatted companion when she needed assistance?

Stumpy's snigger punched another gust of his fetid breath into her face. "Ye ain't so uppity now."

"I believe the lady asked you to release her." The glacial voice that erupted behind her sliced through Stumpy's drink-fueled rage.

Eyes widening, he snatched his hand away at once. "Sorry there, gov'na. No 'arm done."

"Except to the lady's pelisse. Now get going before I demand restitution on her behalf—in one form or another."

As the snake slithered away, Mattie shifted to face the owner of the unfamiliar voice, her surprise heightening at the sight of his emerald-green coat.

Not her earlier shadow, then. Her benefactor smiled at her from below two of the greenest eyes she'd ever seen. Her gaze slipped lower, over the powerful barrel chest to the rapier he still leveled at the departing Stumpy.

Her rescuer took a polite step backward, sheathed the rapier in his walking stick and tipped his brown silk hat. "My apologies for my impertinence. I couldn't help but notice your distress."

"Please, sir. You needn't apologize. Indeed, I most heartily thank you."

"I don't see your maid. Is she lost, then?"

"Ah, in a manner of speaking."

"Are *you* by chance lost?"

"I—I…" Though her pride itched to contradict so embarrassing a muddle, her common sense suggested otherwise. She offered him a rueful grin. "Yes."

The smile he returned was amiable, not mocking, altering his features from merely ordinary to almost handsome. He sketched her a courtly bow. "Neville Fitzgerald. Perhaps I might be of assistance. What street do you seek?"

"If I knew that, I would be considerably less lost." A couple of raindrops sprinkled her cheek.

His smile broadened. Unlike Stumpy, Mr. Fitzgerald possessed an entire set of teeth. "I can understand how that might contribute to your problem. In what part of the city are you staying?"

"Pardon?"

"Belgravia, Mayfair, St. James," he ticked off the list.

"Near Mayfair, I believe. I've only been staying with these...friends for a day."

"Ah. Well, you do remember *their* names, do you not?" His eyes twinkled with ill-suppressed mischief. "Perhaps I will recognize them."

"DeChambelle."

"The Earl of Chambelston?"

"Yes."

"Rather august company for an...American, is it?"

"Yes, I'm an American." Did that bother him?

Nicky's premonition rose in her mind. At least he'd had the foresight to refuse her money. Several more raindrops splatted against her face. She'd find a room for the night before the storm worsened, then appear, slightly rumpled, at the Admiralty in the morning. Certainly the clerk could direct her to the correct residence. She reached for her reticule—

It was gone!

Fear smashed into her gut and shot bile to her throat. Futilely, she stared down the alley where Stumpy had disappeared with all the money she had in the world.

"Are you feeling well, Miss...?" Mr. Fitzgerald's unexceptional brown brows rose above eyes that studied her face.

"Fraser. I—I think that footpad stole my reticule."

"London is so dangerous these days." He offered her an elbow. "Allow me to escort you to Chambelston's residence."

Was it proper for her to accept his company? Or more to the matter, was it prudent? She hesitated, but as no other options presented themselves, she placed her hand on his sleeve. Her bare fingers brought to mind Lady Chambelston's gloves, now blooming on the ground of St. Paul's garden.

Mr. Fitzgerald set off in what she presumed was the proper direction, the two of them accompanied by a steady drizzle. "So what is an American doing in London, Miss Fraser?"

She eyed Mr. Fitzgerald's elegantly cut coat, his polished boots. "I'm searching for the whereabouts of my brother, an American sailor pressed into your country's navy."

"A terrible practice, impressment. Unfortunately, one must sometimes take exceptional measures when resisting tyranny."

"By committing more tyranny?"

"I suppose it rather does seem that way from your perspective." He tilted his head. "And what ship of ours committed such a dastardly act, Miss Fraser?"

"The *Impatience*."

"Ah." He nodded. Every hair stayed in place, and the unsettling image of Kit DeChambelle and his boyishly disarrayed locks spiked through Mattie's mind. "That explains your relationship with the DeChambelles."

"Then you know the earl—"

"Miss Fraser." A deep, masculine voice slashed through her question—and her composure.

She skidded to a halt.

As if her thoughts had conjured his presence, Kit DeChambelle's frowning countenance emerged from the mist. His gaze lingered on her gloveless fingers resting on Mr. Fitzgerald's sleeve then raked over the rent in his mother's ill-fitting gray pelisse.

"DeChambelle." Fitzgerald's greeting wrapped untold implications into the smoothly spoken name. "I was conveying Miss Fraser to your father's townhouse."

Mr. DeChambelle's frown cut furrows into his cheeks. "I will see Miss Fraser home, Fitzgerald." His precise British speech suited the coldly furious light that glittered in the eyes behind his rain-dotted spectacles. Once again she glimpsed another man, a potentially dangerous man, behind the fissures in his urbane exterior.

Her hand trembled as she released Mr. Fitzgerald's sleeve. "Thank you again for all your help."

"Delighted to have made your acquaintance, Miss Fraser."

She smiled at him, endeavoring to ignore the forbidding aura that swirled from the other man.

Fitzgerald gave her one last distracted nod, then his narrowed green gaze focused on the other man. "When you next see Julian, tell him I am still waiting."

Mr. DeChambelle's shoulders snapped to attention. "I am not your lackey to do your bidding for a coin, Fitzgerald. Deliver your own messages." He clamped his hand around her wrist and whirled her away.

Heat radiated through her arm. They marched side by side in formation for several blocks. When they'd left Fitzgerald well behind, her silent escort lurched to a halt.

"Now then, Miss Fraser, do explain what happened." He cocked his head to one side. Fury yet smoldered in his eyes, suggesting that he had reserved the greater portion of his anger for her. That errant lock of hair dropped across his forehead but nothing erased the intractability in his gaze. It tunneled into her mind, as though he detected more than she could conceal. "Please explain why you drove my mother to hysterics and my sister to tears."

"I got separated from them. And then I got lost." To be sure, an abridged version of the truth. A spark of unease kindled at her hypocrisy. Only last night her anger had flared at his incomplete truths and partial lies.

"How distressing. You must have wandered for hours to discover yourself so far from Bond Street. Allow me to demonstrate an easy method for finding your way back to the house." He flicked a finger at a passing hackney.

The driver steered his horse to the side of the street. "Where to, gov'na?" He eyed Mattie's mangled pelisse with curiosity flickering in his stare.

"Ayton Street." Mr. DeChambelle returned his attention to Mattie and gestured to the seat. "A simple wave, Miss Fraser. So effortless and uncomplicated."

Mattie eschewed his proffered hand and climbed into the cab unaided. "I lost my reticule. I haven't the funds to hire a cab."

His hand locked on the hackney, knuckles white and tight. "Lost, Miss Fraser? Or another of your euphemisms?"

"Stolen then, during the altercation that damaged your mother's pelisse."

"Your belongings seem to disappear at an alarming rate, Miss Fraser."

"Only since I met you."

He bounded into the vehicle and dropped onto the seat beside her, and the driver prodded the horse into motion.

As the cab lurched through a puddle, Kit's fury blazed anew and a thousand questions pounded through his mind. He considered the split in his mother's pelisse. Only a few threads prevented the sleeve from falling completely away. With Miss Fraser's every movement the fabric gaped, revealing the dress beneath. He raked his gaze across her, searching for signs of bruises or blood. Was the attack related to the other incidents that had plagued Miss Fraser? To her purpose in coming to London?

He swiveled on the seat and looked out the back of the hackney but observed only the rain-slicked street and a few hardy souls scurrying to find shelter.

"A footpad attacked me." An icy edge sharpened Miss Fraser's drawl. "Mr. Fitzgerald kindly rescued me, but the fiend escaped with my money."

"Stay away from Fitzgerald."

Surprise registered in the widening eyes. "But, why? He saved me from the assault."

Kit hesitated, but recollections of last night's confession prodded him. His three-day lie of omission about Julian had only deepened her distrust. "Fitzgerald was the first officer on the *Impatience*."

"The *Impatience!* That accounts for his questions about my brother's impressment. Do you think Mr. Fitzgerald recognized my name?"

How could he not, especially since the lieutenant already knew of her presence in the city? But why would Fitzgerald want such details? "Fitzgerald knows you are in London—he was at Julian's townhouse that day I questioned my brother about George Fraser." And Julian had been missing ever since.

Miss Fraser's back stiffened another degree, drawing his attention again to the pelisse's rent sleeve.

"Did you get a good look at the footpad?"

She didn't answer for several long moments. Raindrops pattered against the cab's roof and invaded its interior on a gust of wind. "The sailor from the Captain's Quarters. Stumpy."

"The one-armed man who nearly assaulted you two days

ago?" He smothered his grim satisfaction at this reluctant display of trust.

"The same."

Coincidence? Why had the wretch wandered so far afield from his favorite tavern? "How long has he harassed you?"

"Since the day I arrived. He lost his arm to an American cannonball at Lake Champlain."

But would the rotter treat any other American to the same degree of animosity? Or just one—Mattie Fraser? And then there was Fitzgerald's fortuitous arrival at the scene of the crime. Did the circle of those who knew about George Fraser and the missing orders include the *Impatience*'s first lieutenant? Such a man would be familiar with the dockside taverns where newly unemployed tars gathered.

"I'm sorry about upsetting Caro." The soft brown gaze met Kit's through the gloom. "I'll apologize to her as soon as I next see her."

Her words reactivated his ire. "Before you spend any more time with my sister, Miss Fraser, please tell me—are all your promises equally capricious?"

Grief—guilt?—flashed in her eyes before she jerked her face to stare across the street.

Already he regretted the intemperate words. If innocent, she didn't deserve such abuse. And if she conspired to exploit his family connections, he needed her to remain unaware of his suspicions. "Excuse me, Miss Fraser. My distress caused me to speak disrespectfully."

The pert nose rose a fraction of an inch. "I understand."

Probably—hopefully—not. "Still, it was ill-mannered of me to expend my wrath on you."

"And I am equally at fault for causing her distress. Indeed, I find your concern for Caro commendable."

Kit's pulse quickened at this unexpected praise. And when Miss Fraser rested a gentle hand on his sleeve, his heart raced faster yet. If only he was worthy of such respect. "Don't make me into a paragon. I make mistakes." Deadly ones.

"But when it comes to Caro, no doubt even your mistakes are well-intentioned. How long has she…?"

"Been simpleminded?" His tone was harsh, to match the words. "Since birth. Does her condition unsettle you?"

Shadowed eyes searched his gaze. "I'd always considered it a terrible fate to endure, but your sister doesn't seem to suffer by her affliction."

The hackney turned onto Ayton Street. Kit rapped on the roof, and the driver drew the horse to a halt.

"Caro lives in a world of simple pleasures. She doesn't require fanciful gowns or elevated status or the esteem of strangers for her happiness, only the love and constancy of her family. Sometimes I envy her innocence—she doesn't even understand deceit."

Whereas he'd known little else for ten years.

Pushing such morbid thoughts away, Kit jumped down from the cab, shook a handful of coins from his purse and paid the driver. He extended his other hand to Miss Fraser, not quite expecting her to accept his help, but she fitted her palm to his and those deceptively fragile fingers locked around him. A strong hand. Determined. Dependable. "I never repaid you for your assistance the other day when I, er, lost my money."

"Sir?"

Raindrops sprayed his cheeks. He flipped her hand over and dropped several gold pieces onto her palm.

Her brows drew together as she stared at the coins. "Mr. DeChambelle, the hackney wasn't so expensive. I can't accept money from—"

"Yes, you can."

"Even a simple American like me knows it just isn't done."

"I realize such an offer goes against both your feminine

and national pride, but I cannot leave you destitute. I ask nothing of you in return." He shoved away the oppressive weight of the lie and curled her fingers around the coins. "Please keep them, and we will speak no more of this."

"I—I thank you." She allowed him to assist her from the hackney and together they hiked through the puddles to the townhouse.

Higgins opened the door. As they pulled off their wet garments, Miss Fraser tilted her head, her gaze level. "I haven't yet thanked you for coming to search for me."

He tapped her on the chin. "Try not to get lost again. London is a dangerous place."

Once again ensconced in the cheerful yellow chamber, Mattie tugged the bonnet ribbons loose and pulled the hat from her head. As she tossed the wilted bonnet onto the bed, Betsy arrived with a pitcher.

"Oh, Miss Fraser, we were so concerned for your safety."

"I'm sorry I caused you such distress."

The maid poured water into the bowl. "I put your stockings and shifts in the wardrobe. Oh, and two of your gowns arrived. I pressed the white dress, so you can wear it to the opera tonight."

The opera. In all her agitation over the afternoon's events, Mattie had quite forgotten Lady Chambelston's plans for the evening. "Betsy, you are amazing."

"Can I get you anything else?"

"A hot drink sounds divine. Coffee, preferably."

"Very good, Miss Fraser." The door snicked shut as Betsy withdrew.

Mattie splashed warm water on her cold cheeks. The mirror on the stand reflected haggard eyes underscored with dark crescents. Damp tendrils of hair framed her face. Those ubiquitous freckles—the bane of her childhood quest for beauty—contrasted darkly with her wan complexion. She blotted the water from her face, then her depressing reflection vanished as she turned away, propelled by curiosity to the wardrobe.

She slid open the first drawer and caressed the smooth muslin chemises. How soft they would be against her skin. The next drawer revealed fine silk stockings, and—

Her fingers encountered the sharp edge of parchment. Puzzled, she withdrew the crackling paper. Bold, black print shouted the hateful words at her from a piece a paper twin to the one she'd discovered in her Captain's Quarters room.

Her heart hammered against her ribs as she slammed the drawer shut, locking away her most personal garments. But it didn't matter. She could have excused the first instance as a prank, a toothless threat that expired when she left the inn two days ago. No longer. Her nemesis knew where she was, knew how to reach her, knew her most intimate details.

With shaking hands, she lifted the note and read again.

"This is your second warning, Yank. You will not get another."

Kit poured himself a brandy and sipped it while he waited for the rest of his family. The fine, aged drink slipped down his throat, its sting dulling the lingering edge of his temper.

"Ah, Christopher." Maman swept into the room with Caro on her arm.

"Good evening, Maman. Caro, you look lovely in your blue dress."

Maman glanced about the room. "Miss Fraser is not yet ready to depart?"

"Perhaps she got lost on her way to the salon."

"She does appear to have difficulty with directions."

In more ways than one. Kit raised the snifter to his lips again.

Maman's eyes hardened to match the sapphires at her throat. "Are you certain you should be drinking that?"

"Yes." Anger, boredom and guilt made for a fearsome combination. What would he do when he finished this business? When he once again returned to his aimless existence? The future stretched before him, as dark and bleak as the present. He pushed melancholy thoughts away and took a reverent sip of the excellent brandy. "I am unconvinced as to the wisdom of taking our…guest with us."

"You invited her into our home, Christopher. It is only the opera."

And yet with Miss Fraser even the simplest activities were fraught with danger. The hair on the back of his neck stood on end, alerting him to her presence even before the rustle of silk reached his ears. He pasted a smile over his misgivings and turned to face their…guest.

His hand shook and brandy sloshed onto his shoe.

Miss Fraser hesitated in the doorway, a dress of ivory and green hugging her too-thin form. And yet, despite the sharp edges of her slender frame—a parallel to her sometimes prickly behavior—the gown's proper fit and appropriate colors transformed her from pretty to stunning. Her striking hair had been swept into an elaborate coronet of braids and curls and a few green feathers. Despite their formal style, those tresses flashed fire. Kit's heart momentarily stopped beating—and when it started again, it raced ahead.

A yank on his sleeve hauled his gaze away.

"What?" He looked into Maman's amused gaze.

"Be careful lest you drop your drink."

He glanced down at the vintage brandy soaking the carpet. Suddenly the fire in the grate was much too hot and the drink's bite much too potent. He needed some crisp autumn air to clear his head. The recollection of his calamitous lapse in judgment sobered him to restraint.

"Miss Fraser." Maman swished across the rug, grabbing each of the young woman's gloved hands and drawing her into the room. "You look lovely."

"I'm sorry. I've kept you waiting."

"Only a minute or two. No more."

"Shall we leave?" Kit pivoted to set down his now un-wanted drink and bumped into Caro.

The remaining brandy splashed over the rim of his goblet onto Caro's glove. At least it missed her new dress on its way to join the drink on the rug.

"Kit!" Caro stared at the stain that blotched the snowy satin. Dismay slumped her shoulders and trembled on her lips.

"We still have a few minutes, Caroline." His mother wrapped an arm around his sister's shoulders and guided her to the door. "Let us find you another pair."

They slipped out of the salon, leaving him alone with Miss Fraser. Kit hastily set down the goblet before he caused fur-ther destruction.

"Do you truly think it wise for me to go with your family?" Despite her perfect posture, uncertainty flickered in Miss Fraser's eyes. She fidgeted with the ivory lace that edged the pale column of her neck, white-on-white against her gloved hand. "I feel like an interloper."

Kit tried to visualize those same fingers wrapped around the trigger of the weapon hidden in her chamber. Unfortu-nately the events of the past ten years made once-implausible images seem all too likely. "Caro will be disappointed if you renege now."

"I apologized to her earlier this evening. I hope she under-stood. I never stopped to consider how distressing my actions would be to her—a casualty of needing to answer to no one but myself, I'm afraid. I'll try to be more considerate in the future."

"Caro finds change unsettling. I suppose the world is a frightening place when one sees no reason for the things that happen."

"Your sister is...not what I expected." Shadows crouched in the depths of the dark eyes. "You are very fortunate—in a surprising sort of way."

"Yes, I am, though few understand." Perhaps Mattie with all her loss could see what so many others missed. Kit tugged her fingers away from her neck and clasped them between his. He drew her hand to his mouth and brushed his lips against the inside of her wrist. Mattie's scent wafted through the satin into his awareness.

As he stood above the intricate design of her hair, he inhaled its fresh-washed fragrance. Already the new silk dress radiated with her spicy sunshine scent.

And yet the darkness he sensed in her intensified, surging through his cynicism and provoking an unsettling urge to protect her from further pain. "I will learn what happened to your brother, Miss Fraser—I promise. I can see how very much you loved him."

She wrenched her hand from his grasp. Grief shot through her eyes and blanched the skin under her freckles, then hardened across her cheeks.

Not the gratitude he expected.

More like...fear?

"Kit, shall we—" His mother's smile faltered as she and Caro paused in the doorway.

He clasped Mattie's elbow and ushered her to the other ladies. "Just so, Maman. I have caused us to be late enough as it is."

Elaborately costumed characters paraded about the stage, their silly antics provoking another burst of laughter from the audience. Except for Mattie. The unfamiliar language left her as disoriented as being lost in London. Worse, the meaningless lyrics and bewildering actions failed to dislodge Kit DeChambelle's erroneous conclusion—and the guilt his words provoked.

I can see how very much you loved him.

If only she had been the sister her mother had asked her to be, wanted her to be. Expected her to be.

Mattie closed her eyes and concentrated on the soaring music, letting it suffuse her senses and drown out the rowdy crowd below the box—and her memories of regret and remorse.

The faint creak of Kit DeChambelle's chair, two seats away and flanked on either side by his mother and sister, once again shattered her concentration. She felt him lean toward Caroline—toward her, reducing the melodies to so much noise.

The music accelerated in time with her pulse then crashed to a halt.

Her heart, however, raced on.

"Mat-tie?" Caroline shook her from her trance.

She opened her eyes. "Is it over?" Her voice cracked.

"Unfortunately Miss Fraser, that was only the first act." Kit's deep voice rumbled through her sanity. Despite his smile, his presence crowded the small box and most especially her composure. Vibrations—these having nothing to do with the music or her memories—ricocheted through her.

"How many acts does an opera have?"

"This one has four."

"Four!" They would be here all night. "When does the second act begin?"

"Not for a while. The musicians need to rest, and all here must make sure that friends, acquaintances and enemies have suitably admired their attire. Alas, the night has barely begun."

Mattie rubbed shoulder muscles grown taut with the long moments of sitting. And remembering.

"Perhaps Miss Fraser would enjoy a stroll, Christopher." Mother and son shared a look that excluded the others. Bitterness bubbled in Mattie's stomach, then rose in her throat until she tasted her pain.

I can see how very much you loved him. The disturbing words reverberated through her mind again.

Mr. DeChambelle rose to his feet. "Miss Fraser?"

Even as she started to refuse, his hypnotic stare provoked her unwilling compliance. "Thank you. I should very much enjoy a taste of air." With a deep breath she rose and placed her hand on the severe black of his proffered elbow. The sinewy muscles flexed beneath her fingers, and warmth permeated the sleeve. "What about Caro?"

"She tires easily and the crowds distress her. She'll be happier in the box with Maman."

"Oh." Mattie gave the girl a quick wave. Her legs trembled as Kit led her out of the box into the frenzy of swirling colors and roaring chatter.

He leaned closer, his breath stirring tendrils of hair around her face. "Are you enjoying the opera?"

"It is…different from what I expected."

Amusement tweaked his mouth. "I interpret that as a polite denial."

"No doubt I would appreciate the performance more if I understood what was happening."

"Yes, I can see where that would diminish one's enjoyment. Like most operas, this one is in Italian."

"Does everyone here then know Italian?" Except her.

"Not at all. Most only know the story well enough to understand what scenes the singers are portraying. Besides, Italian sung in such a fashion is virtually unintelligible even to those familiar with the language."

"Which you are?"

"Familiar with Italian? I learned enough so I wouldn't starve if I visited the country. Priorities, you understand."

Oh, she feared she understood only too well. How provincial she must seem. "How many, er, places could you visit without concern of starvation?"

"I can order meals in six languages." He nodded a greeting to a couple who eyed Mattie with blatant curiosity. "Hanville. Miss Wilton."

The heat, the perfumes and the conversations assaulted Mattie's senses as thoroughly as the bustling London streets. So much for that bit of air. Her escort, though, maintained a steady progress as he guided her along some mysterious course among the milling crowd.

"So what is the story?"

"The opera? The count is making, er, improper advances to the reluctant maid. Her betrothed plans to outwit his lord. Very egalitarian, with a villainous nobleman and virtuous commoners. As an American, you should approve."

"And do you approve?"

"DeChambelle." A man in a scarlet uniform paused beside them. "Good to see you back in London."

"Good evening, Major Johnson. Have you met our guest from America, Miss Fraser?"

The officer bowed low. "Miss Fraser, a pleasure. Are you enjoying the performance?"

"It is not what I expected but interesting nonetheless."

"Excellent. Miss Fraser, I offer myself as a willing escort if you would care to experience other noteworthy sights and events while you are visiting."

"Mattie." Kit DeChambelle's deep, masculine voice—possessive with its untoward use of her Christian name—rippled along her back with shivers of awareness. "It is time to return to our box. The next act is about to begin."

"Of course. Major, if you will excuse us?"

"Until our next meeting, Miss Fraser."

Kit clamped down the jealousy that spiked through him at Johnson's last lingering look. Johnson's head bobbed on his skinny neck in a manner reminiscent of a pigeon's strut. Then he disappeared into the crowd.

One could hardly blame the poor blighter for his interest. Mattie's hair caught the candlelight and flamed, burning even Kit's reason to ashes. He drew her through the crush, focusing on the glittering assemblage instead of on her nearness. A futile endeavor, that. Lack of sight heightened other senses, making him even more aware of her. The fragrance of her hair. The soft rustle of her dress.

"You seem to have made a conquest, Miss Fraser."

"A novelty frequently attracts a fleeting notice."

"You do yourself an injustice." Indeed, he found her the most beautiful woman in the building. But his attraction extended beyond the physical to the uncommon loyalty that had induced her to travel an ocean for her brother. And though he knew he trod dangerous ground—again—he knew not how to extricate himself.

The swell of gossip crescendoed around them like a soprano's voice in her death scene. Miss Fraser tilted her head toward him, presenting him with an enchanting study of the slender column of her neck. "Is the audience always so loud during the performance?"

"Louder, at least, in the spring when the *ton* descends on town. Many retire to their estates after June to escape the summer heat and enjoy the autumn hunting."

"I suppose the language doesn't matter so much if no one can hear the performance anyway." She surveyed the crowd again. "It certainly looks as if all of London is here. I cannot imagine more people."

"Do you not have a similar summer exodus in Washington?"

"Indeed, but I suspect our notion of heat differs somewhat from yours."

His chuckle surprised even him. Her gaze flitted back to him, an elfish grin twitching on her lips.

"Miss Fraser." Neville Fitzgerald halted before them and sketched Mattie a bow. "How delightful to see you none the worse for your ordeal this afternoon. Are you enjoying the opera?"

"Immensely, thank you, Mr. Fitzgerald."

"Excuse us, Fitzgerald. Miss Fraser and I really must continue." He brushed past the other man, their shoulders colliding with Kit's haste. And anger.

He could conceive of no good reason for Fitzgerald to be so eager to meet Mattie Fraser. Twice, no less.

Chapter Nine

Kit arrived early at the Admiralty and hung his rain-soaked cloak on a peg. Outside his soot-covered window, gloomy skies all but concealed the approaching dawn. He folded his arms over his chest and watched London awake—uniformed officers marching to meetings, a farmer driving his dray to market, maids dashing on morning errands.

Against the outer office's floor, boot heels tapped an answer to one mystery.

"What happened yesterday?" Kit turned his back to the window as Baxter filled the doorway.

"I did as you asked. I followed the young lady."

"And stood idly by while she was attacked?"

Baxter's eyes glittered with affront. "The man was drunk and unarmed and more belligerent than dangerous. I was going to intervene and then Fitzgerald reached her first. At that point I thought it best to remain unseen."

Kit wasn't pacified. "Go."

"The same assignment?" Baxter glanced at the rain-streaked window.

"Yes." A miserable day for such a task, but after the clerk's inaction during yesterday's crime, Kit could work up little sympathy.

"Will the ladies be going out today?"

The door clicked as Harrison let himself in. Kit gestured him to wait. "I doubt they will venture far to see the sights under such conditions."

"Very good, sir." Baxter bowed, looking askance at Harrison as he strode out.

Kit ran a hand through his hair. "That man..."

"Compassion, my friend." Harrison closed the door and tossed his hat onto an empty chair. "Not everyone was born with your gifts."

"I see *I'll* get no sympathy from you. How is your family?"

"Adjusting."

"I'm sorry about what happened. I never expected the war to follow us home. When I asked Alice to board Mat—Miss Fraser, I never realized—"

"Of course not. I know if you'd suspected something amiss, you wouldn't have brought her to our door. And we'd have missed a delightful guest."

"Who brought destruction to your home. I presume you spoke to Alderston?"

"He's going to make good on our little problem, so Alice will get some new furnishings—something good out of bad. But speaking of bad, about your brother..."

Kit's gut clenched. He dropped into a chair and rested his chin on his fist. "Yes?"

"He's in serious difficulty."

"Gambling? Bad investments?"

Harrison relaxed against the door. "Not that I can discover. I did, however, pick up an interesting tidbit. My source claims Neville Fitzgerald was due to be promoted to captain last spring, but your brother spoke against the promotion."

"Are you suggesting Fitzgerald is blackmailing Julian because of a personal vendetta? Julian selected Fitzgerald as his first lieutenant. I thought…" Fitzgerald's strange words echoed through Kit's mind. What had caused such a significant reversal in their relationship? And what did it have to do with Mattie Fraser? If Fitzgerald did indeed seek vengeance on his former captain, what better way to go about it than to use Mattie to locate the missing orders—and then publicize them. The ensuing scandal would ruin the entire DeChambelle family.

"The word of an officer's captain carries exceptional weight at the Admiralty. And with the war now over, Lieutenant Fitzgerald can consider all opportunity for advancement as defunct as Boney's empire."

"I wish I could find out what happened on that ship." Kit shook his head. "But come. We'll start by finding out *who* was on that ship."

"Where are we going?"

"To search the muster books. The answer has to lie within them. I've never been so grateful for navy bureaucracy."

"Good morning, Miss Fraser." Lady Chambelston glanced up from the breakfast table and greeted Mattie with a smile. "That green looks lovely on you. Did you rest comfortably?"

"Very well, ma'am." Mattie surveyed the array of choices and scooped eggs, toast and trout onto her plate. She carried the food to the table and sat across from the two ladies. "Good morning to you, Caro."

"Mat-tie."

Outside the tall windows, the fog created a feeling of isolation that shut out the rest of the city. "Will we be going out today, my lady?" Mattie pushed out the aristocratic address with difficulty.

"I fear you will find our London welcome even wetter than yesterday, what with this unrelenting rain." The countess helped her daughter get a particularly stubborn piece of ham on her fork. "I thought we would stay home—unless you have pressing business again?"

"Er, no, not today." Heat crawled up Mattie's neck as she pondered a day of freedom, without a concern for her search or safety. How delightful. And disconcerting. And a tad dishonorable. "Where is Mr. DeChambelle?"

"Oh, he departed early this morning."

Mattie's suspicions, so recently mitigated, roused again. Did the matter that called him away on such a dismal morning have anything to do with her? With her search? "Do you know when he'll return?"

"Higgins did not say."

"Mr. DeChambelle told me you also have an older son. A navy captain, I believe." Mattie bit into her toast with carefully feigned nonchalance.

A shadow darkened Lady Chambelston's blue eyes. "That would be Julian. I had three sons, but we lost both Gregory and his son to diphtheria a year ago."

The toast turned to dry wood shavings in Mattie's mouth and caught in her throat when she tried to swallow. She glanced at Caro, now struggling to hold her spoon with fingers that would never grip a utensil in the conventional manner. "I'm sorry for your loss."

"Life oft does not transpire the way we plan, no?"

Mattie considered the troubles that had plagued the Frasers since her mother's early death. Her father's drinking. Her brother's increasing defiance. The final confrontation that shattered an already fractured family and provoked her brother's desertion and…disappearance.

The countess assisted Caro with a glass of milk. Loneliness crushed against Mattie, stealing her appetite for her remaining breakfast. At least Lady Chambelston still had her other children. And her husband. And her elegant homes—all of them—and fine clothes.

Mattie folded her napkin and placed it on the pristine table-cloth. "I think I should like to investigate your library further, if you don't mind, my lady."

"I recommend a new novel called *Waverly*. I think you will enjoy it."

"I tell you, DeChambelle, the *Impatience*'s muster books are not here." Harrison returned another volume to its shelf. A plume of dust shot into the already thick air.

A hundred years of neglect tickled Kit's nose and provoked a sneeze. "They have to be here. Perhaps they are the victim of a clerk with an inadequate understanding of the alphabet."

"We've already searched every document from the past century. If the books were here, we'd have located them by now."

Kit ran his finger along the spines of volumes he'd already checked. Several times. He tugged a random tome from the collection and flipped it open. Spidery handwriting recorded the names and dates of men who'd reported for muster every two weeks.

Harrison stopped him with a touch to his arm. "You do realize what this means?"

Kit snapped the book shut and shoved it back into place. "Someone has deliberately removed them." Someone who didn't want them found. Someone with something to hide.

"Not just any someone. An ordinary seaman wouldn't have access to these files. In truth, many of them can't even read."

Which left the officers, Julian or Fitzgerald chief among them, as the primary suspects. Kit leaned back on his heels and tried to brush the grime from his coat, pondering the ramifications.

"DeChambelle, have you considered that your brother may be in serious trouble?"

"I know he is."

"I don't mean his naval career or his finances or whatever secret he's involved himself in." Harrison's native Yorkshire thickened on his tongue. "I mean his life."

Kit gagged on the dust that gathered in the back of his throat. Julian, who'd once been his best friend, now the brother he scarcely knew. "Are you suggesting Julian has been murdered?"

"He's been missing for several days."

"I feared him the perpetrator of several recent crimes."

"Including my home's destruction?"

"He may have cause."

"And the potential vandal might otherwise be…?"

"I don't know. Fitzgerald, for instance. Or perhaps even Alderston."

"Alderston?" Harrison whistled through his teeth. "The old man's ruthless enough."

But did he have reason enough? After all, Alderston wished for Mattie's success—so long as Kit was there to share in her discovery. Yes, he might wish to make Mattie dependent on Kit, but he'd hardly set disgruntled sailors to attacking her.

"You can continue looking if you wish, DeChambelle, but I need sustenance before I engage in further toil."

"Yes, I can see Alice starves you."

"I'm making the most of the peace." Harrison chuckled and patted the beginning of a paunch, then his expression sobered once again. "Come, my friend. I know you are troubled but the answers you seek are not here."

Did Harrison speak of this situation…or his life? "Where do I find the answers?"

"In a book far older than these."

Kit resisted his customary urge to reject Harrison's preaching. After all, his own attempts at finding meaning had disappointed. But...God? "The accounting of my transgressions would fill all these pages."

"And God will forgive every one of them if you but ask."

Expectant silence lingered like the dust as Kit contemplated the rows of ancient books. "It sounds so simple. Too simple."

"Yes, it does sound simple. And yet, you still haven't succeeded in surrendering your pride."

Pride? How could Harrison accuse him of such when the guilt of his past weighed on his every waking moment? "Come, we must find you that meal lest you starve."

Harrison stared at him—into him—for several uncomfortable moments. Then he gathered the candle and gestured Kit out.

Moments later they bid each other farewell and traveled their separate directions. The rain mingled with the dirt on Kit's hands and turned it to mud. He raised his face to the dreary clouds that reflected his mood. He wanted nothing more than to wash the dust from his throat and the memories from his mind. Drink. He needed a drink—several, in fact.

He needed to become rip-roaring, falling-down drunk.

"I apologize for interrupting your reading, Mattie, but your other gowns have arrived."

Mattie ripped her concentration from a tale of Scottish rebellion to find herself once again in an English library. "The seamstresses must have worked through the night."

Lady Chambelston folded her hands across the front of a burgundy skirt. "I thought you might want to change into something more appropriate in the event we receive callers."

"Callers?" Mattie glanced at the world outside the tall windows. Wet leaves shivered forlornly under the rain's assault.

The countess smiled. "Americans pride themselves on their hardiness, no?"

"And our intelligence. We know the difference between hardy and foolhardy." And introducing Mattie as an honored guest would be the most foolhardy action of all. "I really don't think—"

"I understand." The countess raised a distancing hand, her smile wilting with disappointment. "If you change your mind, you are welcome to join me. Betsy will help you prepare."

Lady Chambelston's slippers swished across the rug as she swept out. Mattie stared at her unfinished paragraph for another quarter of an hour, reading the same words over and over, until remorse for her churlish behavior—especially in light of the countess's thoughtfulness—propelled her to her feet.

She hiked through the maze of halls, stopping once to ask a maid for directions, and reached the yellow chamber some not-so-few minutes later. The gloomy darkness depressed even the room's exuberance. She reached for the bellpull to summon Betsy, then stopped.

If her adversary had left another message the maid might find it when she selected Mattie's clothes. She crossed the soft carpet. The wardrobe drawer scraped as she slid it open and peered—

"Mattie." The harsh whisper sliced through the quiet. "I feared ye weren't 'ere after all."

Heart pounding, she whirled to confront the threat behind her. All three-and-a-half feet of him. Rain sparkled on Nicky's hair, a testament to his recent arrival.

"How did you get in here?"

"Toffs never lock their upper windows. Guess they think we can't climb."

"But how did you know which room I'm using?" She could barely find it herself.

"I opened doors until I saw that." He pointed to her coat, freshly cleaned and brushed and looking as respectable as such a garment could. "They sure 'ave a lot of rooms."

"And most of them empty a good deal of the time. But why did you come?"

"To bring ye a message. Ye must come with me, Mattie."

"Now?"

"That bloke I told ye about?"

"The one who knew my brother on the ship?"

"I promised 'im a crown to meet ye now in 'yde Park."

Hyde Park. Where Lady Chambelston had offered to escort Mattie yesterday. The irony almost provoked a smile.

"We 'ave to go immediately afore 'e leaves."

"I'll get my coat." She yanked it from the peg and thrust her arms through the sleeves. Without a pistol in the pocket the coat felt surprisingly light on her shoulders. Too light, given the weighty events of the past few days. She'd left the weapon behind yesterday, much to her later distress.

A mistake she did not intend to make again.

"Mattie?" Nicky loitered by the door.

"Wait." She clambered under the bed, retrieved the pistol and shoved it into her coat pocket, then collected Mr. De-Chambelle's coins from the armoire. As she crossed the room, she glimpsed her reflection in the mirror. Her coat hid the elegant green dress, leaving her looking like the Mattie of old.

"This way to the tree." Nicky gestured from the door.

"Tree? Why can't we use the stairs?"

"One of them fine folks might see us."

Yes, that could be a problem, not to mention the questions that they would incur should Lady Chambelston or a member of her staff observe their departure.

"'Urry, Mattie. 'E ain't going to wait for us long."

She followed Nicky through the hallway. Several rooms later, he pushed open a door and slipped across the threshold. A beautiful blue coverlet adorned the bed in the otherwise empty chamber. Curtains of a matching hue billowed on the breeze to reveal the open window behind.

Nicky scrambled over the ledge and disappeared. Mattie peered out to where he clung to an oak. A very wet oak. "Come on, Mattie. 'E seemed real scared."

Scared? She was the guest sneaking out of a mansion via a wet tree. She drew in a deep breath and crawled onto the sill. Far below—far, far, below—a garden bench waited for a sunny day.

"Don't look down."

"Right." She stared at the oak for several more seconds while she gathered her courage. If she'd believed in prayer, this would have been a perfect moment to entreat a favor from the Almighty. But God had never granted her past petitions, and she didn't expect him to begin today. She closed her eyes and jumped, arms outstretched to embrace the trunk. A twig scratched her cheek as she passed. She clutched a branch, ignoring the smarting scrapes on her palms.

"Knew ye could do it, Mattie."

Except she hadn't reached the ground yet. She clamped her arms around the branch and swung her leg over. Nicky grabbed her ankle and guided it to the foothold below.

They repeated the process several more times until she heard the soft thud of Nicky's feet hitting the ground.

"Jump, Mattie."

Still afraid to look down, she peeled her fingers off the branch and let herself fall.

"This way." He clasped her wrist and hauled her behind him—through the garden, along an alley and down the street. Without a bonnet to protect her head, the rain pelted her face and drenched her hair.

And then the city ended in a rush of fog-cloaked countryside. Hyde Park. Large trees rose up out of the mist like menacing giants. A stick snapped under her foot, startling her like the crack of a pistol.

The tree canopy, the mist, the inclement weather muffled the sounds and shrouded the sights, creating an uneasy sense of isolation. Eerie, how one could be so alone in a city as crowded as London.

And yet, the prickling at the nape of her neck—

"That's 'im." Nicky pointed to a hulking man propped against a tree trunk. Water dripped from the floppy brim of his hat as he shifted his head from one side to the other. "'Is name is Soggy."

Anticipation and trepidation warred in her. "Soggy? Strange name for a sailor."

"Remember, 'e's expecting a crown."

She'd surrendered all her possessions, forsaken her homeland and traveled an ocean for this moment. What was mere money? "If he tells me what I came to learn, he's welcome to it, and more. You, too, for that matter." She slipped her hand into the pocket, her fingers sorting through the coins.

Soggy's shoulders tensed as he caught sight of them.

Mattie fixed a nonthreatening expression on her face. "Wait here, Nicky."

"I'm going with ye."

The dread clenching around her stomach intensified. "No."

"I don't trust 'im, Mattie." She ripped her stare from the giant to Nicky, whose jaw locked with belligerence.

"Which is precisely why I need you to watch my back."

Nicky hesitated.

"I need you, Nicky. Go!"

With one last sigh, the boy loped off.

Peering through the gloom, she eased closer to the man. "Soggy?"

"Ye the leddy what's wanted to meet me?" He sidled nearer and held out a hand.

Mattie planted a half crown in his palm. "This for agreeing to meet me. The rest after you tell me what I came to learn."

"Yer the Yank's sister. Talk like 'e did." He eyed her shrewdly as he secreted the coin inside a navy blue jacket. The remnants of a uniform?

"Nicky says you served aboard the *Impatience*. I'm seeking information about my brother, an American named George Fraser."

"I knew 'im." Soggy spat on the ground, his gaze darting from tree to tree as if searching for a threat.

"Knew?"

"Aye, 'e's dead."

Mattie braced a hand against the rough, wet bark of a tree trunk as the last hope seeped out of her. Dead. The word plummeted through her mind like a cannonball falling to earth, dropping down until its heavy weight lodged in her heart. And yet, deep inside she'd known she'd never see George again. Known her brother's reckless ways would be his undoing. Known she'd failed in the most important duty of her life. "Tell me."

Those restless eyes gentled. "Are ye sure ye want to know, lass? It weren't pretty."

What had George done that people would lie, cheat and kill to prevent her from discovering? "I have to know."

The tar hesitated several more seconds, then nodded. "Fraser, 'e stole something from the captain."

More thievery, of course. "The captain?" Mattie could only wonder at George's audacity.

"Something real important, miss."

"And the captain had him executed?"

"Not immediatelike. The officers, they wanted that paper back bad, but Fraser wouldn't tell them what 'e did with it."

"Paper? What paper?"

Soggy glanced in either direction before he answered. "Don't know, and not sure I want to find out. I never 'ad much learning. But Fraser, 'e was mightily amused. Bragged 'e would be rich."

And instead he was dead. "So the officers determined to make him talk?"

"Used them very words."

Soft drops of rain bounced steadily against the leaves like the even ticking of a clock. Mattie gathered her courage and composure. The next minutes would determine the course of the rest of her life. "How did they 'make him talk'?"

"Beat 'im."

"The officers?"

"No, no. They 'ad others do it. Under their orders. They whacked 'im with clubs until there weren't nothing left. And then they tossed 'im into the sea."

Mattie staggered as if the blows reached to the present. Her eyes fell shut over her grief, yet her sorrow throbbed in her head like a living being, sucking her strength. Fresh pain contracted around her heart with ferocity enough to crack that lonely, empty organ. Or perhaps the unhealed fissures— left over from childhood—splintered further. Her shoulders drooped with the weight of London's gray skies, and the ever-present smoke burned her eyes. "When?"

"February, right afore we got to America."

This winter past. According to Kit DeChambelle, the ship had patrolled the coast of France until she was tasked with conveying the Treaty of Ghent to America.

Her brother had been murdered—after the signing of the treaty.

"Miss? Ye did promise—"

A pistol shot split the air.

Chapter Ten

"Mattie!" Nicky's scream pierced Mattie's ears above the reverberations from the explosion.

She whirled to see the little boy racing toward her.

No! Right in the path of the shooter.

"Nicky, stop!"

A second blast thundered through the mist.

"Get down!" Mattie yelled, scarce able to hear her own voice above the pounding in her head.

She dashed toward him, sliding on the wet, uneven grass. If only she could reach him before the shooter reloaded—

Something walloped her, pitching her off her feet. Down, down she fell, until her back smacked against the grass.

"Oomph." Stunned, she sprawled on the ground. She tried to find the breath that had been knocked clear of her lungs, but a great weight pressed against her chest. Still, her scattered wits focused on one overriding concern.

Must. Get. Nicky.

She tried to rise, only to realize that the *something* still pinned her down.

A living, breathing someone.

Frantically she shoved at the hard, heavy body atop her but the solid form crushed her against the ground.

"Mattie!" Kit DeChambelle's voice roared in her ears. He shifted ever so slightly, allowing her to breathe again. "Are you hurt?"

"You!" Sharp pains radiated from her side as she sucked great gulps of air into her lungs. Had she been shot? No, that felt like a mere bruise—a London-size bruise—from her fall. She twisted her head and peered through the gloom, but saw only the bare bark of the tree trunk where Soggy had stood. Had he fled, or…? And worse, where was Nicky? He was only a few feet from her when she toppled—or rather, was attacked. He should be here, near her. Unless…

"Are you hurt?" Mr. DeChambelle repeated. The spectacles had fallen off her rescuer's face, leaving her an unobstructed view of the blazing blue eyes.

"Only by you. What are you doing here?"

"I saw you leave so I followed you. What are *you* doing here, Miss Fraser? Must I lock you in a room to keep you from danger?"

"I told you it would be better for all concerned were I to stay at an inn."

"With what funds?"

What funds, indeed. Suspicions raced through her mind. She no longer had any money other than what he had provided. She was completely dependent on the DeChambelles' charity.

By deliberate arrangement?

His brother?

Cold dread congealed the blood around his heart as Kit waited, the interminable moments ticking off, to see if her assailant reloaded and returned. The ominous quiet minced his nerves almost as much as the shooting. Did the villain lurk around a tree, waiting for them to arise?

As the agonizing seconds passed, he strove to determine the origin of the shots but his rage-filled mind could not identify the location. How could he capture the assailant when he didn't know where to look?

"I've got to find him." The mouth two inches from his puffed sweet air against his face.

Him? The shooter? Kit peered through the encroaching darkness as he pushed his weight onto his arms. No bullets grazed his head, so he turned his stare to Mattie's face. "Find whom?"

Her lips pressed together in a flat line of distrust below eyes glimmering with fear and…accusation?

Find whom? His mind leaped across his terror and focused on the seconds before the shot, to the small form in green with its familiar, high-pitched voice. Mattie's little friend, the boy from the Captain's Quarters. Frustration melded with the danger and violence. The anger simmering below his skin threatened to explode to the surface—at her for her heedless escape, at the man who wanted her dead. He shoved it aside for another time and focused on his fear for her. So close. So frighteningly, awfully close. He brushed the hair from her face, savoring the warm, soft skin against his fingertips.

She grabbed his wrist and held it at bay. "Don't touch me."

He yanked his hand away, stung by the harsh words. Her dark eyes aimed anger, even repulsion, at him. The freckles sprayed brown against her pallor, and she rubbed her cheek as if his touch—his rescue—had lacerated her skin. Then the fire in her eyes dimmed and behind their depths flickered shadows of…vulnerability. Grief. Loss?

Simple shock? Or did she lay the blame for her troubles at his feet?

Now that the imminent danger had passed, a crowd of the curious, drawn by the gunshots and a taste for the macabre, swelled around them. Would such a gathering make her safer? Or put her more in jeopardy? He rolled over and rose to a crouch beside her, searching for any telltale red but he beheld only the mud pasted to her hair and clothes.

"You there," he called over his shoulder towards the boldest member of the gathering rabble. "Was anyone injured?"

The man muttered something incoherent and shook his head.

"Did anyone see what happened? Where the scoundrel went?"

Unwilling to become involved, the more cowardly of the spectators began to dissipate into the shadows.

To hunt the shooter now would leave Mattie exposed and alone, but by the time he escorted her home and returned, the trail would be colder than the North Sea in February. He clenched his fists in frustration, imagining for a moment the villain's neck between them. "Come, let us get you home."

"But I must—"

"Now, Mattie! There is nothing to be gained by staying here any longer. If your friend was here—injured—we would know by now. Obviously he fled for safety, and you should, too. It is too dark to find anyone without knowing where to look—we would only further endanger you." He stood and pulled her to her feet. Her hair cascaded over her shoulders and knotted around their entwined hands. Those fragile fingers chilled his palm, as if the icy dread that tightened around his gut circulated to her. She shook with shock—the full reaction to her near death only now settling in her.

He wrapped his arm around her shoulders. She tried to pull away—as if she found even this touch distasteful—but her unsteady legs gave way and nearly felled her. He caught her and pulled her close. She dragged another shuddering breath into her lungs, reminding him anew that his two-second miscalculation had nearly cost her life. Without the poise so much a part of her, she seemed so delicate, a shell of the uncompromising woman he admired.

Even the deepening darkness could not disguise the water, mud and debris that marred her coat. If anything happened to Mattie, he would lose the opportunity to save Julian. Indeed, he would lose his last chance to save his soul from the dark despair that so often shadowed his steps and threatened to obliterate his future.

Her shudders increased until at last he scooped her in his arms and ran until he reached the edge of the park. Frantically he searched for a hackney but the residents here mostly traveled in their own curricles, carriages and coaches.

Where was Baxter? Had he run after Mattie's assailant? Or did he yet stand in the rain in front of his parents' house, watching the front door? But who would have expected Mattie to escape via a rear window? Certainly not Kit, who had seen the maneuver by merest chance when he happened to glance out his chamber window.

Two streets later, Kit finally spotted a cab parked in front of a townhouse. He ran to its side and yanked open the door. "Ayton Street."

"Blimy! Ye can't do that!" The wet driver raised his whip. "I'm waiting for a fare."

"I'll pay you double. Triple if you hurry." Kit shoved Mattie onto the seat and jumped in after her.

The cab shot forward like another pistol shot. The suddenly eager driver pushed his nag into breakneck speed, the hackney wheels frequently parting company with the wet bricks as they careened around people, carts and an occasional dog.

Kit had followed Mattie hoping to discover the evidence he needed to absolve Julian of treason. Now, it seemed, someone wanted her dead.

Cold. Mattie was so cold. So cold, she couldn't stop shivering. The wet chill saturating her clothes penetrated all the way into her bones. She hated the feeling of helplessness, of weakness, but after the horror over George's fate and her angst over Nicky's disappearance her mind had numbed to match her knees.

The hackney driver whipped around another turn, propelling her across the seat and against *him*. She wanted to sob, to shout, to shove him away. And yet the rational part of her mind gently admonished her against holding him responsible for another's crime.

Kit DeChambelle wrapped his arm around her, pressing her shivering form to his warmth. Pinned against him, she felt the hardness of his strength—the strength that had knocked her from a bullet's path. She raised her chin and stared into his eyes while the air around them crackled with the tension.

"Kit." Her voice was but a ragged whisper, scarcely audible over the pounding of her heart. "I—I didn't thank you—"

He stopped her with a finger to her lips. "I thought he had killed you, and that nearly killed me." His rapid, exhausted gasps—earned when he carried her from danger—wafted across her cheeks as his blue eyes stared at her across an impenetrable gulf of class, country and kin.

Intertwined families and divided loyalties.

She'd been alone so long. So long. Longing welled within her and splashed across her mind—the old familiar yearning for someone, anyone who cared about Mattie Fraser's fate, who would offer to shoulder some of her burdens or push her from the path of a bullet.

Then his lips brushed hers.

Her eyes drifted shut to block all but the sensations that flooded her being—unfamiliar sensations almost frightening in their intensity. Her misgivings melted like so much ice under the ache of yearning.

The hackney lurched to a halt before the Earl of Chambelston's mansion. She snapped her eyes open and stared into the midnight sky of Kit DeChambelle's gaze. Was that regret that so quickly shadowed the depths of his stare? Confusion befuddled her mind, but she summoned her pride and stiffened her spine.

He pulled away, leaving her suddenly bereft for something that couldn't be. After he paid the driver the promised sum, he reached for her.

Mattie stopped him with a hand. She couldn't bear it if he held her again. "I—I can walk."

Doubt twisted his mouth but he assisted her without comment, then ushered her to the house, his hand again anchored to her back in a manner at once presumptuous and protective. Higgins hovered by the door, his face impassive despite her wild hair and soiled, rent clothes.

"Higgins, is my mother about?"

"I'm afraid she is out, sir."

"Out?" A frown creased his brow. "She hadn't planned an excursion today. Where did she go?"

"I wouldn't know, sir. Would you like me to check with one of the grooms?"

"No, that isn't necessary. Inform Mrs. Parker that Miss Fraser needs a warm bath and a hot toddy."

The butler nodded. "Very good, sir."

Kit waited until the butler strode away, then turned to Mattie. Water darkened his hair and plastered it to his forehead, and grass stains streaked his rumpled cravat. "You need dry clothes."

"I need to find Nicky. To know if he is harmed."

He folded his arms across his chest, his stare level. "I'm going out to make inquiries. I'll see what I can learn."

"Thank you."

The silence stretched for several moments while they gazed at each other across a rift of distrust, reluctant respect and undeniable attraction. "Mattie, have you considered a workhouse for Nicky?"

"I can't send him anywhere against his wishes."

"You could suggest it to him. He'd listen to you."

"And what happens to the children in those places?" Rumors about the conditions at England's poorhouses had reached even Mattie's ears during her two weeks at the Captain's Quarters.

Kit's hesitation confirmed the reports' accuracy. "He'll die on the streets."

"That's not an answer."

"They are fed. Clothed. Educated in a trade."

"Would you ever send Caro to such a place?"

A tic throbbed on the edge of his jaw. "To save her from starvation, yes."

"Nicky isn't starving."

"Because he steals. Do you realize what will happen to him when he is caught? Mattie, if you truly care for the boy you must convince him to end his life of crime."

"I—I'll speak to him." If she ever saw him again. A chill rippled up her back. From her exposure to the cold rain or contemplation of Nicky's likely destiny?

"You're freezing." Concern etched circles under Kit's eyes. "If you don't remove those wet clothes, you'll catch your death of cold. Do you need me to assist you to your chamber?"

"No, I'll be fine. Thank you."

Indeed, she needed to get away to think without the disruption of those perceptive eyes peering into her thoughts, or that concern—for her!—chipping away her resolve.

She trudged up the stairs, the water on her coat trickling onto the stair treads. At the door to her chamber she paused, hand on the knob. Her chamber? Or her prison cell?

But she was destitute, dependent on the charity and good graces of the one family in England she most wanted to hate.

She opened the door and slipped into the room, dripping more water onto the fine carpet.

The reflection that stared back from the mirror looked much the same as before. Wet, lank hair had escaped its pins and her cold lips stood out in relief against her pale face. She touched her fingertips against her so-recently-kissed lips, wanting desperately to believe she could find a future, comfort, a cure here. With Kit DeChambelle. But already, cold reality had begun to settle in.

Someone had delivered those notes to her room at the Captain's Quarters. To here.

And then there was her able collaborator who'd so recently saved her from gunfire. Kit DeChambelle had seen Nicky with her but once, at the Captain's Quarters. Yet despite the gloomy skies and the legion of orphans that roved London's streets, he'd recognized the boy again today.

The door squeaked as Mrs. Parker entered. "Your hot toddy, Miss Fraser." Steam swirled from the liquid in a display of warmth and comfort. Mattie tore her gaze from the solace of a hot drink, to the housekeeper.

"Thank you."

"Betsy will bring your hot bath."

Despite the warm cup in Mattie's hand, a chill coiled through her as the housekeeper strode out of the chamber. She knew little of Kit DeChambelle, only that his brother had ordered George's death. Indeed, she had only Kit's word he was Andrew Harley-Smith's friend. The threats had begun immediately after her first meeting with Kit, shortly before he'd arrived in the nick of time to rescue her from her eviction.

How convenient, that. Where had he been during her aborted meeting with Soggy? How much had he heard?

She slipped her hand into her pocket, expecting her

fingers to brush the barrel of the pistol she'd brought from America.

It was gone.

Kit raked a hand through his sodden hair, his mind roiling with the implications of his actions. The taste of Mattie yet lingered on his lips, defying him to regret his impulse. He'd kissed a woman whose loyalties lay with an enemy country. A woman whose brother had conspired to sully the reputations of Kit's brother and king. A woman who perhaps, even now, schemed to retrieve stolen orders and convey them to American officials.

But if she were innocent?

So much the worse.

Ironic, but it seemed a few scruples yet lurked inside him. He'd taken advantage of a scared and lonely woman, one with neither protection nor provisions. Alderston might be appalled by Kit's show of conscience, but then Alderston would seduce a woman for mercenary advantage without qualm.

He'd have to apologize—even if he wasn't quite sorry for his behavior. Even if he was secretly glad she hadn't pulled away. Nothing worked quite like fear to compel a man to face his feelings. He stripped off his ruined clothes and forced his mind away from their kiss to the most important matter of all.

Mattie's *life*.

An image niggled in the back of his mind. He was missing something. Something important.

His valet slipped into the room and retrieved a dry shirt.

Kit did not so much as glance at it, but held out his arms. "I need my spare spectacles."

"I'll get them for you."

Every time he closed his eyes he imagined Mattie's contorted body lying in a pool of blood. That it had transpired otherwise, that Mattie was unharmed but for a few scrapes and bruises would not assuage his nightmares.

The woman he had placed in his parents' house could bring danger to them all unless he could determine the secret Mattie knew—or had the potential to learn. And Mattie had been as unforthcoming about her involvement as his brother had. But how could he ask for her trust when he used her for his own ends?

At this moment Kit wanted nothing more than to consign Julian to his fate. His brother was a man full grown. Let him fight his own battles. But an image of Caro ever hovered at the edge of Kit's thoughts, reminding him that battles oft caused casualties beyond the principals involved. As he well knew.

He relived the moments just prior to the shooting, when Mattie stood by her purse-thieving friend and a menacing hulk of a man. In the distance loomed a fourth figure, his features obscured—other than the pistol the specter raised and aimed. Kit let his eyes drift shut and focused on the shooter. Would he see his brother's features in his dreams tonight?

But that made no sense. War had been Julian's livelihood for two decades. He was a crack shot—as evidenced by his very survival. Either Julian was not involved, or else he was not trying to hit his target. And couldn't the same also be said of Fitzgerald?

Shock waves rippled through Kit again at the recollection of that pistol report. And at last, the recognition of the anomaly that troubled him.

The shooter raised only one arm—because the shooter had only one arm.

One arm. Just like the man at the inn when the proprietor had evicted Mattie. Just like the man she'd claimed had attacked her only yesterday and stolen her reticule.

One arm. But two shots.

Unfortunately Kit had paid even less attention to the second

shot than the first, his overriding concern having been to
reach Mattie. And then he'd lost his spectacles in their collision, leaving him only hazy outlines of those present.

He focused his attention away from what he'd seen to what
he'd heard. From where had that second pistol report originated? Not the same place as the first. Behind him, perhaps?

Then who fired it?

And at whom?

Chapter Eleven

Kit exited Turner's hackney and splashed through the muck until he reached the dilapidated Captain's Quarters. Sounds and smells assaulted his senses as he stepped over the threshold. Despite the early hour, legions of hardened men fallen on harder times packed the tavern—sailors, dock workers, vagrants and sundry other miscreants. As his eyes adjusted to the gloom he searched out a likely place to begin.

There, in the corner. Three tars whose eyes gleamed undulled by drink as they met his gaze, then glanced away. He stomped through ale puddles, their odor overpowered by the stench of unwashed bodies. "May I?" He scraped the stool across the floor and dropped onto it before they could refuse.

The men made a point of ignoring him.

Kit would not be ignored. "Do you come here often?"

The man on the opposite side of the table thumped his mug down with a slosh. "Fair piece." A loud belch escaped with his words.

"Can I get somethin' for ye?" A serving maid with unnaturally red hair elbowed her way between him and the neighboring sailor.

"Ale." Kit braced his elbows on the table as the maid

sashayed away. "I've been hired to locate a man who comes here on occasion. A man with one arm."

The three men stared at him for several long seconds. Sailors supposedly always had a yarn to share, but these tars were as garrulous as his brother.

"Ye a Runner?" The man to Kit's left, owner of a scraggly beard, scratched his belly where his coarse cotton shirt stretched across his paunch.

"I didn't say that."

A look passed among the men.

"There be any number of men who lost arms—or legs or eyes or other essential parts—for God, king and country." The man on Kit's right pushed up his sleeves as he grabbed his drink. A long, wide scar sliced up his forearm. "Only to starve when they got 'ome."

Kit drew three half crowns from inside his coat and clanked them on the table where they gleamed against the dirty surface. "I'm certain His Majesty regrets the oversight."

The men froze for a moment, then glanced at each other, the glitter in their eyes rivaling the brilliance of the coins. "The king, or the gent paying ye to ask about us law-abiding citizens?"

"Perhaps service to one renders service to the other."

The third man looked at the coins. "Sounds like 'e's looking for Stumpy."

"Any of you seen him today?"

The same man gulped another swig of ale, then shrugged and replied. "Not tonight, gov'na."

He sensed the serving maid saunter up behind him, and he fought the urge to shift out of her way as she plunked a mug before him. Ale slopped onto the scum-coated tabletop.

Better there than his stomach, perhaps.

From the corner of his eye, he saw Turner swagger to a table to his left and order a drink. Kit pulled out several more coins and pressed them into the wench's callused palm. Perhaps they would be more forthcoming inebriated. "Bring more for my friends."

Her eyes lit up when she examined the coins. "Anythin' for ye, dearie."

"But you *do* know Stumpy?" he prodded his companions.

The bearded man offered him a yellow-toothed grin. "Peculiar, but ye ain't the first gent asking after 'im. A popular fellow that Stumpy's been recently."

"Oh? Someone else asked about him?" Kit raised his tankard and gingerly sipped. The ale splashed into his stomach in a single, cold lump. Snatches of Julian's conversation with Fitzgerald replayed in Kit's mind. Fitzgerald, the man who'd happened to rescue Mattie Fraser—from the selfsame Stumpy, no less—in a city the size of London. "What'd he look like?"

"Brown hair. Kind of ordinarylike. Maybe eight stone, and not much taller than Tessie there." He nodded toward the henna-haired maid slopping drinks onto a nearby table.

"Mouselike," the belcher embellished. "But Stumpy wasn't never much more than a rat 'imself."

Relief uncurled in Kit's chest. Too short and thin to be Julian. Or Fitzgerald, for that matter. Besides, after so many years at sea, in all likelihood either of them would be recognized in this locale. So who wanted to know? "Did Stumpy behave differently recently? Had he come into some unexpected funds?"

"Polly claims 'e 'ad some money the other day, but Stumpy said 'is purse was pinched."

The maid returned with three more mugs of ale. She crowded near Kit's face again as she flung them onto the table.

He turned away. Two tables behind, a beefy thug stared at

him, eyes glowing with malice over the rim of his tankard. Muscles rippled beneath his stained shirt as he slapped the mug against the table, his gaze still glued to Kit. Did he assess him as an easy mark for a few pounds?

Or was it something more sinister?

Mattie.

If *he* were now being followed, how safe would she be at his parents' house? And how safe would his family be with Mattie there? "What time does Stumpy usually come here?"

"'E's usually 'ere by now, gov'na. Don't know 'ow's I remember a day when 'e ain't been drunk already by this time."

As he feared. Kit glanced around the shadowy room. No, there was nothing more he could gain here this night unless Stumpy put in a belated appearance.

Or more likely, dearly departed Stumpy's ghost visited his old haunts.

"Add my personal gratitude to the king's." He plopped a few more coins onto the table. "A pleasure, gentlemen."

Mattie needed a plan.

The warm bath and dry clothes—her new brown gown—halted her shivers but her worry about Nicky remained. She stared out the yellow chamber's window. Roof after roof peered over the walls that circled the Chambelston gardens. How did one go about locating a single homeless orphan in a city the size of London? Especially if he might be…injured.

Nicky.

Was he hurt? Did he lie even now with a ball lodged in his body? A ball meant for *her*. She hadn't been able to save George, either.

Murdered. Murdered. *Murdered.* The word beat in time with the cadence of her pounding heart. No wonder someone wanted her dead. George, killed on the order of…Viscount Somershurst, Kit DeChambelle's brother.

George's face flitted through her memory—his gap-toothed grin when he joked with their mother, the quivering lip that belied his stoicism at her funeral, the shadows in his eyes at their father's neglect, the rebellious sneer when he left forever. How had that face appeared after a beating severe enough to kill?

And then those memories of her brother's features metamorphosed into Nicky's.

The crushing pressure around her heart sapped her breath. She dropped into a chair and buried her face in her hands as the deluge of emotions surged over her.

"Mattie?" The whisper tickled her consciousness. "Mattie?"

She raised her head, expecting some reproachful specter. Nicky's form wavered but remained in the doorway. Real? Hot emotion coiled through her belly, and she raised her hands to her throat as she struggled to restrain the tearful exclamation that would attract the servants' attention. "Nicky? Oh, Nicky, I've been so worried." His coat had taken on an additional layer of dirt and the rain had made tracks through the grime on his face. But he was here. And he appeared fine.

"Be ye all right, Mattie?"

She waved a dismissive hand. "Quite. I looked and then you were gone and I didn't know how to find you. What happened?"

"I went after the bounder what shot at ye, but when I got back to the park ye were gone." Fear haunted Nicky's already too-serious eyes. "Stumpy's dead."

"Stumpy?" For a minute his name and image blurred in her mind with Soggy's.

"The bully from the Captain's Quarters what used to give ye such a bad time."

Chills rained over her with the bitterness of cold London showers as she remembered the one-armed assailant who'd stolen her reticule—was it only yesterday? "How?"

"Someone shot 'im. Mattie, 'e was there today."

"There?"

"The park." Nicky wandered over to the bedside table and picked up the book. He flipped it around several times as if he couldn't decide which direction was correct, then set it down, surprisingly gently.

Mattie's chest tightened as she recognized another unfulfilled desire. But how would a boy of the streets find time or teachers for schooling? "Then Stumpy was the man you chased?"

He shook his head and shaggy, dark hair fell into his eyes. "That fella 'ad two arms, same as me and you. I lost 'im. Then when I got back, I found Stumpy with a bullet in 'is 'ead."

"Oh, Nicky." She bent down and wrapped her arms around him as she tried to put the strange pieces together. Stumpy, who had threatened her on multiple occasions, had been shot near the same spot, near the same time that someone had tried to kill her. What was the relationship?

Kit? Her heart rebelled at such a thought, but, her mind niggled, where *had* he gone after he'd escorted her to the house? But surely had Stumpy been witness to or participant in the event, he wouldn't have lingered long enough in Hyde Park for Kit to locate him.

No, according to Nicky, Stumpy had met his fate too soon for Kit to have been the culprit.

Then where was he?

And what had become of her informant? He'd been nervous for the entire duration of their conversation, as if he'd expected trouble. Because he knew he possessed dangerous secrets?

The door squeaked. Mattie froze, her breathing only beginning again when she identified Betsy, her arms encumbered with Mattie's clothes. "Oh, Miss Fraser. I thought you were in the library. I brought—oh!"

At least the dragon of a housekeeper hadn't discovered Nicky.

"I'll take that." Mattie crossed the room and retrieved the gown.

"Did you want me to take your coat?"

"No, thank you. You may go."

Betsy backed out with one last curious look at Nicky, whose eyes were the size of carriage wheels.

"Well," Mattie hastened to reassure Nicky when his brows drew together in concern at being discovered, "Stumpy's death should make me safer."

He pulled away and reached into his coat. "If ye want to stay safe, Mattie, ye ought to take better care of this." He extracted her pistol from his waistband, and passed it to her.

The pressure in her chest—her heart swelling with love for this boy—forestalled the flow of air to her lungs. "You found it. I wager this is the first item you have ever returned to its owner."

He flashed her a grin that failed to alleviate the concern in his old man's eyes. "Ye must leave, Mattie. Back to America. Yer brother's enemies know where ye be."

"For all we know, the shooter could have been someone Stumpy cheated out of a few shillings at cards." Not a scenario she believed, but perhaps one that would allay his fears.

But Nicky was too streetwise for such suggestions. "Ye can't stay 'ere."

But she had nowhere else to go, and no funds to get there.

"I 'ave other news for ye. That gent yer looking for? Rumor is that 'e's back."

"Viscount Somershurst?"

"That one."

The decision of a lifetime—the quest for which she'd sacrificed her home, her country, her possessions, even her self-respect—loomed before her. She stared at her hands, at the fingers still wrapped around the gun. Doubts appealed to her heart, reminding her of Caro's friendship, Lady Chambelston's kindnesses, Kit's...what?

"Mattie?"

And then she looked at Nicky, seeing in his troubled face a young George Fraser's forlorn features. A captain was the absolute ruler of his ship. An English court would never convict Viscount Somershurst of murder, even should Mattie have him charged. She hardened her heart. She was her brother's only hope for justice.

"Mattie?" Nicky repeated her name.

She, however, would be punished. Most likely a hanging—because the English would find a woman shooting a nobleman to be a far greater sin than that same man having her brother beaten to death.

But then, it seemed someone already wanted her dead.

"What are ye doing, Mattie?"

Her hand shook as she checked the pistol's flashpan. Then she grabbed her coat. The wool had absorbed the afternoon's rain, making it even heavier than usual. No matter. She wouldn't need the garment for long. She swung it around her shoulders and shoved the gun into its pocket. It burned against the side of her body, straight to her cold heart. "I'm going to pay Viscount Somershurst a visit."

"Tonight?"

"Now."

Nicky watched her, apprehension drawing his brows together. "I'll come with ye."

"I..." For the first time since she had sold the store in Washington, she wavered, as concern for Nicky and satisfaction for her brother warred within her. "No, Nicky. I couldn't live with myself if you got hurt."

Pleasure sparked in his dark eyes. "Ye needn't worry about me."

"But I do." Besides, she didn't want Nicky to witness her end. "If you love me, Nicky, please go."

Stubbornness quivered on his outthrust lower lip. "Mattie, please don't—"

"Here." She dipped her hand in her pocket, pulled out the change that remained from her venture with Soggy and thrust the coins into Nicky's hands. "You'll need more but this will get you started. Promise me you'll find a ship. I want you to go to America."

"But Mattie—"

"Go to Washington and ask for Lilla Boyd. She was my neighbor." And the closest thing Mattie'd had to a mother during the past sixteen years. "She'll help you find a job, maybe an apprenticeship somewhere."

"But—"

"Start a new life."

"But I want a life with ye, Mattie," he whispered.

"Go." She wrenched open the door before her resolve wavered. The hall was empty. "I love you, Nicky," she whispered to herself.

Then he turned and walked away, leaving her alone with her gun.

Mattie's fists blasted against the door like gunfire. She waited several heartbeats, then struck the door again.

A faint glow glimmered in the transom, then the door swung open.

"I insist—"

This wasn't an imperturbable butler.

The deep tan that stained this man's face and the stubble

that flecked his chin couldn't disguise his identity. Not when the candle flame glinted on his blond hair and glimmered in his deep blue eyes.

Eyes so familiar another fissure split her heart.

"You must be Miss Fraser. Won't you come in?" Julian DeChambelle, Viscount Somershurst, stepped aside and gestured her into the foyer. Even his voice matched that of his brother.

Well, *her* brother's voice had been silenced forever—because of the order of this one man.

She ripped the pistol from her pocket and leveled it at him. "You've been expecting me."

His crooked smile mocked…whom? Her? Him? "Shall we adjourn to the library for this conversation, Miss Fraser?"

"We have nothing to say to each other."

He was more rugged than handsome, his face weathered brown leather with crow's feet serrating the corners of those DeChambelle eyes. Mattie hardened her heart against his marked resemblance to those who had been so kind—his mother, his father, even Caro. He nodded toward her pistol. "Is it loaded?"

"Of course." Why didn't she shoot him and be done with the deed?

"You should know that I didn't impress your brother, Miss Fraser. That responsibility—seeing the ship is completely manned—belongs to the first lieutenant."

"Your excuses won't change my mind. As captain, you are responsible for all that happens aboard your ship."

"Just so, Miss Fraser. I was responsible, and your brother was irresponsible. Are you certain you would not prefer to sit in the library?"

"No! Nor do I want to hear about my brother's failings." She knew what kind of man he was but he still hadn't deserved to die.

"He stole from me, Miss Fraser. And then he refused a direct order to return the purloined article."

"He wasn't a citizen of your country, and the peace treaty had already been signed." Her voice rose and she paused to collect her composure. "He didn't even belong on your ship."

"Be that as it may, Miss Fraser, we have already agreed that as captain I was responsible for everything that happened on that ship. Everything. And that includes punishment for thievery."

"Of a piece of paper! What was so important that you were willing to kill for it?"

"My reputation."

The gun wavered in her hands. She jerked it aright. He never flinched. "No one can steal a reputation, Somershurst. You gave it away."

"So wise. I begin to see how you have so fascinated *my* brother."

Her heart skipped a beat. She focused on his nose—his unscarred nose—rather than those features so similar to Kit's. She couldn't—wouldn't—think of Kit now. She tightened her finger around the trigger. She would not let his words rattle her, sway her. Stop her.

He stretched out a hand. "Give me the gun, Miss Fraser."

Another twinge of misgiving scratched against her conscience as she hesitated. And then footsteps rustled to her left. A servant? A friend? She whirled, swinging the pistol around to face this new threat. Her fingers tightened instinctively around the stock, the trigger.

The gun exploded in her hand. The shock slammed Mattie into the wall behind her and knocked the breath from her lungs.

"Maman!"

Mattie sucked in great gasps of air and turned her head.

The Countess of Chambelston stood in the doorway, the surprised circle of her mouth almost as big as the hole that opened in her side.

Then she slumped to the floor.

Chapter Twelve

"No! No, no, no!" Mattie's screams reverberated off the foyer's high ceiling louder than any gunshot. White lights flashed behind her eyes as her mind tried to block the horror of what she'd done, but the sulfurous odor of gunpowder permeated her very being, allowing her no escape.

The pistol slipped out of her numb fingers and clattered against the floor. Too late. Too late.

Blood splattered the wall in a crazy pattern, as if a dog had shaken off red rain. One wide stripe streaked down the wall, pointing directly to the fallen Lady Chambelston.

"Mattie? Why...?" Confusion and pain clouded her eyes, then her lashes drifted down to rest on her cheeks. The color leached from her face as the blood pooled below her on the parquet.

Not unlike the strength seeping out of Mattie's legs as bile—bitter, bitter bile—clogged her throat. She braced herself for her coming death. She didn't fear it. She welcomed it. Somershurst would beat her just like her brother—but unlike George she deserved his wrath.

But Somershurst dropped to his knees.

His movements galvanized Mattie into action. Ignoring the ever-widening puddle of blood, she crouched beside the fallen woman. "Give me your cravat! We need something to staunch the bleeding."

He hesitated for two seconds, then his years of military training and experience awakened and he shook off his shock. He jerked the cravat knot undone, yanked the fabric from his neck and hurled it to her. "The wound on her back where the bullet exited will be worse. Start there. I'll get more linen." He vaulted to his feet and raced to a nearby door, his boots pounding against the floor.

Mattie shifted the countess onto her uninjured side, yet despite her best efforts to be gentle the lady groaned as the pain of the movement reached into even her unconscious state. The new position revealed the ghastly hole. Mattie's handiwork. She wadded up the cravat and pressed it to the wound, noting with dismay how quickly the fabric became saturated with blood.

"I—I…Mattie?"

She glanced up at the boy lurking outside the gaping front door, a witness to her evil.

"Nicky!"

Eyes round with shock and horror, Nicky retreated a step, his body coiled and tense and ready to flee.

"Get Mr. DeChambelle and bring him here." Pray God he had returned in the meantime. "Now! Run!"

The lad sprinted away.

The viscount rushed back into the foyer with a linen tablecloth which he commenced to shred. "You seem to know your way around gunshot wounds, Miss Fraser."

"My country was recently invaded by yours."

"War is an ugly business." He passed her the pieces of tablecloth.

"I never meant…" Indeed, would she have even shot Somershurst in the end? She had hesitated so long…but all for naught.

"I know. Will you be all right alone here while I fetch a surgeon?"

Mattie nodded, barely aware of his departure.

The minutes ticked by. Mattie's arms began to ache, yet she held her exhausted body rigid. Silently, she petitioned for the countess's life.

Petitioned whom? The God who'd ignored all her other prayers? She needed Alice and Lawrie Harrison with their simple faith to assure her there was indeed a God who heard, who cared, who loved.

Instead she was alone. Alone with the woman she had wounded. Who might yet die?

At one point Lady Chambelston's eyes flickered in her pale face. "Mattie? Why...?" Her eyes again fell shut against the pain.

Why? Why, why—oh, why? The question pounded through Mattie's mind. Moisture filled her eyes but she dared not release the linens to brush it away. She dipped her face and scraped her eyes against the upper portion of her sleeve—the sleeve of her coat wherein she had so faithfully carried that gun.

"I'm so sorry. So very, very sorry."

"Mr. DeChambelle! Mr. DeChambelle!"

Shouts, footsteps and the shattering of glass reverberated through the house, reaching into Kit's room as he was ripping off his wet, torn coat.

He dropped the much abused garment on the floor and ran into the hallway. Mrs. Parker clutched her bosom next to a shattered Ming vase. Higgins hurdled the stairs in a most undignified manner. Several steps ahead of the red-faced butler a small blur raced up the remaining steps, dodged a footman and a screaming maid, and wrapped itself around Kit's leg.

"Mr. DeChambelle!"

Kit's heart began to pound despite his effort to remain calm for the child. "Young Master Nicky, isn't it?" And if he was here… Kit held up a hand to forestall Higgins before the butler snatched the boy and tossed him out.

Nicky's gasps echoed through the foyer. "Mattie…blood… help."

The muscles in Kit's chest tightened around his ribs until he wheezed along with the boy. He crouched next to Nicky. "Where?"

"S-Somershurst."

"Somershurst's house?"

The boy nodded.

Kit rose. "Mrs. Parker, tell Cook that Master Nicky is to have his choice of anything in our kitchen. If my mother or father return, tell them I'm at Julian's house." Where something dreadful had happened.

"Kit?" Caro stood in the doorway of her room, her eyes fearful and confused. While she oft failed to understand the nuances in the situations around her, she sensed any apprehensions they roused. And angst aplenty swirled around her right now.

Despite his compulsion to flee, he paused long enough to give her a quick hug and an assurance he didn't feel. "Don't worry, Caro. I'll take care of the problem."

He bounded down the stairs and out the door, sprinting along the streets to Julian's townhouse. The rain collected on his spectacles, rendering the landmarks, obstacles and fellow pedestrians all but indistinguishable. Still he raced on, driven by an urgency that conquered fatigue. If Mattie were dead, he'd—

There. He veered onto the last street and counted the shadowy forms until he reached Julian's home. A final discharge of speed carried him the last few yards, then Kit burst into the foyer. And lurched to a stop.

Blood! So much blood. Blood was everywhere—sprayed against the wall, pooled on the floor, running in rivulets along the parquet seams. The stench of it overpowered his senses and wrenched him back in time.

He yanked the pistol from the waistband of his trousers and aimed at the familiar redhead crouching on the floor. "Laura!"

Her head turned, vacant eyes staring through him. Mattie's eyes, hauling him back to London, back to the present. Not Laura. Not France. And the body on the floor, not the young woman he'd killed.

And yet, a frightening echo of that ghastly day pulsed through him, that day he'd nearly lost his life and surrendered his soul. Laura. He'd thought to use the French woman to capture an English traitor—and another had paid the price for his pride and arrogance. He gripped the door frame and fought to keep the nightmares at bay—in the past—as he stared at this new horror.

Memories yielded to reality as the blurry scene sharpened into focus. Tears traced a path through the scarlet streak on Mattie's cheek. Her hands were crimson and large splotches of the same color besmirched her coat.

"Mattie!" Kit dropped the gun in his hand, his terror augmented by fury. As he shot to her side his foot kicked an abandoned pistol sending it skittering across the parquet.

Mattie's pistol.

He plunged to his knees, only gradually becoming aware of the prostrate form beside her, still and silent. A familiar form.

"Maman!" An ever-widening crimson stain discolored her gown. A pale arm peeked from her sleeve, the skin white and flecked with red.

Mattie pressed saturated linens against Maman's back and side. "Can't. Get. It. To. Stop." Her words were stiff and tight—like the hands that gripped the linen, as brittle as her hold on her emotions, reality. Sanity.

"Let me."

When Mattie didn't move, he nudged her fingers away and grabbed the cloth, bearing down on the wound. If only the bleeding would stop.

Please, make the bleeding stop.

"Make way." A blue-clad arm elbowed Kit to the side. Sure and efficient hands seized the linen and peeled back an edge.

Kit's breath caught at the familiar sight he'd hoped to never see again, the jagged edges of flesh around an angry bullet hole. His heart pounded against his chest and the foyer's blood-spattered walls seemed to contract around him.

"Well?" Julian loomed over them. Rain soaked his hair and ran down his face.

"Fortunately the ball missed her organs. We need to get a ligature on that artery and clean out any pieces of her dress but with care and rest she should recover. Let's move her to a bed." The surgeon glanced at Mattie as the three men positioned themselves to lift Maman. "Bring us lots of water."

Julian and the surgeon each took a side while Kit cradled Maman's head. Blood soaked her hair and dripped to the floor like a sign marking their path.

Kit glanced at Julian's locked jaw as they carefully carried their mother up the stairs. "What happened?" And where was that incompetent Baxter that he hadn't prevented this tragedy? Hopefully he'd at least gone after the perpetrator.

"Later, Kit."

Later? And let the would-be killer try again? With horror Kit realized Mattie was downstairs getting the surgeon's water. Alone.

"This one." Julian led them into the first room.

They settled Maman on the bed. So deep was her swoon,

she made not a sound the entire time. Kit positioned her head on the pillow, then whirled to—

"Kit." Julian clasped his elbow.

Kit lunged against the hold, but his brother didn't release his arm. "I've got to get to Mattie. She's—"

"It was Mattie's gun."

Yes, he'd seen it lying on the foyer floor but what did that have to do with… "Mattie's?"

"It accidentally discharged."

But what was it doing here? And where were the men who'd shot at Mattie earlier? "What aren't you telling me? And for that matter, what are you doing here and exactly where have you been?"

"Now's not the time, Kit."

Kit's tenuous hold on his temper slipped. "Yes, now is a very bad time when several hours ago might have prevented a tragedy."

Julian hauled Kit away from the bed. "Very well, if you insist on knowing, I'll not protect you. Mattie came to kill me."

"You?" For a moment, Kit considered finishing the job. And then the pieces aligned to form a picture. A very ugly picture. He swallowed the nausea surging to his throat but the bitterness remained in his mouth.

Memories of another woman bombarded his mind. What a dupe he'd been then. And how history repeated.

"Some assistance, gentlemen."

Kit and Julian sprang apart and hurried to the bed to support the surgeon.

"I need someone to hold her while I stitch these wounds." The surgeon frowned as he focused on the torn flesh. "And I need light—lots of light. It's dark as the grave in here."

Julian struck the flint and lit a candle on the bedside table. "I'll gather some lanterns."

"Miss Fraser—"

"Isn't going anywhere—except to get the water."

Bitterness flowed to Kit's throat like blood from a wound. "Don't wager your fortune on her reliability."

"She didn't flee when given the opportunity." Julian paused in the doorway. "I find her tremendously loyal. To a fault. But if it will ease your mind I will prevent her from leaving."

The surgeon fished in his bag and retrieved a hooked needle. "Slide that candle closer. And where is that water?"

Where indeed? Kit's mind was already leaping to the logical conclusion—despite Julian's assurances otherwise—when Mattie shuffled into the room, her shoulders drooping with the weight of a full bucket. The candlelight shimmered on her hair but cast her face in shadow, leaving her expression unreadable.

"Will this be enough, sir?" She set down her burden beside the surgeon but her head remained bowed like an abused dog.

"Fine, fine." He snipped a length of thread. "Now we'll need lots of bandages. Get me several large strips of linen."

She nodded and crept from the room.

For the next several hours Kit almost successfully ignored her as she moved hither and yon, doing the surgeon's bidding. At one point in their ordeal, Julian ushered Father into the room. Dark hollows underscored his eyes, making him appear decades older than his sixty years.

Words of comfort stuck to Kit's tongue, glued in place by his guilt. He had been the one to bring Mattie Fraser into their house, into their lives.

And she'd repaid their kindness with blood.

Any minute, Mattie expected one—or all—of the DeChambelle men to haul her off to gaol for the oh-so-appropriate fate that awaited her. If they didn't kill her here first.

She hauled the rag out of the bucket again and attacked the foyer wall with renewed vehemence. Over and over, both hands pressing with all her strength. But no matter how much she washed, like Lady Macbeth's spot, blood yet remained, faded blots on the white wall.

Stupid, stupid, stupid. Her father was right after all—about both her and George. At least Father had drunk himself into an early grave before he witnessed her disgrace.

"Don't be so vigorous, Miss Fraser. You'll scour the paint off my wall."

Her heart, which had begun to accelerate, thudded to a creep when she identified the speaker not as Kit but his brother. "It doesn't matter. You'll have to repaint as I can't remove all the stains."

"I appreciate the effort. I sent the servants away several days ago when, ah, I feared things might become complicated."

They certainly had.

"At least when my father comes downstairs again, he won't have to see…" Somershurst studied her face. "You should get some sleep, Miss Fraser. You look exhausted."

She was exhausted but every time she closed her eyes she once again lived the horror of watching Lady Chambelston fall. Bleed. Die?

"I have an extra room if you would like."

"No." Mattie knew that like Lady Macbeth, what she'd done—the blood she'd spilled—would haunt even her dreams. "How is your mother?"

"Resting. Father is with her."

And Kit? Probably talking to a judge right now. Mattie didn't ask. She'd forfeited the right to know when she walked into this house with a pistol.

"Would you care to join me in the library?"

To talk or to… She nodded her acquiescence, tossed the rag into the bucket and dried her hands on her skirt.

He picked up her candle and led her through the hallway to a smallish room where he proceeded to light the twin candles that flanked either side of a large desk. Their meager glow revealed several shelves—not all of them filled with books—and two chairs positioned before an empty fireplace.

"Please, sit."

She backed toward the chair but rather than lower herself onto the upholstered seat, she slid behind, using the curved rosewood back as a shield and support. "I think I would rather stand."

"As you wish. A drink, Miss Fraser?"

"No, thank you." The strangeness of his behavior befuddled her mind enough without the addition of alcohol.

He poured a glass for himself from the decanter on the desk and dropped into the other chair. Rain tapped against the window in time with the gentle clicks of the mantel clock.

Mattie traced her fingers across the patterns carved in the chair's wood frame. "I know it probably means little to you, especially under the circumstances, but I am sorry about your mother. I lost my mother when I was eight." Truly she had lost her entire family that day, only she hadn't known it then. "Your mother has always been kind and gracious. I never heard a harsh word from her, not even about those who behaved badly toward Caro."

"Yes, Maman has demonstrated how to turn adversity into victory, not bitterness."

Mattie reflected on her father's failure to rise above self-pity, even for the sake of his children.

Somershurst stared at the drink in his hands, then lifted his gaze to her, the blue of his grim eyes as shadowed as the night.

She'd wanted the *Impatience*'s captain to suffer, and she'd gotten her wish. After a fashion. A hollow victory indeed.

"I didn't get a chance to express my regrets to you earlier about the loss of your brother. I, ah, lost a brother myself only last year."

"The not knowing. That was the worst." She stared at her white knuckles where they gripped the chair and marveled at their extraordinary conversation. Two people who'd wronged each other, conveying their condolences. "Waiting, and never hearing."

"Kit told me you received a letter from him."

Her nerves prickled. Simple conversation or a desire for information? "Only one, and recently, at that. But I don't have it with me."

The clock on the mantel chimed the fourth hour. Mattie yawned.

"You really should get some rest, Miss Fraser."

As if she could while her mind jumped from thought to thought. "What will happen?"

"Happen?" He took a sip of his drink.

"About…me."

"It isn't my place to decide."

No, she supposed not. That decision belonged to the earl, a man who'd been to America, been to war—and yet seemed to hold no animosity against her. Not before. "Would you… would you deliver a note for me?"

"To whom?"

How did she describe Lawrence Harrison? "A friend of your brother's." Kit hated her now. Oh, she had seen it in his eyes—bleak, deadened, their color consumed with revulsion—every time the surgeon spoke to her. But perhaps Mr. Harrison, with his simple—authentic—faith could find the words to bring peace.

Somershurst gestured toward the desk. "Paper, quills and such are in the top drawer."

She crossed the room, her legs not fully steady, and dropped onto the desk chair. Once she had located the items she needed, she stared at the blank sheet of white. How did one confess to so monstrous an offense?

Silence shrouded the room, save for the steady tick of the clock. She started a note, crumpled it up and began again.

"I owe you another apology, Miss Fraser."

She glanced over her shoulder. Somershurst yet wore the same clothes—a dark coat over a white shirt, now spattered with rusty stains. "Another?"

"When Kit first told me of your presence in London, I... did some things of which I am not proud."

"The eviction?"

"Eviction? What eviction?"

If not Somershurst, then whom? "Never mind. You were saying?"

"I had notes delivered—first to your room at the Captain's Quarters and then again at my parents' house. I thought I might frighten you into calling off your search. I was concerned my reputation would suffer if word leaked that I was so careless with..."

"The paper my brother stole?"

"Er, yes. Let me just say such actions were cowardly on my part, and for that I am sorry."

"I...accept your apology. Thank you."

A wry smile—smile!—flitted across his mouth. "If I had known then of your tenacity, I would have conducted myself in a different fashion."

"What a tangled web." She finished the note and added her signature.

"If you are done, Miss Fraser, I must be off. I'm going to

my parents' house, so Caro won't wake to find her family gone."

Poor Caro. She would never understand this. "What will you tell her?"

"That Maman is sick and will be at my house for a few days until she is better."

If she got better. Mattie stared at the concern that hollowed his cheeks. "You care for Caro." Somehow, that made him uncomfortably human. And her own desires and actions decidedly wicked.

"Someday, when my parents are gone, Caro will be my responsibility." He set his glass down and rose. "I'll ask Mrs. Parker to send breakfast for everyone here."

She shook off the sand and folded the paper. "Thank you."

He glanced at the address as he tucked the note into his jacket. "The Admiralty?"

"I don't know where he lives." Not anymore. Had Somershurst also been responsible for the vandalism of the Harrisons' house? Somehow she thought not. "But Kit said they work together, so I figured someone at the Admiralty should be able to find him."

Somershurst held out a hand. "Like our two countries, perhaps we could declare a truce?"

She stared into those familiar eyes—eyes so like Kit's, it hurt. She and Somershurst would never exactly be friends, not with all that lay between them. And yet, they'd discovered a commonality that advanced them beyond enemies. Under other circumstances... "I should like that." She fitted her hand into his.

After he left, she paced to the window. A faint glow glimmered on the horizon, promising the inevitable beginning of another day, but for now the pre-dawn sky left most of the world in shadows. Like her heart, but without the spark of optimism.

How astonishing to think that only yesterday she had so cleverly questioned the countess about her son the captain. Only to learn now there was a real person behind the object of her hate—a man with faults and foibles and a family who loved him. Not unlike her brother in some aspects. If only George hadn't become bitter or run away or stolen that paper. So many "ifs," so many small decisions, each offering an opportunity to correct the course of one's life.

And what of her? Did she yet have a chance to make amends for the past and alter her future? A daunting prospect, given the magnitude of her crime.

Suddenly Nicky's face rose in the window—his hair wild, his eyes stark and his cheeks smudged. Heart pounding, Mattie jerked back—until she realized the image was not an apparition. She unlatched the lock and pushed open the pane.

"Nicky! What are you doing? You gave me such a fright."

He climbed over the sill. "Sorry, Mattie. I came to see 'ow ye are doing."

A difficult assessment to make at the moment. "Where have you been?"

"Mr. DeChambelle's 'ouse. There's a lady there—Mrs. Parker. She got me a place to sleep. But then I wanted to see ye, Mattie. I was so scared when I 'eard the gun."

"Me, too."

"Did that fancy-pants captain try to attack ye? Is 'e keeping you 'ere?"

"Oh, Nicky, I did something so wicked." She crouched to his level and wrapped her arms around him. His ribs poked through the coat that now carried the metallic scent of Lady Chambelston's blood. Through the haze of regret, she felt his small hand patting her back in an awkward attempt to comfort her. "And you know the irony? The captain claims he didn't impress my brother. Such jobs are done by the first officer..."

Nicky pulled away. "Mattie?"

The first officer? Somershurst hadn't mentioned the officer's name—he'd no reason to. But Mattie knew it.

George had stolen a paper and it seemed someone wanted her dead. Someone—but not Somershurst, she now realized. He could have hauled her to gaol last night and demanded justice. No English court would accept the excuses of a penniless American nobody against the testimony of an aristocratic English war hero. Wasn't that why she had determined to undertake vengeance herself? And yet, Somershurst—who held her life in his hands—hadn't succumbed to the same temptation.

How, in all of London, had Lieutenant Fitzgerald—the man responsible for George's impressment—been in exactly the right place to rescue her from a footpad? Unless he had been following her.

For how long? She skipped back over the memories to the day she'd met the *Impatience*'s first officer. Kit had claimed Fitzgerald knew of her presence in London, knew of her search for her brother.

"Mattie?" Nicky's question arrested her speculations.

"Can you do one thing more for me?"

"Of course."

"There's a man, a naval officer from the *Impatience*. Will you see what you can learn?"

"What's 'is name?"

"Fitzgerald."

"I'll be back in a few hours. Will you be here?"

"I hope so." If she wasn't in gaol.

Chapter Thirteen

The midmorning sun blazed through the window and burned Kit's gritty eyes like a night of overindulgence. What a shame the irritation derived from a lack of sleep instead. At least drink would have dimmed the memories that flamed in glowing, horrifying, infuriating intensity. His fault. His fault he'd brought Mattie Fraser into their lives. His fault he'd ignored the evidence of her duplicitous intentions. He rubbed his hands across his forehead and closed his eyes, but the images appeared again. The muddled pictures tortured his mind—a fearsome combination of old regrets and new terrors.

At least Maman yet lived.

Her complexion matched the pallor of the sheets and her eyes still reflected pain, but her jaw had regained its stubborn tilt. "You will do it for me, Kit, no?"

"Maman—"

"That is what I want."

"What do you want, dearest Maman?" Julian swept into the room with a tray. "Breakfast? Because Mrs. Parker sent more than food. She insisted she come—with Cook. And Cook insists you begin the morning with some of her special broth."

A smile tweaked Maman's pale lips. "I shall be so spoiled by this fussing I will not wish to get well."

"The surgeon said you are to get lots of rest. You will suffer from ennui before we permit you to exert yourself." Julian set the tray on a bedside table.

Maman stared at Kit, one brow raised. "Julian can stay with me while you are gone. No more excuses—go."

"She may not be here—"

"And why not?" Maman's gaze flickered to Julian. "Mattie is here, yes?"

"I believe she is yet in the library."

Kit folded his arms across his chest. "Maman would like some time alone with her. I suggested she wait." At least until they'd hauled the malefactor off to gaol. Maman could send her counsel via the post—to Australia.

Julian glanced at Maman, then studied Kit until he shifted in discomfort. Years of staring into the sun had prematurely etched lines around his older brother's eyes. "Maman is old enough to know her mind, Kit. You speak to Miss Fraser while I assist Maman with her breakfast."

Kit aimed one last look of fury at Julian, then strode to the library. He peeked in—cheered when he didn't see Miss Fraser—until he chanced to spy her curled in a chair. A pity she hadn't run away and afforded him reason to reject Maman's request.

Miss Fraser's chest rose and fell with her deep, even breathing. The sunlight streaming through the window burnished her deep red tresses and her new brown dress matched the color of the freckles crossing her nose. The dark curve of her eyelashes lay on her pale cheeks like black crescents. In sleep she looked young, vulnerable, innocent.

A shame it was all an illusion.

She jolted awake, as if suddenly mindful of his presence even in sleep. Her eyes blinked open, dark and disoriented.

Disingenuous. Then awareness roused, shriveling the smile that had started to take shape on her lips.

"Did you sleep well, Miss Fraser?"

She slumped in the chair, as if the sharp edge in his voice had cut her. "Not…particularly."

He swiveled and presented her with his back. A mostly full decanter of brandy beckoned from Julian's desk. He didn't see a goblet, but no matter. He confiscated the drink and sauntered back to the chair that sat opposite hers. "I see you left me a drink."

Shadows obscured the brown eyes until they were nearly black. "You do seem to have a fondness for the stuff."

"Especially this morning." He yanked the stopper off, tilted the decanter and guzzled straight from the bottle.

"And on other occasions. Have you suffered from this thirst for long?"

Only since the last time his stupidity—arrogance, really—led to tragedy. "I need to wash away the taste of Judas's kiss. Drink dulls the memories, you know."

She stared into the empty fireplace, her form as still as a wax figure. "Only temporarily. Only until the morning."

"Hence the reason I begin drinking so early in the day. I intend to stay drunk." He took another swig of the brandy. And yet, the taste didn't satisfy as much as his first sip. Taut silence constricted around the room and fed his exhaustion, his hurt, his anger. "You do realize what will happen to Maman if infection sets in?"

Her lashes drifted down and her lower lip trembled. "I…I want to tell you how sorry I am, Kit."

"Sorry?" He smacked the decanter against the hearth and surged out of the chair. In two paces he loomed over her. "A fine time to feel regret, Miss Fraser."

She shrank back against the seat. From his anger or the brandy on his breath? He reached inside his coat and whipped out a pistol—her pistol. He dropped it onto her lap. Her head snapped back and a soft cry escaped her mouth.

"How sorry, Miss Fraser?" The black barrel gleamed malevolently in the sunlight. "I believe this weapon belongs to you. Keep it. Cherish it. Remember what you did."

She stared at him, round eyes glittery.

"And if those memories don't drive you to despair and drink, you are more callous than I."

"I..." She tentatively traced a finger over the gun's stock then yanked her hand away, as if it were a feral dog that might bite her. "Is this why you came to see me?"

He paced to the window and stared into the sun's glare, welcoming the throb it brought to his temple. "Partly. Maman wishes to talk to you."

"Your mother is awake?"

"Yes. But obviously not of sound mind."

"Why does she wish to see me?"

"I don't know." Rancor contorted his lips and clenched along his jaw. "Don't upset her. I tried to convince her otherwise, but she insisted."

"And your father?"

Kit rubbed his hand over the stubble on his chin. "Sleeping, last I knew." He glanced over his shoulder.

Miss Fraser gripped the gun between her thumb and finger. "I can't take this into your mother's room."

"It isn't loaded, you know. Not anymore."

She flinched, as if he'd discharged the ball into her. "Will you be coming also?"

"I have more important matters to address."

Miss Fraser uncurled from her awkward position and rose from the chair. Stiff creases wrinkled the gown's hem where his mother's blood had dried on the fabric. She shuffled to Julian's desk and tucked the pistol in the drawer. "I hope the matter concludes to your satisfaction."

He waited until she had trudged from the room. Then he retrieved the gun and dropped it into her coat pocket.

Mattie's leaden feet resisted her every step. What did she say to a woman she'd nearly killed? Who might yet die from wounds Mattie had inflicted?

"Pardon me, Miss Fraser." Mrs. Parker materialized in the hallway. "I must speak to you."

"I'm afraid Lady Chambelston has asked to see me. Perhaps afterward...?"

"I'll only take a moment." The housekeeper aimed singularly grim eyes at Mattie. Did she know of Mattie's offense? Most likely. At least now Mrs. Parker had a reason for her animosity.

"I really must—"

"'Tis about Master Nicholas."

"Nicky? Is anything missing?"

"Only the lad, but he gave Betsy a message requesting you meet him at the gate to Hyde Park."

Alarm screeched through Mattie with the volume of an opera singer. Nicky had promised to return *here*. He knew the danger—he would never ask her to leave the house. "Thank you, Mrs. Parker."

"I will send Betsy with you when you are ready."

"That won't be necessary. I won't be able to make the appointment."

Mrs. Parker's lips compressed into a disapproving gray line that matched her steel-colored hair. She stepped forward, her fierce face some inches above Mattie.

Mattie tried to retreat but bumped against the wall.

"Miss Fraser, you cannot leave that young lad to wait for you. Master Nicholas might be in serious difficulty."

Mattie stared at the adamant Mrs. Parker. Suspicions surged through her mind. If she were to leave now, were to give the

DeChambelles the impression she was intent on escape, they would of a certainty order her arrest—and disbelieve her very real declarations of regret. The walls of the narrow hallway closed around her like a prison cell. "I wouldn't worry about Nicky. No one knows London better than he does. He'll return when he gets hungry."

Mrs. Parker's gray eyes heated to the temperature of smoke. "Very well, Miss Fraser."

Mattie sagged against the wall as the housekeeper marched away. A test? Or a threat?

Either way, the true trial was yet to come. Mattie forced her reluctant feet up the stairs, one impossibly high riser at a time. Once on the landing she raised an arm as heavy as her feet—and her heart—and tapped on the door. It swung open to reveal Somershurst on the other side. His lips curved into a weary smile that lightened her burden. Strange, how her relationship with this man had evolved so unexpectedly in the past twelve hours.

He gestured her into the room and leaned over to whisper, "There's a chair next to the bed. Don't stay too long." Then he squeezed her shoulder and slipped out, pulling the door shut with a gentle click.

Against the snow-white sheets, the grayish cast of Lady Chambelston's face bespoke a long recovery. And yet when her gaze flickered to Mattie, an inner glow lit her countenance. Like staring into the sun, the radiance hurt Mattie's eyes. And heart.

She trekked the five paces, the weight on her shoulders, on her soul, pressing harder with each step until she reached the bed and fell to her knees.

Burying her face in the sheets, she could only murmur, "I'm so sorry" over and over.

And then a whispered caress smoothed her hair. Mattie

peeked up into gentle blue eyes. "I had Julian bring a chair for you."

She scrambled from the floor and settled in the chair.

"Did you eat this morning, Mattie?"

"I...haven't much of an appetite."

"I did not ask if you were hungry. I asked if you have eaten since yesterday."

"No, ma'am."

"Please, help yourself to whatever you find." Her gaze swept past Mattie to the breakfast tray. "I know that sick feeling in your belly when you've done the seemingly unforgivable."

That sick feeling sloshed around in Mattie's stomach, but she buttered a piece of cold toast for Lady Chambelston's sake.

"I once..." The countess's fingers twisted around the top of the sheets. "There once was a young couple who were compatible, but their relationship lacked depth and commitment and spirituality. When troubles came—and troubles always come, Mattie—the wife became withdrawn. Angry. Bitter. The husband responded in the manner of most men in his class by finding a woman who was always cheerful and always available—for the right remuneration, of course. The wife escalated with infidelity of her own. And Caro was the result."

Mattie jolted in the chair, her back straightening with her astonishment. "I..." How did one respond to such a revelation?

"I have shocked you."

The countess—so peaceful, so sympathetic, so...perfect. Or not.

"We committed grievous sins against one another, each offense escalating to something worse than the previous. Only when we sought God's mercy—and offered pardon to each other—did we end our destructive behavior and begin to heal our marriage. It has been neither fast nor easy—such changes never are—but thanks be to God we are no longer the people we were then." Lady Chambelston's gaze wavered, darkened. "Alas, our actions had far-reaching consequences—and innocent people suffered because of our transgressions. We deeply injured our children. Our oldest daughter removed us from her life and has not spoken to us since. Julian joined the navy, and we have scarcely seen him these two decades. There is a reason why vengeance is to belong to God."

"But what about justice?"

"Justice demands we turn you over to the magistrate for a punishment of either transportation or death. But mercy allows me to forgive you." The pain-shadowed eyes stared levelly at Mattie, as if reading her soul. "I forgive you, Mattie."

"But…" That was all? Mattie slumped in her chair, rebellion and regret and…relief warring in her mind, in her very being. She dropped her gaze to the forlorn slice of toast still in her hand. "Are you suggesting I should have forgiven your son?"

"I am only telling you what God does for all those who repent. Are you greater than God?" Lady Chambelston's fingers relaxed, though the sheets remained crumpled from her grip. "Tell me, Mattie. Did you truly seek justice? Or revenge?"

"Can't they be the same? And—and, besides, why should I offer forgiveness to someone who isn't even sorry?"

The sheets rose and fell with the countess's steady breathing. "We are no longer talking about Julian, no?"

"I…" Mattie bit her lip and looked away. Outside the window autumn had begun to paint the leaves of a nearby tree. Soon their colors would darken to lifeless brown as they dried up and blew away. Dead, like her father and brother, forever beyond remorse and leaving her only with the guilt and pain of failure.

"Clinging to your anger warps you and injures others. I discovered so—as have you." Lady Chambelston placed her frail hand on Mattie's and gave her a weak squeeze. "Ask for forgiveness of those you wronged, beginning with God. Offer mercy to those who ask it of you. And turn the rest of your hurts over to God to deal with in His time."

A gentle breeze caused the leaves on the tree to dance. Deep inside, Mattie felt a similar stirring that shook off the darkness in her soul. "Your son and I, we've made our peace."

"I did not mean Julian, either. You have other hurts you need to give to God, yes? But I am glad your healing has begun." The hand on Mattie's relaxed, and then went limp. The countess's lashes drifted down to rest on wan cheeks.

Mattie's heart clenched in the seconds before she registered the pulse yet beating in Lady Chambelston's neck—weak but steady, like the woman's words which now pulsated in Mattie's mind. For long moments Mattie remained in the chair, watching the countess sleep and contemplating the wrong-doings and wounds of the past. Her father. George. Viscount Somershurst.

Kit DeChambelle.

The hinges squeaked as the door swung open to reveal the Earl of Chambelston standing in the portal. Mattie whisked her hand out from under his wife's.

He shuffled closer until he stood before her, loomed over her.

"I—I'm so sorry. I—"

"Yes, I can see that, Miss Fraser." Ever the English gentleman, he extracted a handkerchief from his coat and passed it to her. "I'll stay here. There is someone downstairs who wants to see you."

Kit? Mattie dabbed her cheeks dry. "Yes, yes. Thank you." She virtually floated out the door and down the staircase.

Until she reached the library.

Somershurst made polite conversation with Lawrie Harrison. Both rose when she entered.

"Mr. Harrison. I'm so glad you received my note."

Somershurst gave them both a nod. "I'll check on Maman and leave you to your conversation. Miss Fraser, I had a room prepared for your convenience. You should get some rest."

Mattie waited for Somershurst's steps to fade away. She paced to the fireplace and lowered her head against the mantel. "Oh, Mr. Harrison, I did a terrible, terrible thing last night."

"Yes, I heard." He moved to the opposite side of the fireplace, his homely face filled with understanding. "What can I do for you?"

For *her?* "Kit is…" She glanced at the bottle yet on the desk. "Troubled. And you seem to have answers."

"It's not so much having the answers as knowing where to find them. Yes, I'll talk to DeChambelle, if he's willing to listen. But I think you asked me here for something else."

"Would you…would you pray for me? It sounds so real when you pray. I've never heard anyone address God the way you do. I almost feel as if…God actually listens when you pray."

"I believe that."

"But how can you be certain when there is so much evil in the world?"

"Evil caused by human greed, indifference and vendettas?"

Like her brother. Her father. Her.

"God allows us to make choices. Even you, Mattie." He took her hand and held it between his. "Fortunately, He has made a way for forgiveness. Do you want me to pray with you, Mattie?"

"Would you?"

They settled into the chairs that flanked the fireplace, and Mattie followed Lawrie Harrison's gentle prompts and leading. She blinked when they finished, for somehow the room seemed different. Brighter. Changed.

No, the change had occurred within her.

She shook her head, bemused. "This wasn't the reason I asked you to come."

"Accept it as evidence God knows what you need before you do." Harrison lifted a book from the desk. "I brought this for you. I marked some pages where you might wish to begin."

"Thank you."

"How touching." An acerbic Kit DeChambelle sauntered across the room to join them. His blue eyes glittered behind the spectacles, hard but clear. At least he hadn't consoled himself with more brandy. "Glad you're here, Harrison. I wanted to discuss a matter with you."

"I'll, ah, leave you gentlemen to your business." Mattie scooped up the Bible that Harrison had provided and retreated from Kit DeChambelle's scowl.

Kit crossed to Julian's desk and hefted the decanter. "Brandy?"

"None for me. Judging by the amount remaining, it looks to me as if someone has already imbibed rather heavily."

"It was a long night." And longer day.

"Did the brandy bring the relief you crave?"

Kit glared in response to Harrison's gentle nagging but as there were still no goblets he returned the decanter to the desk and retreated to the empty chair. "I appreciate your coming. How did you know?"

"Your American sent me a note."

Not *his* American. "That prosaic? I was afraid you might say God spoke to you."

A secretive smile twitched on Harrison's lips. "I suppose in a way He did."

"I never did understand how Alderston managed to convince the most honest man in all England to join a profession based on lies and deceit. How do you live with the regrets?"

"I pray a lot, just like I did during the war when I would ask God to show me what to do, what choices I should make to minimize suffering."

"I made enough wrong choices for all of us."

"And you still do—you insist on living with the guilt of the past."

Silence descended over the room like autumn fog on a London morning.

Kit instinctively reached for a glass, only to remember he had decided to forego another brandy. "Baxter is missing."

"Baxter? Since when?"

"I last saw him yesterday morning."

"When you assigned him to observe Miss Fraser?"

"Yes. I arrived home after our futile search for the muster books in time to see her escaping through the alley behind the house. I don't know if Baxter also followed her. Two people shot at Mattie in Hyde Park."

"Two?"

But had both shot at Mattie—or was one man aiming at her guard? Baxter? Or even... Kit's fingers curled around the chair arm. Could *he* have been the intended recipient of one of those shots?

He inventoried the list of those who knew about the orders. Julian. Alderston. The Prince Regent. Himself.

And Fitzgerald?

"You know, DeChambelle, Baxter may be fine. He may

be trying to track down one of Miss Fraser's would-be assassins."

"Baxter?" The man had displayed little competence thus far.

"But I'll notify Alderston for you. You have enough troubles to occupy any man."

"Thank you. He'll want to know." Indeed, Alderston might set more guards to protecting Mattie until such time as the orders were recovered. Kit reached again for a glass that wasn't there, his hand hovering above the empty table. Had he become so reliant on drink? Harrison's warning about becoming a slave to drink's power suddenly seemed frighteningly possible. And yet a life without its mind-numbing qualities seemed frighteningly…real.

He stared morosely at the decanter on Julian's desk, not certain if he should feel desire or revulsion.

Harrison followed the line of his stare. "I worry about your craving for drink."

"I don't desire the drink. Only the oblivion it brings."

"Perhaps, for now. But that will change, you know. You've embarked on a path that will lead to your destruction. Only God's forgiveness will bring you peace."

"Some deeds are unforgivable." And unforgettable, at least without copious quantities of brandy. Or whiskey.

"Are we discussing your failings of last year? Or Miss Fraser's of last night?"

"Does it matter?"

Harrison tapped a finger against his knee. "You hurt because you loved Mattie—and she betrayed you. A relationship not unlike God has with us."

"Loved Mattie? I fear you vastly overstate the matter."

"You cannot deny you greatly admired her."

"No, I admired the woman I thought she was." Loyal to her loved ones, tenacious in the face of indifference and adversity.

With such a woman at his side, a man would willingly face an army. With such an illusion, a man would willingly yield to hate.

"If you loathe her so, why do you tarry in seeking justice? Mattie wronged you. You have cause."

The mantel clock ticked through silent seconds while Kit stubbornly held his tongue. And his anger.

"It isn't Mattie's fault she didn't live up to your ideals or that you didn't live down to your cynicism. Her deeds are no worse than yours."

Kit shoved himself out of the chair and paced to the window. But his deeds, his past, followed him.

"Mattie expresses her regret."

"If she is to be believed this time."

"She had the chance to run away, but she remained to accept whatever punishment your family deemed to mete out." Harrison leaned forward and rested his elbows on his knees. Under his thinning hair, his head gleamed in the afternoon sun that streamed through the window. "Accept her contrition as genuine. Mattie made her peace with God and your mother, but until you do likewise you'll never be able to offer her the forgiveness she wants from you. And you might discover God heals better than brandy."

Mattie woke with a start. Even after she identified the unfamiliar walls as the guestroom of Somershurst's townhouse, a sense of unease crawled through her. Hunger? She glanced from the afternoon sky to the small clock on the fireplace mantle which gave the time as four o'clock. What had she missed?

Nicky.

Fear sliced through the empty pit of her stomach. He should have returned hours ago. Mrs. Parker's strange insistence that

Mattie meet Nicky in Hyde Park flashed across her memory. She hadn't gone—and now he was missing.

One little boy, somewhere in London. Would he yet appear, like last night? The ache in her heart felt like that day seven years ago when her brother had left. She'd never seen him again. But this was far worse than when her scapegrace brother had absconded with the family coffers. Unlike George, who had rushed headlong to his destruction, Nicky had acted for her.

Guilt stabbed her like a knife, carving fresh wounds into her heart. Would her folly forever condemn her to misery?

Not this time.

Ignoring the hopelessly wrinkled state of her gown, she ran to the stairs, whispering prayers in time with her steps. She tried the library first, but found only Somershurst in residence.

"Ah, Miss Fraser." He rose from the desk chair. "How may I be of service?"

"Is your brother about?"

"Kit? I believe he is resting. Would you like me to wake him?"

She laced her fingers together in front of her. She hated to disturb him—especially given their last encounter. But what other choice did she have? Somershurst had never met the boy. If Kit wouldn't seek Nicky, she'd have to conduct the search herself. "Yes. Please."

"Immediately, mademoiselle." He snapped his heels together and bowed in such a deliberately silly, formal manner as to almost trigger a smile from her.

She paced to the window while she waited to see if Kit would come. Outside, the low-hanging sun sparkled on Somershurst's garden. Weeds grew among the rosebushes. Tall weeds, testifying to the plot's long neglect. She stared at a lonely pink rose, stubbornly blooming out of season.

"Miss Fraser?"

Mattie held her breath and turned to view the door. Kit leaned against the frame, his hair delightfully sleep-tousled. His shirt gaped open at the neck where he'd removed his cravat. She tried to read his eyes, tried to determine his level of sobriety—and revulsion—but the sunlight glared against his spectacle lenses. "My friend Nicky promised to meet me here hours ago, but he never came."

"The urchin who came to get me last night when…"

"Yes."

He ran a hand through the already mussed hair. "Julian tells me Mrs. Parker has disappeared as well."

"Mrs. Parker!"

"Yes, our housekeeper. She's been part of the staff since the Norman invasion. I can't imagine why she would leave without word."

"I—I know. It's just that Mrs. Parker insisted Nicky left a message for me to meet him in Hyde Park." What was the connection?

Kit stilled, the angular planes of his face freezing for several long, silent moments. "And you didn't go." Hesitancy replaced the earlier harshness in his voice, offering Mattie hope.

"No. I—I was so certain Nicky would come here rather than put me at risk, I disbelieved the message. Do you think he's in trouble?"

"Oh, Mattie. He lives on the streets—he creates trouble. If trouble does not find him, he will find it—if not today or tomorrow, soon."

"But this time, what if I caused his troubles? What if his involvement with me endangered him? Despite his street-smart ways, he's only a little boy." She paused to gather her thoughts. How could she make Kit understand, surrounded as he was by a family that loved him, how very lonely life could be for the orphans of the world like Nicky? Like her? "He has no one who cares about him. No one except me." And...God? The newness of faith in a harsh world burdened her with fresh doubts.

Kit ambled across the room and met her gaze from the other side of the large desk. "I'll look for him."

She leaned against the windowsill and stared at his face. Concern and fatigue underscored his eyes and hollowed his cheeks. "You don't have to do this for me. This is my fault. I—"

"I'm not doing it for you. I'm doing it for him."

She closed her eyes and swallowed the pain his words caused.

"Mattie." The rough edge of his voice gentled. "You can't leave the house, most especially at night, for the places where Nicky is likely to be. It isn't safe for any woman, but especially not for you."

"I—I..."

He prowled around the desk and stood directly in front of her, so close she could see through his spectacles to his eyes. He raised a hand as if to touch her hair, her face. But he stopped, his fingers hovering only inches away. "That's why you brought this problem to me, isn't it?"

"I...hoped." The words tripped awkwardly from her tongue. For sixteen years life had taught her to trust none save herself. "If you refused, I would look for him myself—and I wanted you to know I wasn't running away."

"You are many things, Mattie Fraser—but no coward. I promise to do everything I can. And besides, Nicky may know something about Mrs. Parker's disappearance."

The intensity in his gaze, the strength in his jaw, melted some of the cold fear in her heart. "Thank you."

No sooner had he vanished, though, than her relief transformed to a greater worry. Had she just put Kit in danger?

Chapter Fourteen

"I am looking for a young lad called Nicky."

The rotund gaolkeep stared so long that Kit's skin crawled. As the beady eyes registered the cut of Kit's coat and the cost of his trousers, a leer curled the corners of the man's fleshy face. "We got lots o' Nicks. Ye know which one?"

One with no surname, no known residence. Did Nicky even know his age? Despondency and cynicism warred to replace his anger as Kit calculated the odds of locating the boy or even his body. One in a million. Still, gaol was the most likely venue apart from a pauper's grave. "He is about this tall." He held his hand about four feet from the floor. "Dark hair. Dark eyes. Last seen this morning, so he would have arrived today."

The gaoler scratched a bristly cheek. "I *might* be persuaded to remember such a lad—if ye understand my meaning."

Kit withdrew a coin of small denomination. "Perhaps this will purchase your memory."

"Why, now that ye mention it, I think I do remember him. Nick, ye say? Small lad. Ain't been well fed."

"That describes half the children in London." Kit made as if to leave.

"This one was wearing a greenish coat."

"I want to see him."

"Well, sir, I'd like to 'elp ye. Truly, I would, but it really ain't allowed."

Kit's anger fired hotter as he extracted another, larger coin. While Nicky endured in prison, this swindler practiced legal thievery.

"Perhaps we can make an exception." The scoundrel seized the blunt, retrieved a collection of keys and shuffled his bulk through the maze of corridors that comprised the gaol.

Kit trailed behind, his senses assaulted by putrid odors of human waste and suffering. The windowless walls dimmed hope grayer than the darkening skies beyond until night and day became as one.

"We 'ave a lad like that in 'ere." The gaoler gestured toward a door.

As Kit peered through the bars, the fulsome odors intensified. The weak light revealed a menagerie of prisoners crowded into the tiny space. Surly-faced men reclined on boards covered with a few wisps of stinking straw while several young boys cowered in a corner. Kit tried to picture Mattie's reaction to this nightmare and gagged on the thought.

The gaoler pounded on the metal. "Nick?"

With a sob, a small boy stepped toward the door into the faint light that filtered between the bars. "Nicky?" Kit's heart raced as he studied the tear-streaked cheeks. The boy's coat had disappeared leaving only a ragged shirt to protect him from the cold, dank air.

"Mr. DeChambelle?"

"Let me in," Kit ordered the gaoler.

"Now see 'ere, sir. I can't do that."

Kit pulled out yet another coin and flipped it to the gaoler. The sluggish man missed, and the coin dropped to the floor. He dropped to his knees amid the filth and scooped up the money.

"Can you let me in *now?*"

The gaoler hesitated as he studied the coin. His sly glance roamed over Kit's apparel again, but when it landed on his frown he extracted a key and fitted it into the lock. "Always glad to oblige a friend."

The hinges shrieked as the door scraped across the floor. Kit stepped into the cell, and Nicky hurled himself against him with such force Kit staggered and nearly fell. As he wrapped his arms around the child, Nicky's rapid breaths pressed prominent ribs against him. Kit stroked the dark hair, murmuring insensible words of comfort as the boy's cold hands locked behind his neck.

Behind them the door clanged shut. Invisible bands constricted Kit's chest as if the sound, the mere thought of being locked away in here, ripped the breath from his lungs. How much more horrifying to a child.

He lifted the boy in his arms until the two were of an eye level and pulled his cloak around Nicky to warm him. "Tell me what happened. I need to know so I can get you released."

"Nothing, sir. Truly. I know ye won't be believing me, sir, but I didn't take nothing."

"Where were you?"

Nicky's huge brown eyes stared into him, all the larger because of the room's murkiness. Gone was the cocky lad who spoke and acted older than his years, replaced by a frightened, lonely child. "I was in front of the captain's 'ouse. I'd gone there to see Mattie. A fella accused me of stealing and 'auled me 'ere."

"What fellow? Can you tell me what he looked like?"

"Fine gentleman, 'e was. Talked like ye."

Fitzgerald, perhaps? A draft of unease wisped along Kit's spine. Did the lieutenant linger outside Julian's house waiting for Mattie, hoping she would leave for a sham appointment in Hyde Park? "What is your full name, Nicky?"

"I told the man I was Nicky Fraser."

"Fraser?"

"It's Mattie's name. I knew she would look for me."

Yes, in all of London only Mattie Fraser cared enough to find this orphan, just as she sought the fate of her brother. The ache in Kit's chest concentrated around his heart as if it sought to soften that hard lump. "I'll get you out of here but you must promise me you won't describe this place to Mattie. She loves you very much. She would be hurt and unhappy if she knew the truth."

"I love 'er, too."

Kit swallowed the lump in his throat. "I know. Now I need you to be brave and wait for me. I'll be back for you no matter how long it takes."

"Yes, sir." Nicky's stare, laden with so much trust and even reverence, pierced Kit's heart with cuts so deep the scars would last a lifetime.

The tightness in his chest forced the last remaining air from his lungs. As Kit called for the gaoler, he released Nicky and stripped off his cloak, then his coat. The sleeves nearly dragged on the ground as he wrapped the garment around the boy. "That should keep you warm enough until I get back." He pulled his cloak back over his shirt.

The door clanged as the gaolkeep fitted the key into the lock. Once outside the cell, Kit began to breathe again.

"Anything else I can do for ye, gov'na?"

Vulgar words jumped to Kit's tongue, but he swallowed them before they escaped and the offensive man loosed his anger on Nicky. "What did you say your name was, my good man?"

"Wilkie Fodgel, sir."

"Well, Wilkie, see the lad still wears that coat when I

return, and I'll see you well rewarded." With the recompense the man deserved.

Kit whirled and strode out of the building in silence save for the slap of his heels against the floor. Once outside Kit drew in a deep breath of London's air. Smoky as always, but sweeter than the putrid scent of the gaol.

But where to now? He hadn't a pigeon's sense of the criminal court system, having worked for Alderston who was a law unto himself.

Alderston—the man who seemingly knew more about Mattie Fraser than she did. He would have the wherewithal to attain Nicky's release.

Kit's boots pounded the bricks with renewed purpose as he pointed them toward the elegant Mayfair house.

Moments later the director of clandestine services welcomed Kit into his study. "Kit." He gestured to a chair. "I trust your presence indicates you have met with success?"

"Not yet, sir." He eyed the chair but kept to his feet. "In truth, I don't believe Miss Fraser has the connections to help us."

"Brandy?"

"Ah, maybe not tonight."

Alderston nodded and poured a single drink. "Why do you think so?"

"She had not seen her brother in some years."

"But I wager few people know that. Certainly not those who would steal this paper to embarrass our country at this delicate time." He sipped his drink. "You do realize that if you are not successful, your brother's reputation—your family's reputation—will be forever tarnished."

As Kit stared at Alderston's cold, unrelenting eyes, a shiver swirled up his spine.

"But what brings you here tonight, if not news of your most recent success?"

"I need to get a boy out of prison." Briefly Kit explained, leaving out a plethora of details including Nicky's past successes in crime.

"What was this boy—Nicky, I believe you said—doing in Mayfair?"

"He works for me." The lie flowed easily from Kit's lips, too easily. He had lied on many other occasions during that interminable war and justified them with reminders of his country's peril and his own small part in England's survival. Never had he lied under such circumstances.

For himself—to Alderston of all people. And yet, not for himself. For Nicky. For Mattie.

Alderston stared at Kit for long moments, as if reading the meaning behind Kit's words.

"Come. If we are to get the lad out tonight, we'd best be about this business as quickly as possible."

Alone in the library with only her fears, recriminations and Harrison's Bible for company, Mattie read and reread the same Psalm, trying to calm her frantic thoughts. A fire now burned in the grate, and yet a chill wrapped around her heart.

Twilight had darkened to evening, and still no Kit. What if he returned without Nicky? Her imagination vaulted from one terrifying scenario to the next. What if? What if?

Footsteps scraped against the floor. Mattie held her breath and lifted her head in hope, only to feel her heart drop as the earl—Kit's father—shuffled into the library. He advanced several feet into the room, then spied her and lurched to a halt.

"My apologies, Miss Fraser. I didn't realize the room was occupied."

She popped to her feet. "I was just thinking I ought to retire to my room."

"Don't leave on my account. Stay."

She lowered herself onto the seat again. As Lord Chambelston dropped wearily into the other chair, she tried to read the emotions in his cloudy gaze. "It seems I've apologized to everyone but you, sir. I wish…"

"As do I, Miss Fraser. I want to hate you, but I, of all people, understand better than any." He stared at the flames as if mesmerized.

"Sir?"

"I was a young man when my father bought my commission. Too young to order other men into battle or make decisions over life and death. But with the cockiness of youth, I knew best. And two hundred other men paid the price for my foolishness." He dragged his gaze from the fire to study her face. His lips twitched into a cynical semblance of a smile. "So you see, Miss Fraser, I am yet one hundred ninety-nine to the fore of you."

A log shifted, sending sparks dancing up the flue. "My father ran away from home to join the army when he was fourteen." Not unlike her brother who'd fled at a similar age, she now realized. For similar reasons? Had generations of Frasers repeated the same pattern of bitterness and obstinacy? Lady Chambelston's advice to turn her hurts over to God took on new meaning.

"Julian was about that age when he joined the navy. A better choice because he spent years learning to lead men before assuming responsibility for so many others. Not that he didn't still make mistakes. He, ah, told me a little of what happened to your brother."

"I suppose my brother knew the risks when he continued to sail during war time." And when he stole what did not belong to him. "How—how is the countess?"

"Somewhat better. Julian is with her now." The earl leaned

his head back and let his eyes drift shut. "Would you read to me?"

"Yes, of course. Kit's friend—Mr. Harrison—marked a few passages for me. My father didn't encourage Bible reading or church attendance. I think he was angry with God."

"If there's one thing that serves a man no purpose, it's to be mad at God. It's rather like kicking a boulder. Hurts your toe and doesn't change the rock at all."

Mattie chuckled as she opened the Bible to the Psalms. Over the next hour or so, she read aloud the poignant words that had so eloquently spoken to men's hearts for thousands of years. Sharing the passages with another hurting person brought calmness to her soul. At one point Cook brought tea, which Mattie gratefully sipped to soothe her weary throat.

"My lord?" One of the Chambelston footmen stepped into the room, a silver tray in hand. "A message from Higgins."

"Thank you." The earl broke the seal and scanned the note. "Well, Miss Fraser, it seems Mrs. Parker has been found."

"Is she well?"

"Some broken bones and bruises, but she should recover in time. A carriage struck her near Hyde Park. She was unconscious and unidentified for some hours, but now that she has awakened, she's been moved to Chambelston House."

What was the housekeeper doing near Hyde Park?

Lord Chambelston rose. "Thank you for reading to me, Miss Fraser. The words were comforting, but now your voice is hoarse—how selfish of me not to have stopped you ages ago. I'm going upstairs to check on my wife."

"Good night, sir." She set the book on the table and rested her eyes. And prayed—for Nicky's return, for Mrs. Parker's healing, for Kit's safety.

In the midst of her petitions, the front door squeaked. She leaped from the chair and ran to the foyer.

The night fog swirled around Kit as he entered the townhouse. Water droplets twinkled on his broad, cloak-covered shoulders. Then, as if sensing her presence, he glanced to where she waited in the doorway and an infectious smile lit his face. The fog dissipated, leaving only the mist that glittered in his hair and on his lenses.

"Nicky?"

"I found him." He dropped his arm over the shoulders of the boy beside him.

Nicky looked at her and attempted a wavering smile. Then he shrugged off Kit's arm and a coat more suited to a small giant than to a young boy. He sprinted to her and threw himself into her arms. Mattie staggered, then wrapped her arms around him, feeling the shudders that wracked his body.

She glanced over his head and observed Kit as he removed his cloak—baring himself to his shirt. She started and glanced at the heap of dark fabric Nicky had discarded, then her gaze darted to Kit's face again. His features blurred from the moisture that flooded her eyes and wet her lashes.

Nicky's arms tightened around her. "I thought I'd never see ye again, Mattie."

"I was so worried. You weren't hurt?"

He shook his head. "I love ye, Mattie. I'm sorry ye were scared." And yet, he looked less sorry and more thankful. That someone cared for him?

As Mattie stared into Nicky's trusting brown eyes, something cracked inside her. Maybe it was her heart, because pain pierced her breastbone and tightened around her chest until she could barely breathe.

When had she last heard those words? Not from her father, who had turned to the bottle after her mother's untimely death. Not from her brother—the greedy cad who had stolen what was left of her father's spirit when he ran off with the family funds.

No, only her mother had used those words, last uttered the

same day the dying woman had charged Mattie to take care of her little brother.

A responsibility at which she had failed—just as she'd nearly failed again with Nicky.

She met Kit's glance over the top of the boy's head. "Where?"

"Gaol."

"Prison!" She tightened the embrace until Nicky protested and withdrew.

Kit picked up his discarded coat. "Nicky, have you had anything to eat today?"

"Not since I filched an apple this morning."

"Why don't we find Cook?" Kit held out a hand and the boy gripped it with a dirty palm. Mattie followed behind, her feet dragging with concern.

Cook smiled when the trio entered the kitchen. "Mister Christopher. What are you doing here this late at night?"

"I brought some guests to try your tarts. But first, Master Nicky needs to wash."

Cook examined the greasy fingers. "Come along, Master Nicky. We'll find the pump—and lots of soap."

Nicky cast one last pleading look at Mattie before shuffling off with Cook.

"I think Nicky finds the idea of soap more traumatic than gaol." Kit gestured Mattie to take a seat at a scarred wooden table. "By the by, he knows nothing of Mrs. Parker."

"We do. Your father received a message. She was struck by a carriage and is recovering at Chambelston House."

"A carriage? What was she doing on the street? And for that matter, what street?"

"Near Hyde Park."

"Hyde Park! Didn't Mrs. Parker claim Nicky was to meet you there?"

"I didn't go."

The ache in Kit's chest intensified as he observed the remnants of tears that still wet Mattie's lashes like dewdrops and shimmered in her eyes like sunlight on a lake. The same jumble of emotions spiraled through him—anger, admiration, antipathy, affection. Harrison's assertion that Mattie's actions were no worse than his own echoed again in his mind and rebuked his stubborn heart. He slid onto the bench opposite her and tapped her hand.

"But someone wanted you in Hyde Park. Or near to it. Unlike you, Mrs. Parker had no reason to suspect the message fraudulent. What if upon seeing you decline Nicky's appeal, Mrs. Parker determined to go in your stead?"

"Mrs. Parker?"

"Don't let that battle-ax demeanor fool you. She loves children. Believing Nicky to be in trouble, she walked to Hyde Park, only to be struck by a carriage meant for you."

"Are you suggesting the accident wasn't an accident?"

"As I said, someone wanted you on that street."

"But to mistake Mrs. Parker for me…" Under other circumstances Mattie's disgruntled expression would have amused him. "Her hair—"

"Hidden by a bonnet."

"But the form—"

"Obscured by a coat."

"Surely my clothes are not so similar to Mrs. Parker's. Why, I've never seen her wear any color but gray."

Gray. "Like the borrowed pelisse you wore the day you, ah, ventured to St. Paul's?" The day she had encountered Neville Fitzgerald.

Mattie's neck bobbed with her swallow. "Your mother insisted. Unfortunately, my altercation with Stumpy rather damaged the sleeve."

And she hadn't worn it since. But Fitzgerald wouldn't have known such. Grimly, Kit determined to pay the erstwhile lieutenant a visit. Perhaps Julian would care to accompany him.

Mattie's lashes drifted over her troubled gaze. "How did you get Nicky out of gaol?"

"I used a...family connection. I told him Nicky worked for me." The past five years of his life had been a lie, so why did one small tale for a good cause bother him so? Had not Alderston used *him*, because of his connection to Mattie and Julian?

"What would have happened to him?" Mattie's voice snapped him from his thoughts.

"Given his age, he probably would have been deported."

"But he's only a child!"

He'd used the same excuse to justify his actions to himself. "Stealing is a capital crime. He could have been hung."

"So the poor are allowed to choose between a slow death by starvation or a quick death by execution?"

"Mattie."

She braced her elbows on the table and rested her chin in her palms. A cloud obscured the emotion in that haunted gaze. "I'm sorry. I allowed my fear and anger to result in rudeness. What happened to Nicky is my fault."

"I think we're all exhausted." He stared into Mattie's eyes, all the way to her soul. A man could lose himself in those eyes. Perhaps he already had. Perhaps, as Harrison suggested, that explained why her actions so aggrieved him. He'd lost his heart to a woman who'd wanted only revenge, not him. His lungs ached as if he had run forever.

"How did you find him?"

"A little luck and a lot of insight. Really, Mattie, prison was the most logical place to assume." At least he had persuaded Alderston to use his influence to have Wilkie Fodgel replaced. Perhaps some good would yet come from Nicky's ordeal. "Take heart. Nicky is fine, a little shaken perhaps, but he will be right as rain after a meal."

As if to demonstrate the truth of Kit's assurances, the boy bounced back into the kitchen and slid onto the bench beside Mattie. His freshly scrubbed cheeks shone in the candlelight. "Cook says I can 'ave an entire meat pie. But there aren't any oranges."

Kit poured three glasses of milk. "We'll see about getting you one tomorrow."

The boy grinned, displaying surprisingly good spirits despite his ordeal in the grim environment of the gaol.

Mattie took a sip of her milk. "What happened, Nicky?"

"Found that gent's 'ouse, just like ye asked, but it looked like there weren't nobody there. I climbed in a window, and 'e was dead—right there by the front door."

"Dead!"

"I ran back 'ere, and that's when some other gent 'auled me off and arrested me."

Kit paused, glass halfway to his lips. "What dead gent?"

"The one what was an officer on the ship Mattie was asking about, the *Impatience*."

Mattie stilled as Kit DeChambelle's eyes flickered with recognition.

"Lieutenant Fitzgerald?" he asked of Nicky.

"Aye, 'e's the one."

"And you say he's dead?"

Nicky shrugged. "There's a bloke in 'is 'ouse with a bloody 'ead. Don't rightly know if it's the same fella."

"Mattie, may I see you in the library?" Kit DeChambelle's deep voice filled the kitchen with quiet menace. Beneath the beautiful, almost feminine lashes, his brilliant eyes flashed with very masculine anger.

"But Nicky—"

"Cook will make him a place to sleep here." Kit rose and tugged her along with him, out of the kitchen and through the house. The walls of the hallway tightened around her, like his grip on her wrist.

"Kit, I really don't think—"

"I want some answers." He hauled her into his brother's library. A few glowing embers were all that remained of the fire. He used one to light a candle and then jabbed the taper into a holder on the desk. The light gilded his hair and created enigmatic shadows over the harsh planes of his face. His hands fastened around her arms, making escape impossible. "I want to know why you have been using that boy, that boy who loves you, for your own purposes. Using his love for you. Using even his fear for you."

The soft, dangerous tones weren't a question so much as a statement. An indictment. And to her shame, an accurate assessment. How could Nicky love her to the point he would risk imprisonment, transportation, even death? Heat radiated from Kit's palms through the sleeves of her dress, burning away the excuses she couldn't justify to herself.

"Now I understand why you believed his disappearance was your fault. It *was* your fault. And here I was almost convinced you'd changed."

"I did! I have! That was before…" But only time—and a changed life—would demonstrate the transformation that had occurred within her today.

"Why, Mattie? What haven't you told me? Why do you act without regard to yourself or to those who care about you?"

Anguish from her double failure ruptured through her as the pieces of her heart shattered and crashed to the floor. She yanked herself free of his grasp—but not his accusations—and tumbled into a chair. "My mother died when I was eight."

Kit dropped into the neighboring seat. "How old was your brother?"

"Six." She stared at the glowing coals. Her mind to drifted back to that dreadful moment when her mother's emaciated body gasped its last. Her mother's final whisper echoed through Mattie's mind, a constant companion and reminder of her failure. "She told me…her last words instructed me to take care of my brother."

"You? You were eight years old. What about your father?"

"He tried, but he missed my mother dreadfully. After her death, he turned to whiskey for companionship and started drinking in the evenings." And then the afternoons. And then pretty much the entire day long.

Kit propped his elbows on his knees and leaned forward, his chin resting on templed hands. The sleeves of his shirt stretched over the bulges of his arms. "Go on."

"Without a father and mother to guide him, George began to…get into difficulties. Eventually, my father found out, which only made the situation between them grow worse. With each new provocation from George, my father reached further into his whiskey, and nothing I tried would bring him back."

"You were just a child yourself, as was George."

"Finally Father caught George stealing a particularly large amount of cash from the store and threatened to press charges, so George ran off to sea on the *Constance*."

"Mattie, Mattie. I'm so sorry."

"I wasn't. Don't you see? When George absconded with the family coffers, I felt only relief. Not regret, relief. His thievery had long been suspected by the neighbors. Whenever calamity or larceny befell our community, all eyes looked to George. Then he ran away. And I thought that finally we would be spared the suspicions and censure of our neighbors."

"You are not to blame for another's choices, Mattie."

"But I'd promised my mother I'd take care of my brother."

"And you did, as much as you were able, until such time as George reached an age to make his own decisions." The blue eyes glittered behind their glass shields. "You didn't fail him. You couldn't live his life for him, Mattie."

That boy who loves you. Under other circumstances, Kit's words would have warmed her. Instead, they sent a chill up her spine at her callous disregard of Nicky. And Lady Chambelston. And Caro. And Kit. Truly, she had been no better than her father, who'd wallowed in his own pain, oblivious to the needs of his son.

No better than her brother, who had loved only himself.

But there *was* a difference. As of today, she was forgiven—and learning to forgive. She couldn't undo the past but with God's help she would not continue the old patterns.

"How many years has it been?"

"Since I last saw my brother? Seven."

"Seven years? I thought he was impressed shortly before war was declared."

"George was gone four years when we learned from the *Constance*'s captain he'd been pressed into the British navy. I found my father the next morning. I don't know whether he died from drink or despair."

"And your brother never came home at all in the years prior?"

She stared into Kit's eyes, the angry fires now banked to little more than embers of…sympathy. "I guess he didn't have a reason to return."

"He had you."

Mattie rose from the chair and paced to the window. Night screened the rosebushes in shadows. With the darkness before her and the gleam of the candle behind, the glass pane reflected her face like a mirror. She stared at her reflection, searching for a likeness to George Fraser. "As I said, I guess he never had a reason to return."

A chair spring squeaked. She felt Kit's approach, and then he wrapped his arms around her. He cradled her face against his chest, smoothing the hair from her temples and the grief from her heart. Emotions, pent up for so many years, burst forth in a torrent. All the terrible, wasted, lonely years. Years of waiting for her father, for her brother. She buried her nose in the soft linen of his shirt and inhaled his scent, his strength.

"Funny thing about war." Kit's voice rumbled in his chest, against her cheek. "It oft changes a man. Your brother sent you a letter, no? Perhaps he would have yet gone home had he lived."

Perhaps. Or perhaps not. She'd never know if George had also discovered the secret to altering his life.

"How old would your brother be now?"

"Two and twenty. All I wanted, all I've ever wanted, is to find out what happened." And exact her revenge.

He rested his chin on the top of her head and stroked her back, his fingers soothing as they caressed her spine. "That's why you asked Nicky to try to find Fitzgerald."

"Last night your brother told me that it was the first officer's job to see the ship fully manned."

"And you thought it a little too coincidental that you happened to meet Fitzgerald the other day."

"London is a large city, larger than anything in my previous experience, too large for such a meeting to be accidental. And then there was his demeanor that day. He acted as if he knew neither the *Impatience* nor George. But an American on one of your ships wouldn't be easily overlooked. Everyone I've met knows my birthplace the minute I speak."

"So you asked Nicky to follow Fitzgerald?"

"More like see what he could find out. Because he's mostly lived near the docks, Nicky knows a lot of the sailors. He can find out almost anything about any ship or crew."

"I could have used his services the other day when Harrison and I searched the pay records for information about your brother." She felt Kit's smile against her hair, then his arms stiffened. "Nicky was there at Hyde Park the day someone shot at you."

"He discovered the whereabouts of one of the sailors from the *Impatience*, a seaman called Soggy, who claimed he knew what happened to George."

"Of course he knew what happened to your brother, Miss Fraser." Mattie wrenched free of Kit's embrace and whirled to face the man in the doorway. Kit's brother.

Somershurst leaned against the frame. Proximity emphasized the similarities between the two brothers. The same taut mouth. The same blue eyes. The same tawny hair—Kit's slightly longer and more rumpled, Somershurst's bleached by the sun.

"I'm sorry to distress your further, Miss Fraser, but Soggy wielded one of the clubs that killed George Fraser. Under Lieutenant Fitzgerald's orders."

Chapter Fifteen

Kit let his empty arms fall to his sides. "Jules!"

"I came to talk. It is past time, you know."

Past time, but five minutes too early. Kit looked at Mattie.

Her eyes had grown bleak, like the dead brown leaves that littered the ground in November. Then her lashes dropped over her eyes, shuttering his view of her grief. "Why would this Soggy lie to me?"

"I don't know that he did, Miss Fraser." Julian strolled into the room and joined them. "From what I overheard of your conversation with Kit, Soggy told you the truth. Just not the entire truth."

"But why?" The sob ripped from her throat, and anguish etched deep lines around her mouth.

"Who hired Soggy to meet with Mattie is the more appropriate question." Kit glanced at Julian over the top of Mattie's burnished hair.

"I did." Mattie gripped the window sill. The weak candle-light shimmered on her hair, but cast her face in shadow, leaving her expression unreadable. "Nicky promised him a crown if he'd tell me what he knew. I paid him half in advance. But then the shooting started, so I never gave him the rest."

The shooting! Kit focused on the murky details of that day. Mattie had stood near the sailor at the time. Two shots. Two targets? "Do you know what happened to this 'Soggy'?"

"No, I didn't see him when we left the park."

"Probably ran." If he wasn't caught. Kit shot his brother a look. He and Julian needed to talk. Now. Alone. "Mattie, you should get some rest. I'll walk you to your room."

Her gaze flickered from him to Julian and back—but she acquiesced to his suggestion with a nod.

He proffered his elbow. For several seconds he feared she wouldn't take it. And no wonder, given the recriminations, distrust and dreadful deeds that lay between them.

Then she rested her hand on his arm. Through his shirt he felt the coldness of her chilled palm as he led her to the staircase.

Silence accompanied them to the top of the steps, then her fingers tightened on his sleeve. "What you said, about Nicky and how I used him—"

"I had no right to say those things."

She paused before her door, her eyes luminous in the darkness. "No, I needed to hear them. You made me face some ugly aspects of my character. Of course, I've already realized I need to make some changes in my life."

He held up his hand. "Mattie—"

She pressed her palm to his. "No, let me finish. I did form a friendship with Nicky for what he might gain me, but along the way…"

"You fell in love with the imp. I know that." Sadness etched her face. His fingers tightened around her hand. "And he fell in love with you, too."

"I am only now beginning to realize the great responsibility that accompanies such a gift."

Kit was silent, pondering what Mattie had told him of her relationship with her brother. Perhaps it was understandable that she hadn't realized how Nicky's love would influence his actions.

"Thank you, Kit. I hadn't intended to dampen your shoulder with self-pity."

"I said a great many things today, things I regret. Mattie, I wish…" His own secrets weighed heavily on his heart as he stared into her unflinching dark eyes. A man could drown there—or perhaps he already had. Longing welled in him. He pressed his mouth against her soft fingertips then released her hand. "Get some sleep. Julian and I will see if we can solve this muddle. Betsy will bring your other clothes first thing in the morning."

She offered him a watery smile, then closed the door. For several moments, he stared at that wall of oak, reflecting on what had transpired, on the changes in her. In him. Then he pivoted and marched downstairs to join his brother.

"I'd begun to think you weren't going to return." Julian stood next to his desk, two glasses of brandy poured and waiting. He grasped one in either hand and walked forward. "Drink?"

Kit raised his palm to forestall him. He had work to do tonight. "None for me, thank you."

Julian's brows rose. He reached behind to him return one of the drinks to the desk, then gestured to a chair.

Kit dropped onto the cushion, staring into the fire Julian had recently stoked. "You've been most elusive these past days."

"I had my reasons." Julian lowered himself onto the other chair.

"Reasons pertaining to a certain document that disappeared during your last voyage?"

"So Miss Fraser does know about the orders?"

"Is that why you tried to hurt Mattie, because you thought she knew about that paper?" Kit swallowed the nausea surging to his throat, but the bitterness remained in his mouth. "A woman, Jules! Did you really believe her such a threat?"

"I say, Kit! What a notion. What do you take me for?"

"A desperate man, on the verge of losing everything. Mattie's troubles began mere hours after I spoke to you."

"I admit to trying to frighten Miss Fraser into returning to America—a ham-handed attempt at best, and as I've since learned, a course destined to fail—but having the innkeeper and Mrs. Parker put notes in her room hardly constitutes physical danger."

"Mrs. Parker!"

"Ah, so I surprised you. The innkeeper demanded a bit of cash to leave the note on Miss Fraser's bed, but Mrs. Parker cooperated with me because she was afraid, you understand, a scheming American would entangle you with her wiles. You always were her favorite."

"Notes are one thing, Jules, but shooting at Mattie is hardly an innocuous warning."

"Shooting? I didn't shoot at anyone."

"But I thought you hired Stumpy…"

"Who's Stumpy?"

Relief washed through Kit at this confirmation of the facts he'd gleaned at the Captain's Quarters. Kit searched his memory for Mattie's account of the man who'd lost his arm to an American cannonball. If Stumpy hadn't operated under Julian's orders, then whose? "Two shots were fired at Mattie yesterday while she was in Hyde Park. One of her assailants was a man named Stumpy, but he had only one arm—the second shot came from another direction. I worried perhaps you…"

"At one time, you looked up to me, little brother." Resentment hardened in Julian's eyes and tightened along his jaw. "And now you think me capable of killing a woman."

Why not? Kit had done it.

Julian took a sip of his brandy. "So this fellow *was* named Stumpy. He shot at Mattie, and now he's dead?"

"I don't know—none of his companions saw him in his usual haunts last night. Not to say I don't want him dead, or wouldn't have killed him myself once I'd collected whatever information I could get from him, but I thought you were the person who would be implicated by anything Stumpy might say."

"Truly, Kit, I didn't seek Mattie's death. I wanted her to stop, but I never wanted her dead." Julian drew a deep breath into his lungs. Lines etched his face—not the patterns produced by a life at sea, but creases of anxiety. "I feared that if she continued, Miss Fraser's inquiries would eventually advise certain people of my failure to safeguard the orders."

Except those people already knew about their disappearance. Undoubtedly, Alderston had spies of his own aboard the *Impatience*. Not a surprise given the ship's mission, but why didn't they know the document's whereabouts, either? "You were conveniently missing for days. I don't suppose you have an alibi?"

"I was in Portsmouth."

"Portsmouth?" Where the *Impatience* was berthed. Kit reached for the missing glass and encountered only a…Bible. He folded his hands over his knee. "What did you find?"

"Nothing—truly, nothing. It seems the Admiralty has conveniently misplaced a ship."

Convenient for whom? "It isn't there?"

"Sailed last week."

"But Alderston wants that paper found." Only someone of higher rank than either Julian or Fitzgerald would have the authority to make such a ship disappear.

"Alderston? Is that how you got involved in this?" Julian stared at Kit as if seeing him for the first time. "I ought to have guessed. You're too adept with languages for our government to waste your talents as a simple clerk."

"You know I can admit to no such assumptions." So Julian knew of Alderston. Not surprising, given his long years of service to the crown.

"I remember one time when you impressed Maman by identifying a visiting Frenchman's home region—simply by the way he spoke the language. Why do I suspect your travels to procure supplies during the war were a facade for other activities?"

"That depends on your definition of supplies." Kit pondered the drink in Julian's hand. "I was a foolish lad looking for adventure—and I found Alderston. Does the knowledge of my ungentlemanly activities offend your sensibilities?"

"Only if you were unsuccessful."

Kit pushed aside the bitter recollections of the past spring. "I won't be in this instance. I need that paper."

"What do you know about the orders?"

"Only that we need to get them back."

"You'll have to talk to Fitzgerald then."

"Fitzgerald!" Cold dread swirled through Kit despite the revived fire.

"He claims he's had them since Fraser stole them in February."

"The blackmail. You stood in the way of his promotion to captain, and he was blackmailing you in revenge."

"Fitzgerald was a loose cannon—too self-serving to be entrusted with his own ship, especially when men's lives, our country even, were at stake."

"And now that we are at peace, there won't be another promotion or another captured ship for decades."

What if the man who claimed to possess the orders didn't have them? Wouldn't he fear Mattie's discovery of them?

Enough to kill her, even.

"I think Fitzgerald's dead."

"Dead?" Julian's hand jerked with such force brandy sloshed over the side of the glass and onto his breeches. "How? When?"

"I don't know. My informant's about seven years old. He claims he saw a dead man in Fitzgerald's house earlier today, although he couldn't say with certainty if the deceased was indeed Fitzgerald."

Julian abandoned his drink and surged to his feet. "I think I shall pay a visit to my former lieutenant."

"I'll come with you."

For a moment, Julian's lips flattened to a condescending older-brother frown. And then he looked at Kit again as if seeing a different man and not the younger brother he knew. Or rather, thought he knew. "Yes, I would appreciate your help. How do we go about this?"

"Dark clothes. Soft-soled shoes. And weapons would be wise."

Moments later, they met at the back door where Julian passed Kit a pistol.

"How far?" Kit tucked the gun into his waistband.

"Perhaps thirty minutes on foot."

"You lead."

Kit followed his brother though Julian's neglected garden. The rain-soaked grass muffled his steps and drenched his shoes, leaving his stockings uncomfortably sodden. A narrow alley beyond the grounds pointed them to the wet bricks of a wider road. Heavy quiet wrapped around them, scarcely disturbed by the gentle rhythm of their footfalls. The fog misted Kit's spectacle lenses and the ever-present smoke dulled the gaslights' glare so that the night cloaked their movements.

Minutes later, Julian gestured to a very dark, very quiet townhouse. No candlelight drizzled through the windows to indicate life within.

"Have you been inside before?" Kit studied the building, trying to determine what room matched the stately windows. A dining room? A drawing room?

"Of course."

"Good, then let's enter through the rear, lest a late-returning neighbor find us skulking below the windows." Kit climbed over the wall into Fitzgerald's untended garden.

Julian's feet thudded softly to earth as he followed. "Ouch!"

Kit glanced over his shoulder, but the darkness obscured all but the barest outline of Julian's form. "What happened?"

"Rosebush snared my ankle." Fabric ripped as Julian freed himself from the thorns.

They inched along the foundation until they reached a pair of floor-to-ceiling windows.

Julian touched Kit's arm. "Drawing room."

Kit nodded and set to work on the latches. He cajoled the right one loose. It swung toward him with a single squeak.

His breath caught in his throat. He jerked the pistol from his breeches and wrapped his fingers around the stock while he waited. Tense seconds passed while the blood pounded through his ears. When all yet remained quiet, he slipped over the sill into the drawing room.

Kit pressed his back to the wall while he waited for Julian to climb in, then whispered, "The front door."

"This way." Julian tiptoed across the room and pushed the door. Unlike the window, its hinges swung silently.

The faint glow of the gaslights beamed through the transom window above the door, illuminating the foyer floor. The very bare foyer floor.

Nobody. Or rather, no body.

"Not here." Kit nearly threw down his pistol in disgust.

"No." Julian crouched down close to the parquet. "But Kit, neither is the rug that was here on my last visit."

Kit drew a candle stub and flint from his jacket.

"You came prepared." Was that admiration in Julian's voice?

"Candles are easy to find. Flint, not always so much." Kit struck a spark and lit the wick.

The dark wood revealed no secrets to Kit's critical eyes. He ground his teeth together in frustration at the lack of evidence for Nicky's allegations. Or was that the answer?

"Give me the candle, Kit."

He passed the light to Julian and watched while his brother examined the wall.

"Last night, when Mattie… Well, afterward, she tried to clean the wall but couldn't completely remove the stains. Stains like these." He held the flame near a faint spray design on the foyer wall.

Kit blew out the candle. "We might as well leave."

"But the orders—"

"Aren't likely to be here—if they ever were."

"You are suggesting the house has already been searched?"

"No ordinary thief would conceal a murder and leave behind the silver candlesticks in the drawing room. This was designed to look as if Fitzgerald left for a short journey."

"To the bottom of the Thames, it seems. So you believe the body was Fitzgerald's? But who…?"

"Fitzgerald was blackmailing you."

"I didn't kill him, Kit."

"I meant there could be others. Blackmailers rarely confine their villainy to a single victim." Except this was too professional to be a frantic victim short on funds and unable to meet his extortionist's demands. Who else wanted the orders? Alderston? If so, Kit would learn of their discovery on the morrow. "Come, there's nothing more to gain here tonight."

* * *

The night had begun to ease, transforming the sky from black to dark blue, when Mattie awoke. Outside the window, birds already chirped their merry morning tunes. She lit the bedside candle, only to remember she'd left the Bible in the library.

Once she'd again donned the no-longer-so-new brown dress. She crept through the silent house, candle cupped in her hand to protect the flame from drafts. A stair riser squealed underfoot and she winced, but all remained quiet.

Only a few scattered embers remained of the previous night's fire. Mattie added some kindling and stoked a few cautious flames to life. Then she settled into a chair and opened the Bible to one of the passages Harrison had marked specifically for her. The sky had lightened to soft gray and she'd reached her third reading of Psalm 103 when the same step squeaked again.

Seconds later, Kit paused in the doorway. "I'm sorry to disturb you. I saw the light. I didn't realize anyone else was awake."

"I woke early." She lifted the Bible off her lap and offered him a wry smile. "I needed reassurance my life can be redeemed."

He shuffled into the room and dropped into the other chair. His shoulders drooped, as if crushed beneath a great weight. "Do you really think there is truth there, or are those merely words we latch on to in desperation?"

"I know that the people I see most at peace—Harrison, your mother—believe them. My father, he believed in a remote God—a God who existed, but didn't care. And eventually, my father lost all hope and purpose for his life. I don't want that. I don't want to be lost and lonely anymore. I want what your mother and Harrison have." A memory of her former self, bent on destruction and apathetic about the future, flitted into her mind. "Without these words, the future is bleak."

Shadows darkened the blue eyes that stared into the flames, as if he saw that same bleakness therein. A brittle stillness lay on the lines of his jaw.

Mattie hesitated, the newness of her faith causing her tongue to feel thick and clumsy. Perhaps she should wait and let him talk to Harrison or his mother. Mattie had so little to offer. And yet, a gentle nudging disturbed her reluctance, reminding her Kit's stubborn heart had resisted the guidance of those closest to him. With a quick prayer and a deep breath, she approached the subject he'd only alluded to in the past. "Yesterday, you told me you drink to forget. Kit, what is the memory that haunts you?"

His fingers curled around the chair's arms. His knuckles whitened, and tendons rose along the backs of his hands. Silence swathed the room save for the occasional crackle of the flames. Then, as if conceding some great battle within himself, he shrugged. "The war is over. I suppose there's no longer any harm in the telling. About a year and a half ago, I was in France."

"In France? But I thought…"

"That I worked at the Admiralty, procuring supplies for ships? In a manner of speaking."

A spy. The man behind the spectacles had been a spy. It was almost too fantastic to believe, and yet… "Your facility with languages."

"Yes. Maman, being French, taught us the language as children, so I speak French like a native—like many natives, in fact. A wine merchant from Bordeaux. A clerk from Paris. A dock worker from Marseille."

That day he'd met her, he'd pinpointed the state of her birth. And then at the Captain's Quarters, he'd spoken much like Nicky. "An impressive achievement."

"Hardly." The harshness in his tones tore through the quiet like a scab being ripped from an unhealed wound. "It isn't as if I used my gifts for good."

"But it was war—"

"Surely, Mattie, you know better than to justify the inexcusable. Were you so understanding when my countrymen burned your city?"

She rested her chin on her fist. "No, you are correct. War takes on a different appearance when you suffer the loss. So what happened last year?"

"We discovered we had a traitor in our midst, someone who was transmitting ship movements to the French."

"An Englishman?"

"Some people will do anything for a fee—a reality that my country has also used to advantage."

Against her country also? Unfortunately, she feared too many Americans were only human and would find gold a powerful incentive. "You went after the traitor."

"We believed he sold the information to a Frenchman in Marseille—an older man who had risen through the ranks of French navy." Kit's glance slid her way. "Indeed, he served under Admiral De Grasse."

"De Grasse!"

"I thought you might recognize the name."

"Of course. My father was at Yorktown when the French helped General Washington defeat Cornwallis's army." Mattie rose and added another log to the fire. The designs cut into the crystal brandy decanter sparkled in the flames' renewed glow. At least Kit hadn't already begun to imbibe this morning. She returned to the chair. "So you traveled to Marseille?"

"As a wine merchant looking for assistance in evading the English blockade. But I couldn't attain the information I needed, so I cultivated a relationship with the French naval officer's granddaughter, a young woman close to your years."

A woman. A lump formed in Mattie's throat. And then another memory flashed to the fore of her mind, her first encounter with Kit DeChambelle. "Laura."

His eyes blinked behind the spectacles. "Yes."

Disappointment crowded into her chest, leaving little room for her breath, only the knowledge of something that almost was but couldn't be. She lowered her gaze to the book on her lap. Hadn't she just moments ago blithely asserted that her life now had purpose? She offered another prayer that the Lord would use her to reach this broken man and then give her the strength to let him go when the time came. "Did you, ah, catch your traitor?"

"Not at first. I convinced myself that every delay added to the toll of men killed."

"Not an unfounded assumption."

"And one that let me justify a wealth of evil. I disguised my conceit as patriotism, determined not to let the villain get away with his deeds—and to earn the glory of capturing one last traitor. I abducted the old man and transported him to an English ship blockading the harbor, so they could question him. He maintained his innocence the entire time. And then..." The blue disappeared from Kit's eyes, leaving only pain-clouded black. "The old man didn't survive the interrogation."

Mattie gripped the chair as waves of anguish radiated from Kit and washed over her. "But with his contact gone, surely you at least stopped the traitor."

"He wasn't the traitor's contact. Laura was."

The room darkened. Or had her eyes fallen shut? Mattie swallowed but the lump in her throat continued to swell as if feeding on the emotion swirling around them.

"We realized our mistake soon afterward when Napoleon escaped back to France. I insisted on returning to Marseille. Pride is the deadliest sin because it leads to so many others. I was discovered, of course, and nearly killed." He yanked off his spectacles and rubbed a finger along the scar that streaked his face. "An innocent young woman—scarcely more than a girl, really—was caught in the crossfire. She didn't survive, either. Days later Paris fell to our army, and I was left to wonder—were my actions worth the needless deaths of two innocent people? An old man who should have died in his bed? A young woman at the beginning of her life?"

Heavy silence again closed around Mattie as if waiting in anticipation for her to utter the wrong words. Kit's elegant blue morning coat and precisely tied cravat created the ideal image of English aristocracy—cold, distant, aloof. So at odds with the hot regret that glittered in his eyes and throbbed along his jaw. "Did you like her, this Laura?" Love her? Did his feelings for her perhaps explain why he had been blind to her activities? And why his guilt so haunted him now, to the point he would surrender his future to escape the past?

"Like her? Miss Fraser, I *used* her."

The sudden reversion back to formal address grated a warning in her ears. "The one does not preclude the other." Not when misguided notions of justice consumed one's soul—as she of all people could testify. Had she not employed Nicky— despite her fondness for the boy—to further her ends of vengeance?

"No, you have the right of that." The hollowness in his words matched the despair in his gaze. "The past few years, I wasn't even certain any longer who I was. So many lies— sometimes I'm still not convinced I know what is true. I had been in and out of France for nearly ten years—"

"Ten years? You must have begun that dangerous game very young."

"Eighteen." His lips twisted into a sardonic semblance of a smile. "I didn't feel so young then. I felt invincible."

"And you were never caught until that last time?"

"A near thing several times. But along the way, I made compromises—compromises I rationalized by convincing myself that my actions would ultimately save more lives than they cost."

"That may be true."

"But I don't know for certain." He stared into the flames that danced on the hearth. "I only know that every action took me down a path further from my integrity until it was too late to find my way back."

Mattie slipped out of her chair. The brown skirt pooled against the carpet as she knelt before him. "Hence the drinking to forget. But Kit, it will lead you to further ruin."

He lifted his other hand, his fingertips but a whisper from her cheek. And then he yanked away, his eyes closing to hide the emptiness she glimpsed within. "And that matters why? I don't want to remember the man I've become."

She tapped her fingers against the back of his hand and rose. Retrieving the Bible from the table, she flipped it open and settled the book on his lap. "But don't you see? You don't have to continue as that person. The promise is forgiveness for the past and redemption for the future—a life with meaning and purpose."

"It's too late for me, Mattie. Whereas you find comfort in those verses, I find only condemnation."

Coldness settled around her heart as the warmth—the hope—left her. Until Kit accepted God's forgiveness, he would continue to cling to his guilt, his bitterness.

There was nothing for her here but pain.

Few people strolled Mayfair's streets so early in the morning, and those who did would never be so gauche as to pay a call at such an unacceptable hour. Kit marched to the front door of an elegant brick townhouse and knocked.

"Mr. Alderston is not home." At least his butler was

accustomed to Alderston's odd assortment of callers and even stranger hours.

"Is he at the Admiralty?"

"I don't know, Mr. DeChambelle. He left last night."

Last night? Frustration throbbed along Kit's jaw. "When he returns, would you tell I must speak to him as soon as possible? I'll be either at the Admiralty or at my brother's—Viscount Somershurst. I'm certain he can find the house."

The butler almost let a smile slip. "Indeed, sir."

Kit pointed his steps to the Admiralty, but found neither Alderston nor Baxter in residence. He prowled around Baxter's desk, searching for clues as to the man's last appearance. Kit hadn't seen him since the day Stumpy—and someone else—had shot at Mattie.

"There you are." Harrison rushed into the room, Julian following behind. "I've been searching half of London for you."

Foreboding tightened Kit's gut. Mattie? He gestured both men away from Baxter's desk and into his office, closing the door firmly behind them. "What's happened?"

Harrison folded his arms across his chest and leaned against the door. "The *Impatience* docked in London last night."

Julian strode to the window and stared out at the street. "That explains why I couldn't find her in Portsmouth."

Alderston. Had he guessed the orders might yet be on the ship? Kit looked at Harrison. A silent message, developed over years and years of working together, passed between them. "Thank you."

Harrison slipped out the door and pulled it shut.

"Now then—" Kit began, then stopped, arrested by Julian's expression. "What?"

"I like your friend, but…" A wry twist pulled Julian's

mouth to one side. "It occurs to me this Harrison knows my brother better than I do."

"Perhaps after this is over and Maman is on the mend, we can try again. It's not too late." He stopped, realizing he'd unconsciously quoted Mattie.

"No, not too late."

Did the same sentiment apply to Kit's life? To his relationship with Mattie even? He shifted his weight onto his other foot as if to escape the implications of his simple statement.

"Kit? What did you need to know?"

He tugged his attention back to the *Impatience*. "What is in those orders that they are so important?"

"Not so much the what, but the who."

"A signature?"

"International treachery, approved by the most powerful man in the kingdom."

"The Regent."

"Who else would be daft enough to direct such a mad plan?"

"What kind of international treachery?"

"A scheme to seize control of North America west of the Mississippi River. Think of it, Kit, all of Louisiana and the continent's most important waterway controlled by fair England instead of the Americans."

"And the Regent agreed to such machinations…" Heat flooded Kit's limbs, as if the tiny room suddenly became hot and oppressive. Until that document was found, Mattie's life would forever be endangered. Guilt clawed at his mind, his emotions, but he shoved it away. For the time being. He must find that paper while she was safe with his parents. He snared Julian by the arm. "Come, we are going to examine the *Impatience* from mast to hold. No doubt that was Alderston's intention if we didn't find the orders in London."

"You think he ordered the ship to London?"

"Who else?"

Seconds later, they hastened out of the Admiralty. As they sped toward the docks, the tranquil avenues of the West Side transmuted into streets teeming with drays, wagons and all manner of pedestrians. They raced through the crowded thoroughfares until they spotted the sleek lines of the ship.

Her masts disappeared into the foggy London sky, and she creaked as she rocked to the water's gentle lapping. Her eerily quiet deck showed no sign of life. Alderston's doing, no doubt. He'd want no witnesses to their search. Kit slowed, stopped, sucking deep breaths into his aching chest. The waste that polluted the Thames tainted the smoky air with scents of putrefying flesh and excrement. He stared at the huge vessel, overwhelmed by the enormity of searching her tons of wood for a single sheet of paper—assuming it was even yet on the ship. Those orders had probably been swallowed by a shark—along with Fraser.

But for Julian's sake—for *Mattie's* sake—they had to try.

Kit turned to his brother as Julian puffed beside him. "I defer to your knowledge of the ship. Where would you like to begin?"

Mattie ambled into Somershurst's dining room to find it already occupied. She suppressed a chuckle at the sight of the earl and the urchin eating together. Nicky's chatter echoed through the room, scarcely inhibited by the meal.

The earl rose from his chair on her arrival. "Good morning, Miss Fraser. Did you rest well?"

"Much better." She chose a slice of ham and toast to begin. "How is Lady Chambelston?"

"Still improving. We hope to move her to our house later today. You, ah, are welcome to join us at our home."

Mattie stared at the food on her plate, her appetite suddenly diminished. The DeChambelles had showered her with every kindness—food, lodging, the very clothes on her back—and she had repaid them with lies, evasions and danger. "Ah, I don't know."

"Oh, but Mattie, ye must." Nicky's eyes glowed with excitement. His elbows rested on the table next to a series of utensils he mostly ignored in favor of his fingers. He shoved a spoonful of egg into his mouth. "I'll be there, too."

"I, ah, promised young Master Nicky a position in my household." The earl's face pinkened under its tan.

Except Mattie didn't have a position. She wasn't family and her actions had been anything but friendly. She was neither guest nor servant, neither nobility nor peasant—only the penniless daughter of a perpetually drunk American shopkeeper with the most tenuous of ties to the DeChambelles. She lowered herself onto a chair and gave Nicky the eternal platitude. "We'll see."

The earl, too, resumed his seat. "You can't continue here after we leave, Miss Fraser, Julian not being married and all. Simply not done."

And not needed if Kit and his brother discovered the secret of that paper. Once they accomplished that, Mattie would be safe. And irrelevant. "By the by, sir, K—Mr. DeChambelle said last night that the maid Betsy would be coming with clothes and such, but I haven't seen her."

"Strange, Miss Fraser." Lord Chambelston frowned above his tea cup. "The other things arrived quite early this morning. Perhaps my man might know what happened."

Nicky bounced from his chair. "I'll go ask."

Kit's accusations from the previous night popped into Mattie's head. "Oh, but..." Truly, how much danger would the boy encounter between the dining room and a bedroom?

The earl smiled as Nicky danced from the room. "Been a long while since we had one with that kind of verve underfoot. Caro's condition makes such activity difficult for her.

Our oldest daughter has a son about that age, but…" Sorrow cut the lines around the earl's eyes deeper.

The daughter who was estranged from the family. Mattie well understood his pain.

"Master Nicky needs clean air, good food and space to explore. I was thinking that our family seat in Somerset might be a better home for an energetic lad than London."

A safer one, for certain. Bittersweet pain wrapped around her heart as she realized soon she would see the imp no more. And yet, a spark of joy lightened her sorrow. George was lost forever to her, but Nicky had a future. Opportunity. Hope.

Nicky raced back into the dining room. "I asked, but 'e says 'e ain't seen Betsy all morning."

Mattie's fingers clenched around her knife handle. "Betsy's missing?" First Nicky. Then the housekeeper. Now the maid—the same maid who had delivered the purported message from Nicky to Mrs. Parker.

"Don't fret, Miss Fraser. She probably ran off with a young man. Young women frequently have their heads turned by pretty compliments and promises. Happens all the time—just pray she was clever enough to make certain his intentions were honorable before she left."

"Ah, yes, I suppose." The vaguely familiar man from their trip to the modiste? Or something more sinister? If only Mattie could recall where she'd seen the man before.

"You and Master Nicky will come with us this afternoon when we take Agnes home."

Kit climbed to the quarterdeck and sucked deep breaths of London's foul air into his lungs. The feeling of hopelessness had magnified tenfold as he and Julian searched the stifling bowels of the ship where sunlight never penetrated. Now the twilight sky revealed he had spent an entire day—a fruitless day—crawling the *Impatience*'s dark, fetid hold and creeping through her shadowy, cramped carpenter's walk.

"It could be anywhere," Julian echoed Kit's thoughts as he stepped next to him.

"Someone knows where it is." Foul-smelling bilge water from the hold sloshed in Kit's boots as he followed Julian to the side of the ship. Kit eyed his brother with new respect. Julian had spent the better part of his life aboard such ships since he was scarce past his boyhood. They leaned against the rail, staring over the side at the rooftops of London. "A pity Fraser—or his accomplice, assuming there is one—didn't think to leave a clue."

Julian stilled, his grip tightening on the rail. "Kit, didn't you say that Miss Fraser has a letter her brother purportedly wrote while aboard the *Impatience?*"

"A rather innocuous note. And he included no date as to when he might have written the thing—just requested her to remember him fondly and…" Kit paused. Such sentiments did not harmonize with Mattie's description of her brother's character. A change of heart because of his travails?

Not likely. Not given that he'd continued his thieving ways right up until his death. Not when he'd written only once in all those years.

Julian braced his elbow on the rail and rested his chin on his fist. "Do you think Miss Fraser would mind if I read her letter?"

The knowledge that he would once again use Mattie to save his family churned in Kit's belly like a bad meal. That first day, she had pulled the note out of her reticule. But he'd found it—along with Julian's threat—under the bed at his parents' house when he'd searched her room. Was that before or after Stumpy stole her reticule?

Her reticule. Stumpy hadn't been after her money. He'd wanted the letter. For whom?

Chapter Sixteen

"No, Mat-tie. This." Caro rearranged the doll in its crib. She sat on her bedchamber rug in Lord Chambelston's house, her brow furrowed in concentration as if precise placement of her toys was the most important event in the world.

"Oh, I'm sorry." Mattie smiled. What did she know about dolls? Her childhood had ended sixteen years ago on the night her mother died. She stroked the doll's satin and lace gown. Fortunately her new playmate was quite forgiving of her incompetence. Mattie picked up a blue-eyed baby with brown tresses that looked remarkably like her playmate. "What about this one?"

"This way." Caro, who had definite ideas about the proper way to conduct such matters, placed the doll in Mattie's arms. "Rock."

Mattie commenced to hold the doll according to Caro's specifications. Caro, with her limited understanding of the malevolence and machinations of others. Was she, perhaps, the one to be envied—the one closest to God's heart of them all? Mattie's problems shrank in proportion to the time she spent with this sister of Kit's.

She would miss Caro—and all the DeChambelles. But it was time for her to leave, to protect them from the threats that dogged her every step. Besides, she must go, if only to preserve her sanity, her future. Kit's hard heart would only break hers. His continuous rejection of God was taking him down the same ruinous path as her father—to a place where she refused to go ever again.

A commotion reverberated from the foyer. Mattie set down the doll.

"No, no, Mat-tie. Not sleeping."

Duly chastised, Mattie retrieved the doll and rose from the floor. Wrinkles pleated the skirt of her last new gown, the pale green muslin. A pity she hadn't followed Lady Chambelston's fashion advice—after the past two days, Mattie could happily never wear brown again. "Shall we see who arrived?"

"Kit?" Caro echoed Mattie's thoughts. Hopes.

Together they hastened to the stairs and peered over the banister. Below, two gentlemen conferred with Higgins in the foyer, heads nodding at the butler's comment. Kit glanced up at their approach and his gaze met Mattie's. The appreciation smoldering in his eyes—discernable despite the spectacles—brought a glow of warmth to her heart. And a whisper of warning to her head.

And then the look was gone, replaced once again with empty nothingness. If only... But no, nothing had changed. Kit hadn't changed.

"Kit!" Caro's smile danced in her eyes.

He mounted the stairs two at a time, his greatcoat swirling with his movements, and stopped one step from the top. Even one riser lower, he towered over his sister as he embraced her. "I missed you, Caro." He tweaked a lock of her hair.

"Missed you, Kit."

"And I missed you, too, Mattie." His brows arched as his stare took in the doll she yet carried in her arms.

"Caro and I were playing."

His face softened with...longing? Loneliness? Then the

line of his jaw grew taut. "I'm sorry to interrupt. Julian and I were hoping you still have that letter from your brother."

"The letter?"

His shoulders rose with his deeply drawn breath. "The *Impatience* is in London."

"Now? But when?" And why?

"She arrived last night. We searched her today, but a ship that large… We thought perhaps your brother might have provided you a clue as to where he hid the stolen paper."

"I don't know. I never read the note with such thoughts in mind. I'll get it for you." She thrust the doll into his hands. "Here. You'll have to rock the baby to sleep. Caro insists."

Tenderness muted the bleakness in his gaze. At Caro, or at…her? Mattie's traitorous pulse began to accelerate despite her recent resolutions. She fled his perceptive eyes and her hopeless wishes.

The yellow bedchamber's warmth exacerbated Mattie's agitation. She wriggled under the bed and located the letter still in its niche between the mattress and frame, along with the other notes, including Somershurst's warnings. She crawled out, scrambled to her feet and tossed the two threats onto the room's low-burning fire. The flames flared as they consumed the paper, then retreated, leaving only ashes.

Like her enmity against their author, Captain Julian DeChambelle, late of *HMS Impatience*.

Two pages left—George's letter and the DeChambelle address in Kit's bold hand. She traced a finger along this reminder of their first meeting, then tucked his directions into a drawer. She'd take the paper with her when she returned to America, a reminder of all that had happened, all that had changed.

When she returned to the staircase landing, she found Somershurst had joined Kit. "Where's Caro?"

"She left to put her baby to bed." Kit brushed a hand over her shoulder. "Thank you, Mattie."

The light caress pressed a heavy weight against her heart. She drew in a steadying breath. Still, her hands trembled as she unfolded her last remaining link to her brother and passed the note to Somershurst. "I don't know that this will be of much help."

"Nevertheless, I, ah, appreciate your showing it to me, Miss Fraser."

She swallowed. George was gone, like her bitterness. It mattered no more.

"'My dearest sister,'" Somershurst read aloud in that voice so like his brother's.

"I pray this note finds you in good health. My life at sea has taken a peculiar turn, and I now find myself aboard an English vessel, the *Impatience*. The food is as bad as I'd feared, but I have made a few friends and collected a few trinkets I hope to someday share with you. I miss you and Papa and even my cramped quarters above the store, which I have come to realize were actually quite spacious compared to a ship. If I do not return, I pray you will forgive me the troubles I caused you and look back on the good times with fondness. Affectionately, your brother, George."

"He complained about the food." Kit tapped his templed fingers against his lips. "Perhaps he hid the orders in the galley?"

"But he also mentioned his quarters—which could mean his berth." Somershurst returned the note to Mattie. "Or his reference to the store could mean the hold. I don't see how this helps. For all we know, he wrote this three years ago when first pressed."

"But he mentions collecting trinkets to share. How many such items could he collect on a ship? He might have meant the orders."

Mattie shook her head, sorrow still weighing heavy on her heart. "Given George's propensity for thievery, he probably, ah, collected valuables from half the men on the ship." Thievery. A memory niggled in the back of her mind.

"I'm not so certain of that." Somershurst's blue gaze narrowed. "You see, when a man dies at sea, his belongings are auctioned to the crew with the proceeds going to any surviving kin. I don't recall Fraser having an excessive number of possessions."

Because he hid them! On the ship—like he had at home. The thoughts whizzed through Mattie's mind; the random phrases at last forming a complete thought. "Take me to the ship. Let me look."

Kit edged closer. "Mattie, you've never even seen the *Impatience*."

"No, but I know how George hid stolen money and other valuables when he still lived at home."

Blue eyes met blue as the brothers shared a look. "We should let her try, Kit. None of us will be safe until we recover that paper."

Kit sighed, but nodded his acquiescence. "Get your coat, Mattie. I'll see to the carriage."

Moments later Kit tucked her into the corner of the private family carriage and settled onto the seat beside her while his brother took the opposing bench. Despite the conveyance's richness, the small confines brought her into agonizingly frequent contact with his cloak-covered shoulder. The silence exacerbated the tension in her belly and accentuated every sound. The squeak of the springs. The rustle of Kit's coat. The scrape of his shoe.

After a rut jostled her against him—again—she sought

refuge in conversation. "Am I to know about this mysterious paper?"

Kit leaned forward and braced his elbows on his knees. The movement seemed to bring him even closer to her. "She deserves to know, Jules."

Somershurst tilted his head back against the seat and waved a gloved hand. "Very well, Miss Fraser. Last winter, your country and mine entered into a treaty to end our recent hostilities. The *Impatience* was charged with conveying that treaty to America."

"Yes, Kit related those details to me when we met."

"During our voyage to America your brother stole a paper from my cabin—the orders relating to the treaty's delivery, to be precise. And therein lies the source of all our difficulties." The muted glow of the gaslights reflected the sardonic gleam in Somershurst's eyes. "You see, this treaty was not binding until ratifications were exchanged."

She shook her head. "I don't understand. We sent representatives to the peace talks last year. I thought they signed the treaty last winter."

"Indeed, but this treaty was…unusual. Prior treaties between our countries—such as that when we granted the colonies their independence—"

"When we won our independence."

Beside her Kit snorted, and even Somershurst smiled.

"Er, yes. The prior treaties went into effect when they were signed. This one had to be ratified by both countries, then those ratifications exchanged in Washington before it took effect."

"So that is the reason the British envoy came to Washington."

"Just so, Miss Fraser. I'd forgotten that you were from Washington and might have heard about such events in your country. I also assume you know what happened at New Orleans shortly before the envoy's arrival?"

She lifted her chin and offered him a sugary smile. "Of course. General Jackson routed the British invaders. The battle was a resounding victory and quite celebrated."

"Two weeks after the treaty was signed."

"No one in America knew the treaty had been finalized. It takes longer than that for news to arrive on our side of the ocean. Besides, your country attacked us at New Orleans."

Somershurst stretched out his legs. "Your defense of your country is admirable. Yes, we attacked and lost. New Orleans was our last offensive—planned at the same time we finalized the Treaty of Ghent."

"But as you said, the treaty had already been signed. The battle made no difference to the war's outcome."

"But it might have, Miss Fraser. Because of the unusual provision regarding ratification, the treaty was signed—but not yet in effect. The British government has long viewed Bonaparte's sale of Louisiana as illegal."

"Of course it was legal."

"Only if one agrees Bonaparte legitimately appropriated Louisiana from Spain. Many in our country—our government—do not. General Pakenham's orders went beyond the capture of New Orleans. He was to liberate Louisiana from the United States and rule it on behalf of Spain."

"And how did your government intend to rule on 'behalf' of Spain'?"

"Pakenham carried a commission naming him governor of Louisiana. And had we been victorious, a nonbinding treaty would not have stopped us."

"Goodness gracious!" Though Mattie's heart hammered furiously, the blood drained from her face, leaving her dazed. "Those orders instructed you to withhold the treaty if you discovered the British had captured New Orleans. Then you would demand a new treaty, ceding Louisiana to England."

"Now you understand our government's intentions." Somershurst nodded, a mocking smile fixed on his face. "Think of it, Miss Fraser. Your country locked against the Atlantic on your east and surrounded by British and Spanish territory to your north, south and west."

"But—but what difference does it make now? The treaty was ratified last winter."

"What difference?" Kit interrupted her whirling thoughts. She chanced a glance at him. Dark anger filled his eyes. "As our treaty with France is not yet realized, our government feels it cannot afford to let the details of this adventure be published. Think what it would do to our negotiating position should any learn of our government's penchant for international duplicity."

It was too fantastic, too utterly unbelievable. Mattie lifted her gaze and stared at Somershurst. "So my brother discovered this stratagem and you had him killed before he could give these papers to the Americans."

"Dear me, no, Miss Fraser. Surely you knew your brother well enough not to credit him with altruistic motives. He tried to blackmail me."

George. Faithless to the end.

"Furthermore, though you may disbelieve me, Miss Fraser, I simply gave the order to retrieve the missing paper. Indeed, I was most distressed when the men killed Fraser in the ensuing scuffle. You may be assured that I, of all people, did not want your brother dead before he revealed his secret."

The *Impatience* creaked with the gentle motion of the Thames. Her masts disappeared into the night, her rigging swaying with the current. She was a huge ship, far larger than the one that had brought Mattie to England.

And very soon Mattie would retrace that path back to her homeland. Her heart, however, would not go with her.

Kit held her elbow and assisted her climb up the gangway. His consideration brought her another wave of longing, another wave of regret. "So how did your brother hide stolen money at home?"

"We lived above my father's store and George had his own room in the attic. Hot in the summer, cold in the winter and private enough to let him get into all sorts of trouble." As Kit assisted her onto the deck, she glanced at Somershurst.

He stood a few feet from Kit and her, very much alone. At her pause, he turned his head and a brief flicker of pain flashed through his DeChambelle eyes before he concealed it again with his sardonic arrogance.

He missed this life, this ship.

Again, she felt the odd connection between them, that of no-longer-enemies-but-never-quite-friends. She, too, already felt the loss of what could be no more.

"Mattie?" Kit's voice forced her to the matter at hand. Time enough for sorrow later. "What did George do?"

"Carved out a hollow in one of the beams of the house, then whittled a false knot to cover it. He hid money and jewels in there until I finally caught him one day. My father had been drinking, and he…" She didn't want to remember any more of that day—the argument, the fight, George's departure.

Her own relief.

And her subsequent guilt.

"So, we might find the paper hidden in a beam." Somershurst spread his arms wide. "Miss Fraser, this is an exceedingly large ship. You do realize that searching for the right beam might well take us the rest of our lives?"

On shore, the lights of London shimmered in the night, hazy from the smoke that hung in the air. Mattie stared at them for silent moments, then shook her head. "No, your ship would have been bursting with men, most of whom would not have taken kindly to an American whittling away the ship. George would've had a limited number of places that afforded him the necessary privacy. We need to think like George to guess which beam."

Kit's arm tightened around her shoulders. "So far, we've suggested the hold, the galley, or his berth."

Somershurst led them to a ladder. "Fraser's messmates never indicated he'd altered anything there. They were among the first of the crew I questioned."

"Could they have been involved?" Mattie asked.

"I doubt it. They were a vile sort—uncouth and unschooled. Unlike Fraser, I doubt any of them knew the value of those orders. Fraser could not have done as you suggest without their knowing it, and not even the offer of a bribe produced information from them. Poor piece of luck that Fraser could read."

"My father," Mattie interrupted without remorse, "being a shopkeeper, thought it prudent that both George and I learn to read and compute."

Kit tensed and Mattie felt his excitement sizzle through him along the hand that gripped her shoulder. "The purser's store, Julian. Can you see the irony? Fraser's father was a shopkeeper. And of all men on a ship, pursers have the worst reputation for corruption."

"Not on my ship." Julian rested his chin against his fist. "Ironic, but not feasible. Too many people about, unless..."

"The carpenter's walk behind the purser's store."

Julian drew in a deep breath. "Possible, if not probable. As good a conjecture as any." He climbed down the ladder to the deck below.

"Good work, Mattie," Kit said as he pulled her against him. Oh, so right, and oh, so impossible. "Just a little more, then we will have this ordeal behind us."

Except the *us* would be behind them, too.

"Let me help you down."

"I've been on a ship before."

A grin tugged at his lips and eased the strain around his eyes. "Just so, my dear."

Moments later the two of them joined Somershurst in the dark, dank quarters. Just being belowdeck amid the overpowering vinegar-and-sulfur odor brought to Mattie's mind her voyage to England.

And the voyage she would soon make again.

Somershurst lit a lantern. The feeble light scarcely cut through the darkness this far below the sky. Below the river, in fact. "This way." He led them to a tiny tunnel, not even as tall as Mattie, that stretched along the side of the ship.

"What is this?" She balked at entering such a dark, confined space.

"The carpenter's walk," Kit's voice murmured in her ear. "It allows the carpenter to make repairs to the side of the ship in the event of a hull breach."

Somershurst and the light began to move away. "Alas, Miss Fraser, sailors frequently make use of it for nefarious purposes."

Hardly a comforting statement. She crouched and followed, Kit's steady hand against her back still burning through her skin.

"Well, the purser's store should be on the other side of this bulkhead from us. Any idea what might have attracted your brother's notice, Miss Fraser?"

She paused beside a heavy beam shaped like an inverted *L*. "May I have the lantern?"

Julian shrugged his stooped shoulders and passed it to her.

She hunkered past several more similarly shaped beams,

then turned and crowded her way past the men to the one behind them and stopped. There was something…

"Mattie?" Kit's voice had tightened. "Do you see something unusual about that knee?"

"If by knee you mean this beam, then yes. Look. There is an extra bolt that the others don't have."

"I say! She's right, Kit." Somershurst withdrew a knife from his coat and pried the "bolt" loose. It popped out of its spot to reveal a small cavity in the knee. Somershurst stared at the article in his palm. "Ingenious. It is only a piece of wood carved in the shape of a button-head bolt and designed to fit over the hole."

"Go ahead, Mattie." Kit's voice was low. "You solved the riddle. You should be the one to recover the orders."

The darkness magnified the lap of waves against the side of the ship, the ragged sound of Kit's breathing, the heavy pulsing of the blood in her ears. A chill permeated the air and curled under her skirt, under her skin. Mattie slipped her fingers into the hole and encountered the cold metal of several coins—and then the smoothness of rolled paper.

"Mattie?" Kit stared into the luminous brown eyes. The flickering lantern threw shadows into them—specters of pain and grief.

"You read it." She withdrew a tube of paper and passed it to him, her hand cold, as skin kissed skin.

Julian edged closer and took the lantern while Kit unrolled the paper and held it next to the light.

"'You are hereby directed, that should General Pakenham's offensive at New Orleans—'" He broke off, nausea sloshing in his belly. His own government, perfidious to the end. He rolled up the parchment again and gave it to his brother. "They're yours."

Julian stared at them, anger hardening in his eyes. "So Fitzgerald never had them."

Fitzgerald!

Kit's senses screamed an alert.

"But if Lieutenant Fitzgerald never had them, who else is so desperate he would kill for this?" Mattie echoed Kit's thoughts aloud.

A muted squeak filtered through the wall from the hold. The creak of a rocking ship? Or the footstep of a skulking man?

Kit shifted the gun in his waistband to the back of his trousers, hidden by the folds of his coat. He leaned next to Mattie, so close the scent of her hair teased his senses, and reached into her pocket. His fingers met the barrel of the pistol he'd shoved there during that pique of anger.

He hefted it aloft—a small, snub-nosed affair, less effectual than the ones Kit was wont to carry but better suited to a woman's hand. Mattie's eyes widened—with fright or betrayal? No matter, he'd apologize profusely when they'd escaped. If they escaped. Another rasp like that of a step rustled against the deck. He pushed her behind him where he could see her no more.

"Once you know who else wants the orders, Miss Fraser," a voice spoke from the doorway to the carpenter's walk, "you will know why I am going to kill you."

Chapter Seventeen

Kit's eyes strained against the darkness. "Baxter?"

The clerk stepped into the carpenter's walk and shuffled close enough for the lantern's light to catch eyes that glittered like a rabid feline's. And the malevolent glint of his pistol. "Greetings, DeChambelle. Fancy meeting you here. Put the pistol on the floor. Slowly. I don't wish to court an accident with a man of your reputation."

Kit stared at Baxter's eager face, reminded of his younger self—full of pleasure, patriotism and pride. How had he missed what was now so obvious? He stooped and rested Mattie's unloaded weapon on the deck.

"Very good. Now you, Somershurst. I'm certain you are similarly supplied. Your weapons, please—including your knife."

"Who are *you?*" Julian eyed Baxter with aristocratic indifference as he lowered his weapons.

"Baxter," Kit answered for him. "Works for Alderston, too. He killed Fitzgerald."

The clerk shrugged. "The man was a nuisance, and his thugs too much of a danger to Miss Fraser."

"So Fitzgerald hired Stumpy. I'd begun to suspect as much when I realized his real objective in stealing Miss Fraser's reticule was to recover her brother's letter. When that failed, he set about finding a more permanent solution."

"You ought be ashamed, DeChambelle. You almost lost Miss Fraser that day in Hyde Park."

"How gratifying to know you weren't entirely remiss in the duties I'd assigned you." If only Kit could keep the man talking. "I presume you dealt with Stumpy—after you missed in the park."

"Missed?" Baxter lifted his chin, scorn tilting his mouth. "I could hardly shoot him in front of an audience. But I knew how to find him."

"Because you'd made inquires at the Captain's Quarters the night before."

"After a certain event, Alderston was no longer convinced he could trust you to complete this job adequately."

Alderston, the man whose loyalty to country exceeded all else. Kit's friend, mentor and now betrayer. And for what? England's honor, or the Regent's avarice and pride? "And how does Alderston foresee this job being completed?"

"You may live, DeChambelle, and your brother also, as a reward for your great services."

"And because Alderston knows I will never divulge so shameful an action by my country."

"Just so. However, since we cannot trust similar assurances from Miss Fraser, she must die. Fortunately, as an American nobody, she won't be missed."

Except by him. And Caro. And a street urchin named Nicky. "We cannot kill a woman, Baxter."

"Why ever not? It isn't as if we haven't done it before for our country, DeChambelle."

Not this time. Not this woman. The last time had nearly cost his sanity—this would cost his soul. "The war is over."

He glanced at Mattie's face, pale in the lantern's glow. The freckles stood out across her nose. Her dress peeped out under her cloak, the hem now stained with grime from her adventure aboard the ship.

Would this be the image he took to his death?

Only hours earlier he'd chuckled at her self-conscious attempts at play with his sister. And yet, the sight of Mattie Fraser cradling Caro's doll had filled him with indescribable longings. Even hope for a future. For him. For them.

For the past year and more when he'd despaired of the futility of life, death held the promise of welcome relief. Now face-to-face with his own mortality, knowing he might have to sacrifice his life to save Mattie, he at last began to understand a love so great it would surrender all, forgive all.

He tried to catch Mattie's eye but she stared at Baxter, her lips pressed together in a tight line. "You killed Fitzgerald yesterday, but Betsy was gone this morning. If you've been working to keep me alive, how was she involved?"

"She thought to sell her services to both Fitzgerald and me, reporting your movements to both of us. She has been dealt with."

Kit sidled in front of Mattie while his mind sprinted at racehorse speed. The weight of his pistol—primed, loaded, ready—pressed against his back, waiting for the perfect moment. He would have only this one chance.

One shot. In the murkiness of a single lantern.

At this range, he was certain to hit his target. But then, the same applied to Baxter. He had to get Baxter to turn his weapon on him. There'd be little hope for his survival but he could save Mattie.

"Now give me the orders, Somershurst."

Kit tensed as he heard, nay, *felt* someone moving across the dark orlop deck.

Friend or foe?

He glanced at Julian, then at Baxter. His brother's eyes flickered, then stilled again.

"Mattie?" A small, dark head slid around the doorway. *Nicky.*

Mattie's breath caught in her throat. She stared at the door where Nicky stood. London's finest pickpocket. The little boy who'd stolen her heart.

Baxter spun around, pistol winking malevolently.

"Nicky, move!" a voice screamed. *Her* voice.

Nicky froze.

A flash of movement swirled next to her. Then Julian, Viscount Somershurst, crashed into Baxter at the moment a pistol shot—nay, *two* pistol shots—exploded in the small space.

Bodies ricocheted against the ship's hull and thudded against the wooden deck. The stench of gunpowder bombarded the small space and stung her eyes.

"Jules!" Kit dropped his still-smoking pistol and lunged to his knees, allowing Mattie an unimpeded view of the writhing limbs and spurting blood where Somershurst and Baxter lay tangled on the deck. He touched the inert form of his brother. "Jules?"

Somershurst's eyes flickered, then focused on Kit. "Just a flesh wound."

Mattie's legs folded and she sank to the floor beside the men. "Let me see it."

"Mattie," Kit warned. *"Stay back."*

Too late. She had already seen the cavern where Kit's bullet had tunneled into Baxter's chest. An expanding circle of crimson saturated the clerk's once-white shirt. The bright red blood gushed across the deck and polluted the air with its acrid metallic odor.

Somershurst's groan ripped Mattie's gaze from Baxter's sightless eyes to Kit's brother. The feeble lantern light emphasized his pallor. He pressed a hand against his upper arm, but the blood flowed freely between his fingers. Blood from the bullet Baxter had meant for her, from the bullet Kit had intended to take for her.

She retrieved her handkerchief from her pocket and brushed Somershurst's bloodstained fingers away. "Let me." She pushed the cloth against his wound.

A whisper of a smile tweaked his pale lips and one pain-filled eye winked at her. "I'll warrant you never thought you'd patch me up after a bullet wound, Miss Fraser."

"I have a soft spot for fools who are crazy enough to charge an armed man."

"Yes, well, remind me to duck lower next time." He glanced at Baxter's lifeless form. "By the way, good shot, Kit."

"Of course it was a good shot." The unfamiliar voice floated to them from the carpenter's-walk entrance. Muffled footsteps eased across the deck, then a fourth man joined them in the narrow passageway. "I taught DeChambelle everything he knows."

The sloshing in Kit's stomach intensified. He rose and shielded Mattie as he stared at Alderston. His old mentor's arm wrapped around Nicky, the deadly end of a pistol pressed against the boy's temple.

Kit had feared it would come to this the minute he'd seen Baxter. Alderston wouldn't leave to chance a situation of this magnitude.

"I guess Baxter's failure means you can't slip away, leaving another with the bloody hands."

"I don't want to hurt you," Alderston said.

"But you will."

"Only if I have to. Now step aside."

"You can't shoot the boy, Alderston." But Alderston would. Even as Kit gave voice to the denials, his heart recognized the ruthlessness—the frightening absence of compassion—in his mentor's eyes. Alderston's single-minded devotion would dare anything. To think, Kit had at one time admired such dedication—until it had nearly robbed him of his humanity.

"He's only a street urchin, Kit."

"But he's one of ours, not French or American."

"I don't *want* to shoot the boy, but it isn't my decision. Miss Fraser? Which is it to be? You or the boy?"

"Don't move, Mattie." Kit kept his gaze glued on his former idol. "He can't kill us all."

"How do you know I didn't bring an army, DeChambelle?"

"Because every additional person increases the likelihood that some rumor escapes your control and finds its way to our enemies."

Alderston's lips curled in a deadly smile as he cocked the pistol. "Miss Fraser?" He tightened his arm around the boy with enough force to squeeze out Nicky's stoicism and force him to gasp in pain.

"Stop!" With a sob Mattie slid to the side, out from behind Kit, her fingers stained with Julian's blood.

Alderston's grip on Nicky relaxed. He leveled the pistol at Mattie's heart, just as Kit's own stuttered to a halt. If only—

Nicky whipped out a knife and slashed. His indiscriminate attack—more desperation than design—sliced down Alderston's cheek like a trail of red tears. Alderston's roar echoed off the hull, then broke off, buried beneath an explosion of gunshot.

"No!" Kit whirled, heart racing and stomach heaving. "Mattie!"

But she just stood there, eyes blankly staring at some frightening apparition behind him. Kit glanced over his shoulder as Alderston slumped to the deck, a stain of scarlet blooming in the middle of his chest.

"Sorry, Kit." Julian's reedy voice whispered from the deck. "Know the man was a friend of yours."

Kit sank again to his knees beside his brother. A curl of smoke yet wafted from the barrel of Julian's pistol—the one he'd thrown to the deck on Baxter's order. The same blood that coated Julian's hands now stained the gun's stock. Love for this brother welled in Kit's eyes, in his soul. "Thank you. As you said, he'd been a friend. I don't know—"

"Some things a man shouldn't have to find out."

Kit gently removed Julian's coat, then disentangled the cravat from his brother's neck and pushed aside his shirt. "Looks like the bullet went through the muscle. So far as I can tell, it didn't hit the bone, so it didn't lodge in your arm."

"Just a scratch."

"An ugly one. You need a surgeon, Jules." He folded the cravat and flattened it against the wound.

"Mattie." Nicky's voice was little more than a whisper but it screamed in Mattie's conscience.

She leaped from the deck and ran to him. She wrapped her arms around him, his face crushed against her shoulder. His small body shuddered with his sobs.

"Shh, Nicky. It's over," she whispered against his head.

"I—" he hiccuped. "I was so scared for ye, Mattie."

"But you acted with courage despite your fear. That's bravery." She stroked his hair, dark against the pale skin of her fingers.

"Put me down, Mattie." He squirmed again and she surrendered to his desire for independence. He pointed to Baxter's prone form. "That's the bloke what threw me in gaol."

"Him? But…why?" She looked to Kit for confirmation.

"Nicky saw Fitzgerald's body, remember? Baxter may have feared he witnessed more than that."

"You mean, Fitzgerald's murder?"

"Baxter went to great pains to hide the evidence. No doubt

Alderston didn't want Fitzgerald's family inquiring into his death so long as the orders were still missing. Now, let's get Julian out of here."

"I'll check for the carriage, gov'na." Nicky's words were strong, despite the absence of his usual cockiness. He stepped over Alderston's prostrate body and slipped out of the narrow passageway.

"Can you walk?" Kit asked his brother.

"It's my arm, not my leg, Kit. Of course I can walk." Julian pushed himself to his feet, swaying slightly. Once he'd secured his balance, he glanced again at the orders still clutched in his fist. "Technically, these belong to our government. Do you want to give them to the Regent?"

"No. He gave up that consideration when he ordered Alderston to kill Mattie."

Julian nodded. "Thought so." He made his way up the ladder that led to the upper decks.

Kit motioned to Mattie and she climbed toward the fresher air above. Julian might claim his legs were fine, but her feet trembled as she placed one after the other on the rungs.

Once at the carriage, Kit helped the three of them—Julian, Nicky and her—into the cab, then snapped the door shut.

"Kit?" Mattie said.

But he looked past her to his brother, his mouth set in a grim line. "I've got some final business."

Somershurst's lips thinned. "You needn't wish him well on my regard."

"You will find a secure location for those orders?"

"I've even less desire than the Regent for their existence to be known. But I will if I must. The scandal at their disclosure will hardly fall on my shoulders alone. After all, I was merely the courier, not their author. Remind him of that for me, will you?"

"I'll see he gets the message." Kit stepped back, and the carriage lurched forward.

Tense silence hung between Mattie and the man in the rear-facing seat for several awkward moments.

"Now what happens?" she asked at last.

"*Uti possidetis,* Miss Fraser—each side keeps what it holds. Kit and I keep the orders and our silence, and our government leaves us in peace. It behooves no one to disturb the balance. And so, Miss Fraser, we are at what chess players term a stale-mate."

She glanced at the orders in his hand. Blood ran down his arm and stained the parchment. "Would you really publish the existence of those orders?" For her?

"I don't wish to, but I will if I must." His lips thinned with grim determination.

Publishing those orders would forever tarnish his reputation, and by extension his family's, but Somershurst had already proved he would go to great lengths to protect those dear to him. If she needed confirmation about the rightness of her decision to leave, she read it in his hard, weary eyes. After all, Alderston had claimed she was the threat. With her gone, perhaps the DeChambelles could live in peace. "Can you get me a ship?"

"A ship, Miss Fraser?"

"To America. I'm afraid I can't pay you immediately, but I will reimburse you in time." Eventually.

The carriage bounced across a rut. Somershurst's face paled and his mouth tightened with the pain of the jolt. "Have you spoken to Kit?"

"It's the right thing to do, considering all that has happened." A lump lodged in her throat, one that would remain a very long time. She prayed her new faith would give her strength and peace in the months and years ahead. "Kit will live in constant fear for me so long as I remain."

"Perhaps having a purpose for one's life is no very bad thing." Did he speak of Kit? Or himself?

"He needs to find that purpose for himself, without me." Like she had. "I'm only human. I cannot be his savior."

Silence thickened in the carriage like the heavy fog outside the windows that shrouded them from the city. "Very well, Miss Fraser. When do you wish to leave?"

"Soon. Preferably the next ship leaving for America."

"If ye is going to America, Mattie, I want to come, too."

Dear, precious Nicky. "But Lord Chambelston promised you a position—"

"No." His lower lip protruded stubbornly. "I don't want a position. I want ye, Mattie."

Warmth filled her aching heart. She didn't know how she would support herself, let alone a small boy, but if he was threatening to return to his life on the streets… "Very well. Lord Somershurst, can you procure us two passages to America as quickly as possible?"

"You give precious little consideration to an injured man, Miss Fraser."

"Oh. Yes, I'm sorry. I—"

"Never mind. I will send out inquiries immediately when we arrive, before the surgeon has a chance to thread his needle. But I wish you would speak to Kit before you make your final decision."

"I've already made my final decision. But if I promise to let him know, will you give me your word you'll not interfere?"

"My *word?* After what lies between us, you want my word?" His brows arched above impassive blue eyes. "Very well, Miss Fraser, I give you my word that I will not be the instrument of Kit's further misery."

Kit paused by a streetlamp and perused the note again— somewhat unnecessarily as the words were already engraved on his heart. Mattie's words. Words of heartfelt simplicity and heartbreaking finality.

Dawn had begun to blush above the roofs of nearby tenements and the light fog had already started to lift, unlike the clouds in his head that darkened all thoughts but despair. Alderston was dead and Mattie was leaving. Kit had arrived home after his late-night meeting with the Regent to find the note in his room. Mattie's farewell.

An unsettling quiet filled the streets and exacerbated Kit's feeling of solitude. The vices that thrived by night had retreated, yet few of the workers and tradesmen had thus far ventured forth to begin their day's toils.

Despite the early hour, the happy racket of waking children reverberated through the walls of the Harrisons' new home. Loneliness coiled through Kit at this reminder of all he was about to lose. And yet for the first time in long months he no longer wished to forget. He wanted to remember.

He refolded the note and gathered the courage to walk to Harrison's door. And to knock.

The door swung open to reveal Harrison's befuddled face. "DeChambelle? Is something wrong?" Yesterday's stubble still shadowed his jaw and spikes of his sleep-tangled hair projected in all directions.

"Alderston's dead." And Mattie was leaving.

Harrison glanced over his shoulder to where Alice watched them through wary eyes. He nodded to his wife, then slipped over the threshold and eased the door shut. "Come. Let's walk."

Kit fell into step beside his old friend as they strolled the narrow street.

"I'm sorry about Alderston. Whatever else one may say of the man, he was devoted to his country."

"Perhaps too much so." Kit clasped his hands behind his

back. "I've been thinking about what you said. About my pride."

A smile wisped across Harrison's face. "And does your pride make it difficult for you to admit this?"

"As a matter of fact, yes." A sparrow scolded them from a nearby rooftop. "The events of the past few days have forced me to reexamine some unpleasant aspects of my character."

"Growth often produces pain, but it also brings great potential for taking us to a better place."

"God knows, I don't like the place I'm taking myself." Small wonder Mattie preferred a life alone in America to a future in England—with him. Or rather, the man he'd been working to become.

Harrison paused and tilted his head. "You dropped God's name into that sentence rather effortlessly. Does that mean…?"

"Yes." Kit pondered an approaching dray cart. "As I stood there, looking at Alderston, I realized that to preserve my sanity, I would have to continue forth in either of two directions. I could either enslave my body to drink in order to forget the past, or I could harden my heart against human emotion in order to discount the past."

"Like Alderston."

"He was going to kill Mattie, you know. And he wouldn't have suffered a twinge of regret. To him, she was merely an obstacle." Whereas to Kit, she was…the future. He shook his head to free himself of the terrible images. "I want to choose a third way, Lawrie. I want forgiveness from the past. Would you help me? I'm ready to listen now. I'm ready to change."

Ready to surrender.

A tentative knock tapped against the door of the yellow chamber. "Miss Fraser?"

Mattie glanced up from the Bible on her lap. "Yes?"

A shy maid—not Betsy, of course—stepped into the room and curtsied. "Viscount Somershurst asks if you would attend him."

The ship. Mattie set the Bible on the armoire's polished surface. "Of course. Could you escort me to the room?"

"This way, Miss." The maid guided Mattie's heavy feet through the halls and paused at a door. "Here."

"Thank you." As the maid left, Mattie rapped on the door.

"Enter."

"My lord?" She cracked open the door to the room where Kit's brother convalesced. Afternoon sunlight filtered through the window panes and bathed the room in a peaceful glow. "You have news for me?"

Somershurst looked up from where he reclined on the bed and frowned. "Egad, Miss Fraser, don't start."

"Oh, I'm sorry. I didn't mean to press about the ship. I—"

"Not the ship. That 'my lord' nonsense. I'd hoped for better from an American, especially after all we'd been through. You know my name. And all my secrets."

Mattie forced a light smile to her face though her heart felt heavy. "I doubt all of them...Julian."

"To tell the truth, when I hear anyone say 'my lord,' I still look over my shoulder for..." His lips flattened and shadows darkened the blue of his eyes.

"Your mother told me about your brother and nephew." She waited while he regained his composure.

"Well, come in, Mattie." He gestured to her with one bare arm. White bandages swathed his other sun-browned shoulder, but the color had returned to his face. "And close the door behind you. Your being in the room is scarcely more scandalous than standing in the doorway, and a great deal less likely to attract notice."

She slipped into the room, fighting to appear nonchalant despite his provoking comments. "Did you—"

"Yes, I did." He scooped a paper off the bedside table and passed it to her. "Here are the details. The *Gallant*. She's an American ship so she won't offend your sensibilities. But she leaves tomorrow, so you'll need to board in the morning. The captain is expecting you."

"Thank you."

"Have you spoken to Kit?"

"Not since he left the ship last night." But she'd learned all she needed to know yesterday. She couldn't tie herself—let alone a child like Nicky—to a man bent on destruction.

"He deserves to know."

"I wrote him a note detailing my reasons." More than that—a face-to-face confrontation—beyond a few brief words of farewell, would be unnecessary. Painful.

"A note? A rather cold parting. Are you certain—"

"Yes."

"Then take this with you." He tossed her a purse.

The coins inside chinked as she caught the pouch. She hefted its weight in her hand. "What...?"

"Enough for you to begin a new life."

"I can't accept this. Why, you've already arranged my passage."

"It is little enough. Fitzgerald would have extorted far more over the years. And you'll need funds to feed and clothe and educate young Master Nicky. I owe him my life."

As did she.

"I'll be returning to my townhouse today. If you need me, send one of the footmen."

"I will." Mattie strode to the door, then stopped and turned to face Kit's brother one last time. "It's been..." Not a pleasure, exactly.

Sympathy flecked those blue DeChambelle eyes. "I understand."

Ah, George. His specter haunted her still. When she returned to America, she would forego the painful reminders of Washington and go elsewhere, perhaps to the West. With the funds Julian had provided, she could open a store of her own. The Indiana Territory might well be a new state soon—a good place for a new beginning. She hesitated, then asked, "Do you think Kit will be penalized for what happened?"

"I think you have the wherewithal to make it worthwhile to him. Consider this decision carefully. You needn't rush— there will be other ships, you know."

"This is the correct decision. Farewell, Julian."

"God go with you, Mattie. I wish you every happiness."

Mattie paused at the top of the staircase, willing her unsteady legs to carry her to the bottom. No doubt the carriage would be arriving forthwith to take her and Nicky to the docks. She reached for her bags, only to stop. How odd to be leaving empty-handed but for the Bible in her hand, her bags having already been taken to the ship.

"Ah, Miss Fraser. There you are." The earl smiled as he met her on the landing. An elegant black cloak enveloped his shoulders.

"Sir?"

"We thought we would go with you, to see you off."

"How kind of you, my lord." *We?* She hadn't spoken to Kit since… Where had he been these past two days? Had he even read the letter she'd written? The idea of seeing him one last time delighted and dismayed her.

"Would you step into my wife's chamber a moment?" The earl gestured, and Mattie followed him through the hallway.

Lady Chambelston reclined on her bed, her cheeks at last

beginning to glow again with health. She smiled when they entered the room.

Mattie's throat ached from her effort to fight back memories and tears. "Was there something you wished to say to me, ma'am?"

"Something I wished to give you, rather." The countess nodded to a velvet box. "For you."

A gift for her—the woman who had brought so much misery to an already suffering family? Mattie popped open the box. Twin earrings of diamonds and emeralds winked at her from their bed. "Oh, I could never accept these after all you've already given me!"

The countess raised a hand to stop her protests. "My son tells me you saved his life."

And had nearly taken Lady Chambelston's through her quest for vengeance. "An exaggeration, to be sure, ma'am. The credit goes to Nicky."

"Keep them, Mattie. Please. To remember us by."

Mattie looked again at the sparkling stones, now wavering through the moisture that filled her eyes. "I'll never need jewels to remember you and all you've done for me, but... thank you." She closed the box and clenched it until her fingers ached.

"Then share what you've learned here, Mattie. With Nicky, and with others who need to know."

"I will."

The countess gestured her closer. Mattie leaned over and accepted the woman's embrace. Fragrances of comfort and faint perfume unsettled Mattie's senses.

"Mat-tie?" Caro called from the hallway.

"Are you certain this is what you want?" the countess said as she released her. "You will always be welcome in our home. You may stay as long as you wish."

No, it wasn't what she wanted, but... "This is for the best.

For all of us." She forced her mouth into one last smile then joined Caro and her father in the hallway.

No Kit, though. Relief warred with regret, even though she knew 'twas better this way. Or easier, at least.

"Where's Nicky?" she asked as the earl aided her into the carriage.

"He was so excited, we let him go ahead with the bags. He should be on the ship waiting for you."

"Oh, dear." She hoped someone had checked the silver.

The carriage bounced over the bricks until too soon it stopped at the docks, not far from the spot where she had first landed on English soil. How long ago that seemed. Today the sun poured down with aching brightness. As she alighted from the carriage, she stared at the *Gallant*'s masts rising up to a clear blue sky, a sky as blue as Kit DeChambelle's eyes.

"Goodbye, sir," she said to the earl.

He patted her shoulder awkwardly, his eyes even more brilliant than normal. "Send us a letter when you are settled, Mattie.

"I'll do that, sir."

"I've always wanted to see America again. Peacefully."

A hysterical giggle bubbled in her throat at the notion of entertaining an English earl in the wilds of Indiana. "Goodbye, Caro."

"Goodbye, Mat-tie." Caroline embraced her, then stepped back, her eyes shimmering with moisture.

"Hurry, miss!" a crewman called.

Mattie turned her face away and forced her uncooperative legs into motion. Once on the ship she joined the other passengers at the rail as they shouted farewells to friends and relatives. She lifted her hand, then froze as a third person joined Caro and the earl.

A breeze ruffled his blond hair and her heart stopped for

the second it took her to determine that a sling immobilized his left arm.

Julian, not Kit.

Her disappointment tasted bitter in her mouth.

"Mattie!" Nicky joined her at the rail.

She coerced her face into a smile for his sake. "What do you think of our ship?"

"I 'ave a room and a bed all to myself."

"A berth." She tweaked a few strands of his dark—clean—hair. "You're on a ship now. The captain won't take kindly to landlubber talk."

"I ain't met the captain yet. But I talked to the cook. Want to meet 'im?"

"Perhaps later." In the distance, St. Paul's dome winked a farewell in the sunlight as Mattie allowed herself one last look at London. One last link to Kit DeChambelle. A great weight pressed against her—against her heart, against her shoulders—as she fought to raise her hand for one final wave. Then she left to find her cabin. And solitude.

Moments later she slipped into her room. Somershurst hadn't scrimped when he'd made the arrangements. The muted light filtering through the tiny porthole bathed the space in shadows. She opened the precious velvet box but the emeralds stared back dully, their fire dimmed by the gloom as surely as her spirit. She snapped the case shut and stowed it in her pocket, then glanced at the same coat that had seen her to England. Plain brown wool—coarse and practical. Like her. She brushed her fingertips along the scratchy fabric, letting it remind her of who she was and what she had come to do.

A woman consumed by her own notions of vengeance.

Fortunately, she did not return the same woman. And at least her ill-begun quest had yielded two worthy results. Nicky would have a home and a family—her. And no matter what cloud of suspicion lurked over the DeChambelles, Kit had freed Julian of *his* burden.

Bands of pain tightened around her chest until she could scarcely breathe. She dropped to the bed, buried her face in her hands and let the sobs come. They wracked her body and purged her soul until there was no feeling left inside.

She reached into her coat pocket for a handkerchief, but only the velvet box caressed her fingers. Perhaps in her bags. She looked at the satchels in the corner of her cabin—

Unfamiliar bags, not hers.

Obviously the crewman who'd led her to this cabin had erred. As most of the passengers still waved at the rail yet, she could rectify the situation with none the wiser.

She slipped off the bed and exited the cabin.

"Ah, there you are. Come, you don't want to miss your last view of London."

The clipped English voice, *his* voice, set her heart pounding. Slowly, she turned. *"Kit?"*

He stepped from the shadows until he stood before her, so close she could detect his scent over the foul-smelling Thames and London's ever-present smoke. His warmth radiated through his clothes and curled around the cold, melancholy places inside her.

"But—but, what are you doing here?"

"I came to talk to you."

"I've already said my piece."

"But you haven't heard mine."

What was left to say, but goodbye? Unless… Hope thrummed in her pulse. "Why did you tell your mother I saved your life?"

He blinked puzzled eyes. "I didn't."

Julian. But Mattie supposed, in a way, she had saved him from his lieutenant's extortion and his government's suspicions.

Kit circled his fingers around her wrist and drew her to the ladder. "Come, let us enjoy the view from the deck. We have one last matter of business to settle before we leave English waters."

Mattie followed him to the upper deck. Already other passengers abandoned their positions at the rail as the ship floated down the Thames, leaving London's buildings growing smaller in the distance. The spectators at the dock—Kit's family among them—had shrunk so as to be indistinguishable.

Kit hefted a bag onto the rail, then reached inside and withdrew her pistol.

The Thames's stench caught in her chest, choking her.

"Here. Hold this."

She whipped her hands behind her back. "I told you before, I don't want it."

"Just for a moment, for one last time."

Reluctantly, she accepted the weapon. Simple wood and iron, yet with so much power to destroy.

He reached into the bag again and withdrew a goblet of finest crystal. "You were right about many things, Mattie— including the dangerous path I trod. That night on the *Impatience,* when I wasn't sure any of us would leave alive, many things—things I'd stubbornly ignored for so long— suddenly became clear to me. I don't want to be the man I was, or worse, the man I was on my way to becoming. And with God's help, I won't."

A wild swirl of hope coiled through her. "Kit? But…"

"I've spent the past two days getting my affairs in order— beginning with my heart. I've surrendered everything—my pride, my past, my future. My life. I am a new creature, embarking on a new life."

He drew back his arm, then catapulted the goblet into the air. It winked in the light as it arched upwards. And then it plunged down, down into the dark, churning waters of the river.

"My past is forgiven. Buried." He turned his face toward her, his eyes light and boyish, his smile erasing the strain of self-reproach. "Go on, Mattie. Bury the past. Here—in England."

She looked at the gun one last time, then hurled it into waters. "Thank you."

"I've learned we cannot look to the future until we cast off the shackles of the past. Mattie."

She drew her gaze from the river to his suddenly serious face. He reached inside the bag one more time, and when he extracted his hand, a circlet of gold set with emeralds and diamonds gleamed up at her from his palm. How did they reflect the light when her earrings hadn't?

"It looks like the earrings your mother gave me."

His lopsided grin slipped through the debris of the walls around her heart. "As it should. My mother thought it would make a splendid wedding ring, and it would be a shame to divide the set. It belonged to my grandmother."

Mattie Fraser—and heirloom jewelry? "But…"

"Marry me, Mattie." Wistfulness clouded his blue eyes to gray. "Else I will be lost, living in America without you."

"America? You intend to sail all the way to America?"

Amusement softened his cheeks. "That is why I am on this ship."

"But I thought… You can't leave your home, your family, your country. Your life is in England."

"I don't want a life in England without you."

"Me?"

"I love you, Mattie. More than country. More than family. More than life itself. I want to watch the glow of the sunset against your face and see the brilliance of the sunrise reflected in your eyes."

She closed those eyes against the unattainable pictures he painted. And yet, clenching her lids shut gave her mind free rein to conjure images to match his words.

"I want to hear my name on your lips."

That lump had lodged in her throat again. And yet this time it swelled with hope. "Don't tease me, Kit. Not about this."

He captured her hand again and held it while his gaze bored deep into her heart. The warmth of his palm seeped into her and filled her with tenderness. "I love you, Mattie Fraser, and I will ask you again—and again and again until you are so weary you finally say *yes*. Will you do me the honor of becoming my wife? We'll take what we've learned and make a new life for ourselves."

Her eyes stung until his face blurred. "Oh, Kit. If you truly want this, then yes. Oh, yes with all my heart."

"Come, let us find the captain. He can marry us once we are underway. That sunset I spoke of? I want tonight to be the first."

Kit stared across the churning gray sea. His cloak billowed behind him, whipped by the icy wind that lashed his face with coldness and hurled the ship westward. He met the wind defiantly. It tossed salt-flavored spray against his face where the drops mingled with the salt-cured tears that pooled in the corners of his eyes.

Somewhere beyond the horizon now, the misty island of his birth rose above the waves, shrouded by approaching twilight. He and Julian would never have that chance to reconnect after all. It was indeed too late. A warning, perhaps, that he should never again postpone an opportunity for reconciliation or transformation.

"Mr. DeChambelle!" Nicky's excited voice rose above the gale. "Come look."

The boy clutched his hand and tugged.

Kit stared down at the dark windblown hair, and his pensive mood dispersed into the mist.

"What did you wish to show me?"

"Look!" Nicky drew him toward the other side of the ship where Mattie waited, her gaze focused westward. She gripped the rail, her finger encircled by the emerald wedding ring.

His wife.

Rays of waning sunlight speared through the clouds, painting the sky a brilliant scarlet and dyeing the churning sea with red.

He paused next to Mattie. She'd regained her poise, but a new sense of understanding—of experience—softened what had previously been a confrontational tilt of her chin and smoothed the sharp edges in her speech. She never turned, but she knew he was there—she clasped his other hand between both of hers. Joy swelled inside him, pushing aside those last lingering feelings of loss.

His wife.

"It's a sign, you know, a red sky at night."

"A sign for fair weather on the morrow," he murmured.

He withdrew his hand from her grasp so he could wrap his arm around her shoulders and pull her closer. So close, he inhaled the fragrance of her hair in the sea-scented air.

The three of them stared in silence at Heaven's pageant of light and color until the twilight dimmed to night.

His tomorrows promised to be fair indeed.

* * * * *

Dear Reader,

The Regency has become a favorite setting among American readers, a curious development given that America was at war with Britain during those years. As a lover of both Regency settings and American history, I wondered…could I combine the two? And thus began the inspiration for Mattie Fraser, an American wounded by her brother's impressment and the British invasion of Washington—and bent on revenge.

My research into the War of 1812 led to an interesting discovery. Until the American victories at Baltimore and Lake Champlain, the British peace commission demanded territorial concessions. Even after the commission abandoned its demands, the treaty, signed on December 24, 1814, contained an unusual clause that prevented it from going into effect until the two countries exchanged ratifications.

While the nonbinding treaty crossed the Atlantic, the war in America waged on. On January 8, 1815, General Pakenham (brother-in-law to the Duke of Wellington) attacked at New Orleans, but the Americans under the command of future president Andrew Jackson soundly defeated the British forces. British peace commissioner Julian Baker arrived in New York to news of Pakenham's death and an American victory. Ratifications were exchanged on February 17, 1815, thus officially ending the War of 1812.

One wonders, though, what Baker's orders were had he arrived in New York to news of an American defeat. Well, you know my theory.

I love to hear from readers and can be contacted via my website cjchasebooks.com.

May God grant you fair winds and following seas.

QUESTIONS FOR DISCUSSION

1. What is the difference between forgiveness and reconciliation?

2. Mattie and Kit expressed remorse for the things they had done, but others (such as Mattie's father and brother) never did. Can you forgive people who never express regret for the things they have done? Can—or should—you reconcile with those who are unrepentant?

3. According to Mahatma Ghandi, "The weak can never forgive. Forgiveness is the attribute of the strong." Do you agree? How was this true in the lives of Mattie and Kit? What caused the change? How have you observed this in your own life?

4. In Matthew 18:15-17, Jesus outlines the steps for dealing with the forgiveness and reconciliation of fellow believers. In what way is this similar to God's relationship with humanity? In what ways does it differ?

5. How does the older brother in the parable of the Prodigal Son (Luke 15:11-32) illustrate the need to go beyond forgiveness to reconciliation? Do you have any prodigal "brothers" with whom you need to reconcile? What do you need to change in your life and attitudes to make this reconciliation possible?

6. Lady Chambelston suffered because of Mattie's sin, and yet because of her willingness to forgive she was able to use her pain to point Mattie to God. What events can you use from your life to point others to God?

7. Kit looked at his future and saw a life of developing alcohol dependency. Mattie saw a future of punishment and execution. Have you ever contemplated what your future might be if God didn't redeem your life from destruction (Psalms 103:4)? How would your life have been different?

8. Kit's spectacles correct his vision, but his pride keeps him spiritually blind. What behaviors and attitudes sabotage our spiritual vision? What "corrective lenses" can we use to keep our spiritual life in focus?

9. Because of his past actions, Kit feels unworthy of God's love and forgiveness. However, his friend Harrison suggests the problem is actually Kit's pride. These seem to contradict. What do you think was blocking Kit's reconciliation with God? What events did God use to reach Kit? Do you have attitudes that put stumbling blocks in your relationship with God? What events has God used to bring you to Him?

10. Many Christians feel guilt for sins they have long ago confessed. Why do you think that is? How can you find release from the guilt of old sins?

11. Kit not only relinquishes his guilt and pride but he also leaves his country and family. Has God ever called you to leave behind things you hold dear? What did you gain by following His calling?

INSPIRATIONAL

Inspirational romances to warm your heart & soul.

TITLES AVAILABLE NEXT MONTH

Available September 13, 2011

REQUEST YOUR FREE BOOKS!

2 FREE INSPIRATIONAL NOVELS
PLUS 2
FREE
MYSTERY GIFTS

Love Inspired
HISTORICAL
INSPIRATIONAL HISTORICAL ROMANCE

YES! Please send me 2 FREE Love Inspired® Historical novels and my 2 FREE mystery gifts (gifts are worth about $10). After receiving them, if I don't wish to receive any more books, I can return the shipping statement marked "cancel". If I don't cancel, I will receive 4 brand-new novels every month and be billed just $4.49 per book in the U.S. or $4.99 per book in Canada. That's a saving of at least 22% off the cover price. It's quite a bargain! Shipping and handling is just 50¢ per book in the U.S. and 75¢ per book in Canada.* I understand that accepting the 2 free books and gifts places me under no obligation to buy anything. I can always return a shipment and cancel at any time. Even if I never buy another book, the two free books and gifts are mine to keep forever.

102/302 IDN FEHF

Name _____ (PLEASE PRINT) _____

Address _____ Apt. #

City _____ State/Prov. _____ Zip/Postal Code

Signature (if under 18, a parent or guardian must sign)

Mail to the **Reader Service:**
IN U.S.A.: P.O. Box 1867, Buffalo, NY 14240-1867
IN CANADA: P.O. Box 609, Fort Erie, Ontario L2A 5X3

Not valid for current subscribers to Love Inspired Historical books.

Want to try two free books from another series?
Call 1-800-873-8635 or visit www.ReaderService.com.

* Terms and prices subject to change without notice. Prices do not include applicable taxes. Sales tax applicable in N.Y. Canadian residents will be charged applicable taxes. Offer not valid in Quebec. This offer is limited to one order per household. All orders subject to credit approval. Credit or debit balances in a customer's account(s) may be offset by any other outstanding balance owed by or to the customer. Please allow 4 to 6 weeks for delivery. Offer available while quantities last.

Your Privacy—The Reader Service is committed to protecting your privacy. Our Privacy Policy is available online at www.ReaderService.com or upon request from the Reader Service.

We make a portion of our mailing list available to reputable third parties that offer products we believe may interest you. If you prefer that we not exchange your name with third parties, or if you wish to clarify or modify your communication preferences, please visit us at www.ReaderService.com/consumerchoice or write to us at Reader Service Preference Service, P.O. Box 9062, Buffalo, NY 14269. Include your complete name and address.

LIH11B